Killer of Giants

A Rogan Novel

Also by Steven L. Shrewsbury

Along Come Evening
Mojo Hand
Last Man Screaming
Born of Swords
Within
Philistine
Hell Billy
Overkill
Thrall
Stronger Than Death
Tormentor
Hawg
Godforsaken

King of the Bastards*
Throne of the Bastards*
Curse of the Bastards*
*(with Brian Keene)

Bad Magick**
**(with Nate Southard)

Bedlam Unleashed***
***(with Peter Welmerink)

Beyond Night+
+(with Eric S. Brown)

COLLECTIONS
Blood & Steel: Volume I
Thoroughbred
Bulletproof Soul
Depths of Savagery
Nocturnal Vacations

Killer of Giants

A Rogan Novel

Steven L. Shrewsbury

Cover art: Hugor and Hugorky Rodriguez

Cover art in this book copyright ©2022 Seventh Star Press, LLC.

Editor: Stephen Zimmer

Published by Seventh Star Press, LLC.

ISBN Number: 978-1-7368125-5-6

Seventh Star Press
www.seventhstarpress.com
info@seventhstarpress.com

Publisher's Note:
Killer of Giants is a work of fiction. All names, characters, and places are the product of the author's imagination, used in fictitious manner. Any resemblances to actual persons, places, locales, events, etc. are purely coincidental.

Printed in the United States of America

First Edition

Acknowledgments

Thanks to Brian Keene, who gave me the overall push for this work with one line. Rogan, here he is in a youthful adventure and tale of horror, so, it's all your fault…as usual.

Thank you always to Brady Allen, Bob Freeman, Peter Welmerink, Ronald Kelly, Angie & Chris Fulbright and Kristin Staggs for always listening & encouraging me.

Also to Angela Bodine, Stephen Zimmer, Donnise Parks, Tod Clark, Christine Whitehead, Dave Barnett, Julie Lauth, Julie King Rice, and Dean Harrison for being awesome folks.

Special kudos go to Adriane Rinehart for being there and providing inspiration for Aliene. You rock.

And lastly, thanks to my family. You know who you are. But most of all, John & Aaron who never stop believing in their dad.

Shrews

Rural Illinois

Dedication

For my barbarians
John & Aaron
And my godson, Mark Jr
And my niece, Amy
I lerv her

VOICES FROM THE PAST:
INTRODUCTION

By Brian Keene

I've known Shrews (the nickname I've always used for author Steven L. Shrewsbury) for twenty years or so. I've known his character Rogan for about the same amount of time. I've watched Shrews's sons grow from babies whom I held into remarkable young men. I've watched Rogan and his saga grow, as well.

Shrews has populated his books with plenty of memorable recurring characters -- the fascinating Gorias La Gaul, the Celtic warrior Lucan Mac Aliester, psychic archeologist Elijah Blackthorn, and many more. But Rogan was always my favorite, because of the love and passion Shrews has for the character. All creators have certain characters they feel that way about. And as a reader, you'll tend to find that -- when they are writing about those characters -- the creator will often deliver some of their best work. You see it reflected in everything from Manly Wade Wellman's Silver John to F. Paul Wilson's Repairman Jack to Mary SanGiovanni's Kathy Ryan to my own Levi Stoltzfus.

There's a lot of Shrews imbued in Rogan -- enough so that

when I read the character's dialogue, I always hear it in his voice. And enough so that when Shrews suggested to me that he and I collaborate on a novel about Rogan's senior years, I hesitated at first. After all, this was his character and his world -- set in that antediluvian period between the Garden of Eden and the Great Flood. Shrews put that second concern to rest by pointing out to me that we'd already given little Easter Egg nods to each other's fictional universes in previous works, and besides, my Labyrinth mythos allows for the inclusion of all of space and time, so why couldn't one of those levels of reality be Rogan's pre-Biblical world?

Okay, I argued. That was all well and good. But Rogan was still his character and spoke with his voice, and it wasn't a voice that I was sure I could say anything with.

Then Shrews suggested that I was staring down the barrel of turning fifty, and several of our friends had already died, and the rest of us were starting to feel our own mortality, and beginning to realize we were no longer quite as vital or as energetic as we'd once been, and it took us a lot longer to heal, and that was where Rogan was in this trilogy, and he was pretty sure I had something to say about all of those things.

And he was right. I did.

And so did Shrews.

And that trilogy -- KING OF THE BASTARDS, THRONE OF THE BASTARDS, and CURSE OF THE BASTARDS -- is the result. Rogan still spoke with Shrews's voice, one hundred percent. But the books were about something all three of us wanted to talk about.

This novel is talking about different things. KILLER OF GIANTS is a novel about a much younger Rogan, a man with different attitudes and concerns and appetites than the one in the Bastards trilogy. But his voice is still the same. It's still Shrews. It's a voice from the past, talking about things remembered -- of how things used to be. As a creator, I'm not sure if the wellspring is Shrews's own memory or if he's perhaps looking at the world through the eyes of his sons, but either way, the results are remarkable and entertaining.

Also, there's a really cool scene in which Rogan leaps off the back of a wooly mammoth and piledrives a sword through the head of a giant.

I'll bet Shrews could have done that twenty years ago.

Let's listen.

-- Brian Keene
Somewhere along the Susquehanna River
October 2021

"Are you prepared to meet your master, the Devil?"

ROBERT E. HOWARD

CHAPTER ONE

Never Say Die

"Spear the living ones you find up higher, Thyssen, that's where the heart lies. I thought you a soldier before you were a slave?"

The squelch of the death blow meted out by Thyssen's lance curled about in Rogan's ears. He didn't dare breathe or move his long frame compressed by dead men. Through the stink of the lifeless warriors atop him, Rogan could smell the pyres nearby smoking with human flesh.

Eyes closed tight, he hoped with some humor that the cadaver dogs searching the battlefield wouldn't notice him. The light of day came near to dying, but the voices of those clearing the battleground still persisted in their tasks.

Eyes open again, Rogan plotted his escape from his position under the dead fighters he'd signed on to fight with against King Nungal, and a few of those who died killing them for Kalama-ur. He prayed to Wodan for the evening darkness, not that his god cared or intervened ever.

"Move faster, Thyssen, bring up the dogs," the voice of the taskmaster rang out again. "…or I'll sell your big ass for fodder to that Nephilim asshead Azrag before he rides south." The rough voice threatened an unseen man. "Pray to your foreign gods he doesn't drag you to Irem for a feast with Marduk and the demon Zazaeil."

Rogan heard the muttered curses of Thyssen to his overlord, calling him, "Yes, master Jakmurph, you ignorant bastard." He also overheard the searching dogs barking, but they sounded farther away.

The light of the day came to him scarce, which proved good as they couldn't find him that way with any ease. He wondered how much daylight remained for him, for the darkness would be his friend if he were to escape this mound of the dead. Rogan could perceive the bodies on the battlefield being dragged then dropped by the sounds of their chainmail armor and weapons falling against the ground. In his mind's eye, he could see the slaves who labored to lay the bodies out and strip them of anything useful.

He remained as still as one of the dead though, blessed or lucky slapped by the gods that he fell in such a way to hide him. Rogan hoped the murky touch of the evening would aide his escape, but those searching might find him before the blackness arrived.

Not every strike from the spearman made much of a sound. Sometimes, the blows fell like heavy thuds, and other times, the reaction came to Rogan's ears like a boot pulling out of the mud. However, a few times a horrific squeal accompanied the wet sound. *He found another guy hiding…*

Though his mind told him evening had to be encroaching, a light rushed in on the bearded face of the youth Rogan. He glared at the one who uncovered bodies over him, but it couldn't have been the one the master cursed as Thyssen. A grubby faced woman Rogan guessed to be between thirty and forty summers old raised up some bodies using a bronze pole as a lever. Face to face with her, Rogan blinked and felt his heart sink. She moved her neck about, chaffing a little at the slave collar under her chin.

The one Thyssen cursed as Jakmurph cussed loud, saying,

"Bodyne? You addled-brained bitch, get to work. Are you revolted? After all you've seen in my service, I would doubt it very damn much."

The dirty faced woman frowned at Rogan, blinked, and lessened her hold on the lever covering him again. He breathed in some relief, but again felt the revulsion of the battlefield stank. Rogan had smelt innards and guts of various kinds all his life, but the shock of how much a battleground reeked of feces didn't cease to surprise him.

Jakmurph railed again at his slaves, saying, "The Kelts are easy to spot in the mound, bloody savages, as their hair is fair. If you see the color of their eyes, green or blue, you might be in trouble as they die hard." He then coughed and said, "Mercenary bastards."

Rogan shifted, moving away from his position flat on his back and rolled over, letting the bodies rest softly on his back as Bodyne moved on. He could perceive her well through a gap in the bodies. Her eyes looked back to where the living fighter hid, but she didn't betray him. He saw her move nearer to a huge man, also wearing a collar sporting a chain down his back. Another figure moved into Rogan's sight, a tall man wearing a chainmail shirt, sporting a sword at his hip and a flask in his right hand. Balding, but vibrant, his body surged and swelled up in his barrel chest.

"Jakmurph," Rogan grunted in a whisper, as his eyes scanned the field all about, seeing no other opposition aside from the dog handlers. "Shynar prick." His hand gripped the pommel of his pinned sword. "Your ass is mine."

His sword failed to pull out from the bodies sucking it down tight better than a scabbard. Rogan vowed to retrieve his father's sword, but only after he cleared the air.

Jakmurph's back looked as wide as a wheat crib door for a target, but when Rogan rose up and threw off the bodies, the man started to turn and the objective shrank as thin as a serpent. A blink of the eyes, and this illusion broke, as did the buckler of the shield Rogan tried to pick up and brain Jakmurph. The young Kelt fighter stumbled from the bodies, empty handed and face to face with the taskmaster.

"What?" Jakmurph's mouth gasped, his black eyes wide at the sight before him. The man remained still and didn't go for his sword. Some sour liquor from his flask spewed out of his lips as he cried out, "Thyssen!"

Rogan's boot drove into the crotch of the taskmaster, disappearing into the short kilt but connecting with something soft. His right fist arched, swinging down as Jakmurph bent, reacting to the low blow.

The balled-up bludgeon of bone and skin smashed into the left eye of the taskmaster, breaking the ball into jelly, smearing the thick liquid across Jakmurph's nose. Only a moment passed before Rogan's left arm curled about Jakmurph's head in a headlock. Another second didn't drop before Rogan's right thumb jammed into the broken eye socket and delved in several inches.

"Master?" Bodyne exclaimed in terror, then froze. Her expression changed as the warrior that arose from the dead men gripped Jakmurph's face, his thumb unseen.

The taskmaster's stout frame jerked in Rogan's grasp, then he fell back to his buttocks, legs kicking. Though Jakmurph cried out once, hands clutching his face, the fight left him and he flopped on top of more corpses.

Thyssen stepped closer, spear in hand, looking at the body of the taskmaster along with Bodyne. He then eyed the tall youth who struck down his master.

"Master of none, no more," Rogan declared. "My little sister could have taken that bloated man down."

Rogan turned, dug into the dead bodies for his sword, and pulled it free after he braced his boot on a body. He faced the two slaves and said, "Hold out your hands."

Dropping to her knees, fast, Bodyne willingly spread out her wrists over a space of clear ground.

Rogan leaned back and swung the heavy blade down. The

great sword passed through her chains and she cried out, her breath gone for a moment.

"Helluva sword," Thyssen commented as he knelt by the body of the taskmaster. He stood, working on his collar with a key and soon the binding dropped. "Ya must be strong as an ox to swing it, much less carry it all the fuck over the world."

"My father is a helluva man," Rogan related, looking at those who handled the dogs not far away. These men gaped at them, but made no move. No other taskmasters were near, nor did any note their actions in the grim evening.

"Did he make that big-assed blade?" Bodyne wondered as she rose to let Thyssen undo her collar.

"Yes," Rogan confessed, near to irritated by her obvious question. "Far away from here, though."

"You pick up it like a common blade." She said, "I can't believe you can fight with that thing using only one hand."

Gripping the leather-wrapped hilt as Bodyne stared at the weapon, Rogan eyed Thyssen. "By that reddish hair and your pale skin, you aren't from around these nations, either." The towering youth then faced north, squinted, and shook his head. He turned the blade down with some grace, like he'd done it countless times before. "So far away from home."

"No, I'm not, bright boy." Thyssen's gaze followed his. "You won't want to run that way, Kelt. Ya might be strong as a devil, but yer brains are crap."

Rogan smirked at him. "Screw off. I can see remnants of those I rode in with over there beyond the creek. The blue and yellow banner is that of my captain, Lybeck and that red-bearded bastard has to be Urell, the field colonel under our commander."

As the youth started to take a step forward to his fellows a half-mile in the distance, Thyssen put his spear across his path. "Look closer, kid."

"I'm no kid, ya damn slave," Rogan sneered at him, but did trail his gaze. Rogan's mouth fell open. "Are they prisoners?"

Thyssen said, "Those men with them are officers of this

army you fought. Their colors are red and white, that of Nungal. That fat one is Ransim, one of the squad commanders. I think that tall one with short hair is called Harland."

"Who cares?"

"A real dickhead."

"How do you know that?"

Thyssen shrugged. "He kinda looks like one, no?"

Anger boiling over, Rogan swept his blade across the air as if could kill them all and snapped, "What in hades are they…"

Bodyne joined them and said, "They look awful chummy."

"The backstabbing bastards," Rogan hissed, eyes full of confusion. "What in all of hell did they…"

Thyssen stepped forward, his face close to Rogan's. "You are the last survivor and I don't understand what happened in this battle of the war between the Shynar Lords. Nonetheless, we need to get out of here."

"We?" Rogan gave him a smile. "You have some speaking balls for a freed slave, spearman."

Thyssen gestured over at the wagons gathering up the clutter from the field. "Night is nearly here. We are cloaked enough as it is from those men." He knelt and pulled the cloak off his dead master. "Wrap this around yourself and those pricks over there will figure you the taskmaster."

"I've gotta get outta here," Rogan said, but took the cloak and swung it about his shoulders, putting the hood up over his shock of auburn hair. "Where are the horses?"

"Huh?" Thyssen near to laughed.

"The place smells like horseshit, or whatever those beasts of war they brought through," Rogan stated and then frowned. "Of course it does."

"Monsters from the Dark Continent with big horns of Nungal," Thyssen said. "When the Calvary of Kamala-ur swept through and saw them, they ran. They didn't much clean up after their mounts."

Unsure just how much manure mingled with the blood

and guts around him, Rogan again fell to cussing the situation. Suddenly, he gripped a pouch on his waist belt. "At least I still have the jewels for this fight."

"Congratulations." Thyssen gave him a mock bow.

Rogan's eyes narrowed at him. "I still have my balls, too, spearman."

"Just go with us," Bodyne said quiet, as if they would hear so far away. "We can get out in the night but not that way north."

A few steps into their move, Rogan recalled Thyssen's words...*I don't understand what happened in this battle of the war between the Shynar Lords.* Rogan remembered his father, Jarek, dealing with the kings over that ivory colored mammoth and not being a part of the armed fight. He didn't see his father, his sister Gale, or any of this close kindred in that bunch looking through the evening light.

But he remembered the fight.

Shoulder to shoulder with men from his stripe or similar mercenaries, Rogan had been close to the front that attacked King Nungal's forces. They were all told how bad of a man Nungal lived, something about little boys and goats, and that more gold would be had once his head became propped on a pike.

Rogan and the men around him fought hard, even if the first ranks were hit hard by long bowmen and lances. The barbaric fighters cut through these pike men fast. Rogan recalled leaping up onto one of the long pikes that had been dropped and draped over the belly of a stout fallen soldier. He'd balanced on the great shaft like a beam and cut the top of another soldier's head off.

Their brains were gray, just like a Kelt's but they died easier. In time, his forces were crushed back, overwhelmed by so many men and horses.

Their heads turned as a trumpeting sound echoed south.

She looked up at Thyssen. "We better avoid the south, too."

"We need to get leaving," Thyssen agreed with her. "But I wonder what lies more to the south? Come along, let us look over that ridge. We can skid the edge of the field and get out through the grassy low lands."

Rogan walked with them and muttered, "There is no *we* here."

Thyssen said, "You set us free, but until we get changed and out of here, we are still slaves and you are a lone survivor of a mercenary army."

"So," Rogan nodded once. "Our lives are both worth a bucket of crap?"

Bodyne shot him a look, but kept watching where she stepped through the mass of dead bodies already laid out at the perimeter. "My, my, not dim after all. Sharp one for such a big kid, isn't he?"

"I'm no kid," Rogan corrected her. "I'm twenty-five winters old."

Thyssen smirked. "Me too."

After Rogan scanned Thyssen's lined face, he spat. "Bullcrap."

Chuckling, Thyssen explained, "It's not the years, it's the mileage. I'm from far away from this shithole on the edge of the desert."

"You know I'm not from here and only a part of this army because of the gift to the gods or whatever the hell that hairy beast is supposed to be."

"Gift to the gods?" Thyssen slurred his words. "Why would the damned gods want a hairy elephant?"

"Why do wizards cast spells more than they screw?" Rogan snapped back, near to stumbling over a dead men's legs. "This world is crazy."

Bodyne and Thyssen glanced at each other once and kept looking down as they walked in the dimming light free of the rows of corpses. Bodyne replied, "With hair and eyes that color, no one would take you for a local anywhere near here."

Thyssen said, "Neither one of us are going north."

With a dismissive wave, Rogan promised, "I'll ride right

through those pricks and cut the balls off Lybeck and Urell as I go."

"If you had a horse," Thyssen put in the talk.

Bodyne quipped, "Or a hairy elephant."

"Damn you both."

"You'll be dead, first, if you try that ride or run," Thyssen vowed. "I've thought of escape many times in the past months."

Rogan sighed. "I bet you have. Thinking only gets your brain riled up. Action comes from the soul, not the brain."

"To the west of here is the boundless desert and further south past Irem lies the start of the great southern sea. Our only hope out of this realm is to the east and to skirt about that land north of here."

Rogan looked east. "The land beyond here is the place of giants." He then faced them again. "That's what they told us as we approached."

"Scared?" Thyssen speculated.

"I will tell you once I see one. I don't fear a story."

"I am," Thyssen affirmed as they all knelt before the ridge at the lower portion of the battlefield. "Scared, I mean."

"Yeah?"

"Only a dumbass doesn't fear giants."

Bodyne offered, "He's a brutal man, a Kelt, full of heavy bravado. He doesn't scare easy. His mind won't let him. You heard him."

Rogan gave her a smile.

She smiled back. "He sure isn't scared of hiding under dead men."

"My name is Rogan. I'm the son of Jarek of the Caucus Mountains. I am Keltos until I die, then I shall go beyond to be with my kindred."

Thyssen pointed beyond the valley into the murky light of the half moon, "Good for you, kid. If that prick sees us, you'll not see your happy homeland again. Your dead kindred will kick yer ass for dying stupid, I bet."

"Damn!" Rogan reacted to the sight before them and pushed both of them down for cover. "Ask for a giant, and one shows his face."

"Mercy, goddess," Bodyne prayed and lowered her head to the grasses.

"Well, that's where the trumpet sound came from," Thyssen stated as two teamsters led in a huge creature, four-legged, hirsute and sporting long tusks. They stopped by the giant man who stood flanked by others that fought against Rogan's army.

Rogan sounded confused as he said, "That's the mammoth from our side. I saw her only this morning, that she was to be gift to the gods." His voice fell as horses arrived, carrying Lybeck, Urell, and others of his own band. "Those sonsofbitches…"

"That is a Nephilim," Thyssen said quietly as he saw the looming figure near the elephant.

"I didn't take him for a dwarf."

"Never seen a white-haired mammoth." Thyssen shook his head but didn't take his gaze from the giant. "I don't know if it's Azrag from the south or another. He is supposed to live closer to here."

"Azrag? Doesn't matter," Rogan murmured, staying down lower himself. "He's getting on that mammoth like it's a horse."

Thyssen peeped over the edge and then hid again. "Your fellows are saluting him and taking up saddlebags from the other side."

"Not my fellows, the backstabbing pricks." Eyes closed, Rogan recalled them giving out orders, for flanking moves all that…but they hadn't joined them in the rear guard. *The bastards,* he cursed them, *led to our deaths, and for what? Why kill us all?*

"Huh, wonder how much gold is in there? Enough to pay for your lives?"

Eyes open, Rogan observed them once more close. He thought of how much his body ached from the battle, how that soldier with the axe had nearly killed him, and would've, save for the strength of his father's sword to deflect that blade.

His body surged, hungering for revenge on them all. After he watched a few more moments, Rogan lay down by them to hide as well. He looked deep into the sky at the wispy clouds, barely visible in the encroaching nightfall, and mouthed salty profanities.

"That's some mouth, kid," Thyssen declared, also looking up.

"I don't know why Wodan spared me, but I'll see all of them dead. That will be what I will do."

"Ya make surviving sound so noble," Thyssen said and stifled a liquidy cough. "Ya made it out alive. Run like hell."

"I'm no coward."

"Doesn't make ya brave to live through a massacre only to get cut to pieces by more swords."

Bodyne peeked over the edge and then concealed herself too. "Surely they didn't get all these men killed over a hairy elephant?"

His head moving side to side slow, Rogan replied, "They all died so those pricks could, I don't know. That's insane." He paused, took a breath, and closed his eyes, seeing the battle formations again. "We came to fight. We came to kill. Those pricks across the way, they came to go to work. They had no passion and we would have carried the day."

Bodyne whispered, "But?"

"They fought in boxes, lines, waves for formations, not favoring a head-on fight. That and they had those monsters armored up."

Thyssen said, "You learned a good lesson, then. I can't believe you lived this long in life before you found it out."

"What?"

"My father is a general back where I come from, and real armies have tacticians to figure out ways to beat an enemy, even if it is tougher, and with more passion. Remember that later in life. Use your head, not just your arms and balls."

His eyes glowing in the night, Rogan swore, "Damn, I have

fought like this all my life and it has served me well."

"As I said," Thyssen mumbled. "Lucky to be alive, then."

"Burn in hell."

"Where are your brothers? They are all dead. You are the last one."

"So you remind me."

"Luck favored you or that damn god of yours, however you want it."

Rogan's body seethed as his crouch looked ready to uncoil. "My father. I don't see him or my sister in the camp back there. They had the mammoth." His voice went quiet as he said, "But they had sent him off before we began."

The mammoth trumpeted again and all three jumped a bit.

Thyssen lay his arm over Bodyne and squeezed Rogan's shoulder.

"Get off me."

Releasing him, Thyssen ordered, "Be smart. Don't charge down there to kill them searching for your father and sister. We all will die, too."

"Like I care that much for your lives."

"Listen, dammit." His look intensified on Rogan. "Then have a mind for your own life, fool kid."

"Piss off."

"Take a breath and we shall kill them another day."

His anger seething, Rogan looked at the edge of the ridge like he could see them all at once. His ire burned but he fought it down. Rogan then turned to face the battlefield again. The edges of the war zone appeared in an orderly fashion, so many of the dead laid out, not yet stripped of their armor, gold, and weapons.

The piles of corpses out further were of those ready for the pyre, already stripped and discarded. Further on to where he had hid, the masses were still laid out, appearing to him like scattered rats nests.

In time, someone would come for the taskmaster. Soon, maybe by morning, something would be discovered. Rogan needed sleep, but his legs needed to run even more.

Thyssen continued. "You are angry and it boils in you from your head to your balls, but take a clue and don't do it. Be smart and we…you…can escape."

"And I will." After a few breaths, Rogan closed his eyes, letting his ears and other senses take over. He heard the horses trotting, but their hoof beats faded away from them. He turned about and gazed over the ridge.

"We'll go in a little bit," Rogan told them with a balanced voice. "Let them get along, away from us."

"We?" Bodyne raised an eyebrow.

Rogan smiled. "Yeah, we."

CHAPTER TWO

Hard Life to Love

"I don't see him, Urell," the tall man said as he shaded his eyes from the rising sun that bathed the battlefield. The sound of an abrupt cry made him turn his head.

"Because he's not among the dead, Lybeck," the red-haired man clad in chain mail and leather leggings shouted. He didn't face Lybeck, even though he addressed him. Urell bellowed at a stocky man wearing a slave collar and drew his short axe from his saddlebags. "These scum slaves saw something and I'll wring it out of them."

His voice deep, but gentle, Lybeck again scanned the rows of dead soldiers laid out and said, "What did they see? They couldn't tell one mercenary from another."

"How many Kelts were there in the mercs?" Urell snapped as he stood up, hardly regarding two of their fellow soldiers on horseback who wandered lazily across the scene. As these two looked the lines of the dead over, Urell faced another of the slaves. This older slave, skinny, lean, and a mass of scar tissue, had just let go of his twin dogs to step forward to be questioned.

"Kelts?" Lybeck replied. "Just a few. He was a damn good fighter, too. The others were from all over, as you can see."

"Wasn't his father here, too?" Urell wondered, still studying the bodies, waving at the bodies with the small axe.

One of those on horseback, the chubbier of the two soldiers, said, "Jarek, the father of that Kelt, went off after they brought the mammoth up."

Lybeck stared at the soldier who spoke, saying, "Yes, Ransim, he did. There were no more of those cursed Kelts, a girl with the older man, but they all departed before the fighting began."

"I hate not knowing," Urell stated and then twirled his single axe head about, putting the pointy top toward the dog wrangler's throat. "Did you see any escape? Where are those that walked away from all this?"

"Urell, stop," Lybeck told him, distaste in his mouth as the taller soldier on horseback giggled like a child. "You seek to kill the chickens because a few other hens escaped the rabid coyotes' attack?"

His green eyes flaring toward Lybeck, Urell retorted, "Don't get all complex on me. You know our orders here. All the foreign guerillas had to be purged from the troops out here." He then looked to the laughing soldier and said, "Shut your ass, Harland. I fail to see such humor out of a merc attached to Nungal."

The tall soldier sat up very straight and ceased to laugh. His lips quivered as he failed to stifle his amusement, nor did he try to hide it. Lungs full of air, the man tried to hold himself still in the saddle. He failed.

Urell glowered at him and then faced the bodies again. "Jackass."

Harland whispered to Ransim, "I'll bet you a gold piece that they burnt Rogan's body last night with the first ones and have lost it."

Eyes tighter at that possibility, Lybeck said, "He's not here, that Rogan, and he's just one man, hardly that, a boy."

Urell turned to him. "You are going to tell me what trouble can he be?"

"Oh, not at all. I know where he came from, the tribes and the Keltos folks of the far north. No, we were lucky to have him as a fighter for this long. But he's wild and wanted nothing for this ordered life, just for gold and adventure." Lybeck grinned, a smile half-buried in the curls of his black beard. "Kind of like you."

His eyes wider and his jaw grinding so the pointed red moustache quaked, Urell fired back, "I'm not from those barbaric beasts. You know my kindred hailed from across the great land bridge until the mountains of Zenghaus." His manner softened some and he smiled back. "And yes, money and whores propels the souls of many a man in this world." He turned back to the slave. "Well?"

"Late in the evening," the dog wrangler muttered and then cleared his throat to speak louder. "There were a few slaves that counted the dead out on this field, but I haven't seen them again in our number."

His smile fading, Urell asked, "Are they known to you?"

The dog master nodded. "I could identify them, but they were from far away, the big man out here with the spear to make sure they were dead. That was a bad man. He was from far away from that place called Transalpina."

At that name, Lybeck, Urell and the two on horseback laughed. "Transalpina?" Lybeck repeated. "That's a world away."

Urell agreed. "If it is even real."

"Thynnes or Thyssen, I can't recall his name perfect," the slave said with a shrug. "Big man, built like a barrel. He had old eyes but hadn't lived long enough to get them."

"Poetic," Lybeck consented, scanning the field and focusing on the wagons that came up to remove more of the dead. "Anyone else?"

"One of the women that collect items, I didn't know her. However..." the slave jutted his chin toward a body that lay outside the rows of fighters. "...she served him, taskmaster Jakmurph there."

Urell took a few steps over and eyed the body. "One of the others said he was a master, yet he wears no insignia nor bears keys or cover."

"The body is stripped," the slave offered as he waved his callous hands about. "Another wears his cloak and has used his keys. I gamble if we searched long enough, we'd find collars on the ground in the muck."

Harland leaned off his horse, but gripped the reins tight as he said, "By the goddess's ass, your taskmaster lost an eye."

Ransim's nose flared as he observed this as well, saying, "Looks to be in the back of his brain. Damn that luck, huh?"

The slave regarded Jakmurph once more before he said, "The bugs are nesting in his eye socket well already. That's what happens when we let the bodies lay out too long. He's been dead a while."

Hand to his belly, Harland shifted his horse away from that scene, but no one could escape the stench of the bloated bodies on the battlefield.

After he sighed loud, Urell walked back to Lybeck, who shielded his eyes from the sun and gazed south. "What do you think?"

"Me? I think the Keltos boy Rogan survived and ran away amongst a few fleeing slaves that killed their master. He's long gone by now."

Nodding Urell cursed with color and admitted, "I would guess. Damn. I hate loose ends in any matter."

Lybeck yawned and waved for Urell to join him as he walked. "Leave these slaves to their labors. Grisly business indeed, but necessary in the light of war."

Deflated, Urell did walk on with Lybeck to an open trail leading away from the rowed-up dead men. Those on horseback followed along, Ransim handing a flask to Harland, who drank deep from it.

Eying him, Lybeck said, "He's one mutt from the mountains in this godforsaken world. He hired on to fight so he could get money spoils and get laid. He is probably running on to join up another army and do the same."

"Or starving out there in the badlands," Urell said with some glee in his tone.

"I won't debate his resourcefulness. I knew him a little, kind of a brooding youth, but he could snare a rabbit or snake and live off the land. His life means nothing to us."

"Unless his sword is turned on us with a new army and gets planted in my back." Urell's neck veins seethed as if he saw such a scene painted across the sky.

"If you fear such things for each young man you stabbed in the back like we did poor Rogan, you must not sleep well at night,"

Urell glared at him as they walked. "If I saw him dead, I'd sleep much better, I admit. How in hell do you sleep your own self? Draped in your moral code and love for a goddess best left forgotten in stone idols?"

"I sleep fine, it's the dreaming that the poppy plants help to ease. One tries to be a steady hand, even in this line of work we have. I understand your concern. I'd rather see Rogan dead than hear Rogan dead. However, one cannot always get what one desires."

"Well," Urell shook his head and looked back to the south, "he'll find little peace in that direction."

The two returned to their black horses and they all started away from the main battleground.

Harland returned the flask to Ransim and then pointed emphatically to a ridge overlooking the field. "Look there."

Ransim nodded and smiled. "I see them. Don't act like a dog in heat."

"Their heat is what I wanna taste," Harland said with glee. "I have seen them before in the service of Nungal, but they stay in the shadows. Look at those ladies!"

After Lybeck and Urell did look up, they saw the seven figures on horseback watching the field from a distance. Urell said, "Probably King Nungal's inner guard."

"Inner guard?" Harland grinned. "His has women with swords and bows guard his innards? I bet they guard more than that. Look at them. They are not from here. I can tell by their dark skin and ebony eyes."

Lybeck told Harland, "Watch that mouth or you might be seeing your own innards. The king likes what he likes."

"It's the end of the week." Harland still smirked. "I thought perhaps this was little boy day for the king? Could be, not dark lady day."

Ransim shot him a sour look and hissed, "Watch it, man."

Eyes rolled to heaven, Harland vowed in a fake, grand tone, "I shall behave. Let the heavens help me."

Ignoring them, Lybeck said, "I can smell the lords of Comunale roasting a heavy swine this morning. Let us go have some good pig for an early lunch. These men do brew fine ale. That will get us full and happy for the day."

Nostrils flaring, Urell said, "I wasn't sure if that smell was the pyres for the dead or fine swine."

Lybeck stopped, sniffed the air, and smiled. "They do smell the same. Let's hope they feed us pork."

Hand to his gut, Urell replied, "You are an ass."

Lybeck slapped him on the back. "Fret not on that Kelt Rogan. What trouble could he really be?"

*****

Rogan leapt off the mammoth's snowy haired head, his sword pointed down like a spear, and called out the name of his god. He dropped his complete weight onto the Nephilim and only the growling cry for "*WODAN*" caused Azrag to turn about.

The giant still smiled and locked eyes with the plummeting warrior from afar. The threats, jeers, and filthy words of the giant still in his ears, Rogan drove the sword down into Azrag's left eye as his full mass dropped down. His boots soon landed on the upper thighs of the Nephilim as all his force sent the blade deep into the skull of the giant, piercing and pulping Azrag's eye, driving the weapon on out the back of Azrag's enormous skull.

Azrag twisted, his baritone howl choked as his huge hands clutched Rogan's elbows. The giant dislodged the fighter from his self and he took a few steps. His heavy sandals stomped as his body trembled, still holding Rogan aloft. His twelve fingers fluttered. Rogan landed on his left hip, rolled up and over to his knees, still facing the giant as he landed on his feet.

Thyssen shouted at Rogan, "Forget Azrag. He's dead and doesn't realize it. Get after his damned men!"

Up on his feet again, Rogan saw Thyssen spearing one of the men who had been raiding the small caravan of wagons, but they had paused in their actions as their leader became imperiled. Rogan had no spear to kill as Thyssen did, but his hands went to his belt, pulling out the matching daggers there.

He bent lower and tackled one of the followers of Azrag as he stood transfixed at the giant staggering. Rogan's body block threw the sunburnt man's body into one of the wagon wheels. The two daggers in Rogan's hands made fast work of him, each dagger striking on a different side of the man's body three times: Kidneys, chest, and neck.

"To hell with you all," Thyssen roared, his spear withdrawing from the chest of one turbaned man, to have the bronze ball of the weapon smash back into the mouth of another. Thyssen swung the spear about with perfect elegance, slitting the throat of the smash-mouthed raider. He swung the ball end again, ruining another's mouth in a shower of scarlet and flying yellow teeth.

Bodyne grabbed the whip of one of the dead drivers of the caravan and faced a raider who snapped out of his shock at his master being ran through by Rogan. His amazement lasted too long as Bodyne unleashed the whip and wrapped it about his neck.

Quick to kick him in the groin, Bodyne doubled the man

over. She then pulled a small mallet from her robes, an instrument Rogan guessed could be used to tenderize meat…but Bodyne drove it down into the turban of the raider. The man gagged twice, shook as if cold, and then hit the dirt. He convulsed and broke wind loud.

"He died fast," Rogan remarked as he took up the fallen sword of a raider. "Unlike his giant lord."

Bodyne looked along with Rogan at Azrag's gyrations, shivering and staggering toward the largest of the wagons. This great cart held a large, covered, rectangular box like a transport cart. Azrag's six fingered hands slapped on the doors of the compartment and he wavered on his sandaled feet, yet didn't fall.

Thynnes skewered another raider in the pelvis and shouted, "Why doesn't the sonofabitch fall down?"

"I can smell his brains," Rogan noted, just as the double doors of the cart flew open. "He can't figure out that he's…dead." The sight from within the cart made him stand as still as the raiders that had watched Azrag dying.

A raw voice screeched from the compartment, higher than what he figured a man would produce, but the cry wasn't one of terror nor of a terrified woman. The originator of the tone kicked one of the raiders across the face with leather boots that rose to her knees and then hit another man in the jaw with a left uppercut that Rogan would've been proud to mete out.

The woman, very tall and long-geared, swung a short sword from a gloved right hand. She cut down a raider that came too close, slicing him across the face and twirling his jaw around backwards. His horrid scream would last until he bled out. She then stabbed forward twice, slaying the two men she'd struck on her appearance.

Thyssen stood beside Rogan and said, "We thought they needed saving?"

The woman growled and noted the staggering Azrag. She looked him over and then at Rogan and Thyssen. "Which one of you did this? Whose sword is that?"

Some panic in his tone, Thyssen said, "Oh crap fire and spare the flint rocks, if that's his woman…"

Rogan shook his head. "Why would Azrag's men surround and intimidate a caravan with his woman in it?"

Thyssen shrugged. "She looks big enough to take him. Maybe she's tired of being screwed by him."

His head tilted a bit, Rogan had to grunt his agreement. He spoke up to tell her, "It's my sword."

Azrag fell to his knees at last, eye to eye with the tall woman. One eye, at least.

She reached out, gripped the pommel of the sword with both hands, and placed a boot in the giant's chest for more leverage. Her teeth clenched, she made no sound as the blade slowly slid from the head of the Nephilim. Her eyes wide a moment, they then narrowed, studying the heavy sword.

From behind her in the wagon emerged a hooded form, hunched over, and using two canes to navigate out and onto the ground.

"It's a fine blade, mother," she said to the slow moving figure from the wagon. "Very weighty indeed."

Hood pushed back on the new arrival, Rogan saw the persona indeed that of an elderly woman, sporting a long, withered face and hoary white hair.

"Kill him, Elisa," she stated, facing Azrag.

"I can't," Elisa told her and sighed loud like a girl love lost, not a six-foot-plus killer in battle leathers. "He's dead now."

"Take his head," the old woman told her, her long nailed thumb drawing across her own throat as she still clutched a cane. "We can have some use of it." She then put her canes down and start to rub her palms together. Each took on a glow of orange and she waved them at the giant. The orange hue slapped onto the fallen giant like a liquid and covered over him fast, but never dripped off him. The orange glow grew even brighter and then went away. "He'll be easier to cut now."

Her right foot back and planted, Elisa swung the sword,

connecting with the right side of Azrag's neck. The weapon delved in deep, but didn't pass through. She yanked the sword out, reared back, and swung again. This time she chopped in deeper and struck something that gave out a loud crack.

"Found the neck bones," Thyssen affirmed.

"She's done that before," Rogan figured aloud. "Maybe not to a giant."

Again, Elisa swung the blade like an axe, this time striking the left side of Azrag's neck. Still, the Nephilim kept his head. Her full lips peeling back, she struck again, and again, on the left side of Azrag's neck. Breathing hard a few times, she reeled about and drove the sword into the right side.

Rogan walked up behind Azrag as Elisa stepped back, looking at the sword and then at Rogan.

She snapped, "Who carries a damned oversized weapon like this?" She threw it down and spat at the hilt, but missed. "You'd wear out on the battlefield using it all the time. Damn thing is too dense."

Rogan stepped onto the calves of the kneeling giant and gripped Azrag's long tresses. "He still isn't dead." His knee in the giant's back, Rogan wrenched the head to the left. A sound not unlike a man biting a fresh apple echoed out and Rogan cricked the head from the giant's neck. As he did, Rogan jumped back, still sporting the head, and avoided most of the gouting blood spewing up from the shoulders of the giant.

Elisa and her mother moved back, but cursed in unison as the last beats of the giant's heart ceased, denoted by the jets of blood stopping.

Rogan looked down at the head and then at the two women.

The old woman said, "I'm Yana, we are not from around here."

As Thyssen and Bodyne joined Rogan, he didn't have time to speak, for Elisa blurted out, "You stupid pricks! Why in the hell did you attack them?"

Rogan's mouth remained open and Azrag's head lowered a

little in his grip.

Thyssen offered, "Your caravan was under attack, the raiders were killing everyone out here with you."

Elisa's brown eyes flared. "So out of the goodness of your hearts, you decided to attack them? With a giant along?"

Waving his spear at dead bodies, Thyssen said, "Your period of mourning for your fellow travelers is inspiring."

"Thyssen is putting honey on a boar's ass," Rogan said. He held up the head a bit and then turned to face the huge, hairy elephant. "He had the hairy beast, the great mammoth from my true folk."

"You are a jester if you expect me to believe you intervened for that creature." Elisa blinked, searching for the words. "That monster…"

Yana smiled a dim grin of jagged teeth, "I was peering through the door crack, young man, that was quite a move jumping off that beast's head. And it let you."

"I told you she was mine, and of my people," Rogan reminded her.

Yana asked, "What's its name?"

"Elisa," Rogan said with no humor, but Thyssen burst out laughing at his jest, near to bending in half at the jape.

"Piss on you," Elisa declared, her chest swelling up. "You robbed me of my prize of a giant just to get a damned hairy elephant back?"

Eyes on the head in his hands, Rogan shrugged and threw the head over near the women. "I don't want it."

"You dumbass," Elisa snarled, all sweetness gone from her lips as they peeled back to show a tigress' teeth. "I don't want his head…"

"I think yer mom does." Rogan pointed at Yana. "Nice wizard move, you did there before, ma'am."

The old woman nodded with vigor.

"I wanted his damned life," Elisa shouted, then her tone dropped. Her gloved hands slapped the chain vest over the battle leathers on her chest. "I, Elisa of Larak, the killer of giants."

A smile lurking amongst his unkempt beard, Rogan replied, "I'm Rogan from Lake Asshole of Caucasia, deflowerer of virgins and lover of great capacity."

Yana giggled at his words as she yanked back some locks of Azrag's head, studying the cut on his neck.

Humorless, Elisa shot back, "How many giants have you slain?"

"Who counts?"

She waved her left hand at him, dismissing the fighter. "You have killed none but Azrag and see nothing in it but a dead body to brag over."

Rogan eyed Thyssen. "Who's bragging? Better to get rid of that thing from the earth. I didn't wanna eat his soul or whatever the hell you wanted."

"No?" Elisa shot back.

"Nope. That's fuckin' weird. We just wanna escape this place."

Elisa and Yana both turned to glare at him at the same time. Yana spoke, asking, "Escape from what?"

Rogan hesitated, but Thynnes said, "No big story. We survived that war up north and are trying to get the hell away. Slavery is no easy march for anyone."

While Bodyne nodded in frank agreement, Elisa clucked and said, "They will kill me first before I got under a collar."

Bodyne said, "You will hope so. This is all just wasting time. We have horses and supplies now from the giant's people. Let's get going further and faster." She looked from Elisa to Rogan. "You two can compare cocks later if you wish."

Yana agreed. "She's correct. We need to move on." Her withered hand went to her upper chest and she clutched a thin necklace of tiny objects, closing her eyes. "Others will follow and find these fools and our dead friends."

Rogan looked her over. "Are you a necromancer?"

Eyes open, Yana winked at him. "Why ask an old lady a

thing like that?"

"You wear a necklace of tiny bones and jewels like the shamans of my homeland. They grab them and pray or have visions, too…or at least we fall for it as well."

Elisa spoke up to say, "Mother isn't a damned necromancer, but a worker in many of the magical arts."

Thyssen took a canteen from one of the dead raiders and unscrewed the top. "Could she miracle our asses away from here?"

Though she gave Thyssen an acerbic look, the tall woman turned to the cart. "I'll drive once we gather up what we can."

The old woman opened the doors to the cart and let go of her canes to seize an object inside. Looming behind her, Rogan observed her. At first, Yana tried to conceal the object, then stepped aside, opened her hands, and then covered it up again.

Thyssen asked, "What does she got there?"

Elisa leered at him, saying, "Never you mind."

"What does she conceal?" Thyssen asked Rogan.

"It's a rock," Rogan replied, with a bored look. "Just a black rock."

Yana closed the doors to the cart and went back to the corpse of the giant. She patted Azrag's head lightly. "The body of a Nephilim will fetch a really fine amount in Azar, don't you know."

Thyssen wondered, "Won't his friends or brothers be pissed he's dead?"

"Likely," Yana replied. "Azrag held territories south of Nodd, east of here. We don't want to go that way, anyhow. We should push on more southwest. He was wandering near here, probably headed to Irem with his new beast."

Eyes studying the heavy sword from his own back in the sunlight, Rogan snorted the single word, "We?"

Thyssen was quick to ask, "Why Irem?"

"They all are headed to Irem, city of pillars," Yana told him.

Rogan asked, "Who?"

"The giants, you fair-haired dumbass," Elisa fired back. "They go at the bidding of their Nephilim king, Marduk, firstborn of the fallen. He has given an order for them all to congregate at Irem every so often. Him and that prick Zazaeil."

Bodyne muttered, "Sounds like a place to avoid."

"Yeah," Rogan agreed. "We don't have to go to Irem."

Yana said, "I still remind you all that the head and body of Azrag will fetch pretty monies from those at Azar."

"Azar?" Rogan questioned as he yanked free a turban from a fallen raider. He started to clean off his sword with it as he asked, "Where is that?"

Yana said, "Another days ride to the south east. Azar sits on the sea, north of the Valley of Despair, and on the road to Irem."

Thyssen smiled. "A port city? Good. We can sail away from this damned place." He watched Rogan walk over to the great hairy elephant. "Hey, I really don't think you can sail with that thing?"

Rogan replied, "How do you intend to haul that body to Azar? In the wagon or on a few horses?" He patted the side of the mammoth. "She can carry his body very easy since he rode her like a steed."

Elisa took a few steps near the hairy beast. "She?"

Again, he patted the side of the elephant. "Aliene."

"Aliene?" Bodyne near to chuckled. "That's a pretty name for an elephant."

"Well," Rogan explained. "That's Keltos for *beautiful*."

They all exchanged looked aside from Rogan, who patted the huge beast harder.

Thyssen broke up laughing. "You two wanna be alone?"

"Fuck off," Rogan spat. "You and your girlfriends won't be carrying Ass-rag anywhere without Aliene's help."

Elisa cursed Rogan, but Thyssen only laughed. "Yeah, I reckon the snake handlers and bone rollers in Azar will pay us damn well for him."

Rogan nodded. "So they say."

Thyssen said, "I bet the giants are worth a lot dead, as well."

He and Rogan observed Yana still clutching the bones of her necklace and petting the forehead of the dead giant. "We need to get the hell away from here."

Rogan grumbled in his gut and then stared at the sky

"Yeah?" Thyssen prodded him.

Rogan sheathed the long blade on his back. He fell silent. Eyes closed and head down, Rogan searched his thoughts and ignored the desires of his heart to pray.

He thought only of his father and sister.

Rogan gave a single nod.

CHAPTER THREE
Walk Away

The next morning dawned in the southern Shynar colony city of Comunale to the sounds of tortured screams down the avenue of justice. This street, paved by cut stones and intricately laid out by a previous king than Nungal, provided a good avenue as Lybeck and the soldiers made their way on horseback to the palace of the Lord. The cheers of the crowd, the giggles of children, and the bickering of women in the carnivals of the morning show filled their ears near to what the cries of the dying did.

Lybeck grimaced at the display, but Urell smirked, saying, "We all celebrate in our own way."

"These are supposed to be civilized folk?" Lybeck said, rolling his eyes at the men hung up by their hands on ropes, their feet nailed to the wood platforms and genitals stretched with metallic pinchers. "And they call those I employ as mercenaries barbarians?"

"All a matter of degree," Urell shrugged. "They let their hair down out here, and revel in the violence as long as it isn't unto their own people."

"A few of those men *are* their own folk."

Harland spoke up to say, "Traitors and a few rotten failures, thus be it to such malodourous scum, aye?"

Lybeck again wore an indignant look. "I'll be glad to head back northeast with my men, they are just happy to be clean, filthy in a whorehouse, and then cleaned up again."

"As we all," Urell agreed. "It's been a day since we saw that battlefield and I shall be smiling when I leave here."

A glance over his shoulder, Lybeck asked, "Where are your men? My dozen underlings are not far behind us."

"I sent them south yesterdays to recon after that Kelt, if he lives."

Sighing, Lybeck turned his head to avoid seeing the blood spurt as a traitor's head popped off from a noose. "Rogan's body wasn't among the dead and I'd sooner he was gone than in my path."

Urell laughed as they rode on past the festivities and to the first gate of the palace of Nungal. "You should relax more, friend. I doubt he'd put it together you sold them out as a part of all this."

"Sold them out? You make me sound like such a firebrand traitor. I never anticipated all of them dying like dogs and that it was all over…"

"A hairy elephant and whores?" Urell laughed again as they all four dismounted. "You were paid well beforehand to supply the forces for the game amongst kings. You are to retire and give up all this, so this last payout was your legacy."

Lybeck climbed off his horse and winced. "The aches and pains are getting to be too much. I had not sanctioned a slaughter when bringing this together. I hadn't thought the scales would be so uneven in the battle."

His red beard grinding, Urell gave him a tapered look. "Don't play fragile on me, old man. You wanted them all dead and yourself clean of it. Your balls are hanging low because you think that Kelt survived and might understand you were the one who suckered his countrymen into it all."

Killer of Giants

Ransim cleared his throat and said, "There were but a few Kelts and their neighbors. Rogan wouldn't possibly hold such anger over a few lives."

"They live by the blood feud, those wild-assed men of the ice and snow," Urell turned and looked north. "You should hope he returns to the unkind mountains and not ever chooses to cross your path."

Looking at his hands, his fingers quivered. Lybeck made tight fists and said, "Let's hope for that."

Harland glanced about the crowd. "Where are the whores?"

Ransim took a draw off his canteen and scanned for what Harland asked for, but their search came up short. Two escorts from the king emerged from the alcove by the entrance. Both women wore shimmering kilts colored gold, which contrasted their obsidian skin. Naked to the waist, the barefoot girls took each Lybeck and Urell by their elbow and walked with them.

Their dire looks to Harland and Ransim told them to stay outside the gate of the palace. They then insisted the two they led take off their boots before they stepped onto the lush carpets that trailed through the palace. The two men exchanged a look and tried to breathe steady. Seeing as they were in the king's palace, they readily complied.

After they traversed the vast dining areas of the first floor of the brick palace, the escorts took them out onto a vast, but enclosed, courtyard, replete with small pools. Lybeck noted a few ponds were for bathing or copulating, and a couple other shallow ones were for tiny swimming fish. He figured in a pinch, these royals would mix and match.

In a shaded corner, being fanned by two more black women holding giant leaves, sat King Nungal and another older man, dressed in similar shiny clothing. Both soldiers had seen King Nungal before, but never at such a close meeting. Though he had skin tanned by the sun, it shined in the light with an oily quality Lybeck guessed an application. Though unable to guess his advanced age, Nungal's eyes sat weary, even if he smiled a mouthful of good teeth. The other man remained unknown to Lybeck, but Urell stepped away from him and took a knee with sudden respect.

"Kamala-ur, your servant, Urell," the red-headed rough man said as he bowed his head in reverence.

Lybeck stepped nearer to the scene, his feet irritated a bit by the grain of the stones under them. When Kamala-ur turned in his seat to face them and give a nod to Urell, Lybeck's mouth fell open.

"What is it?" Kamala-ur asked. "You expected me to be a pampered little prick like Nungal, here?"

Blinking and searching for words, Lybeck gave a quick bow to the thick-muscled man, also a king.

Kamala-ur laughed once, bare feet tapping like a dancer, but his huge shoulders gave off the threat of a man ready to tackle anyone near him. "Don't fear any anger from Nungal. He knows he's a spoiled prick."

Eyes glancing to Nungal as Urell stood again, the king smiled and sipped from a ceramic goblet.

"One doesn't get a face like this from an inheritance," Kalama-ur informed them, raising his rough chin and pointing at both sides of his face. Indeed, the ruler sported coarse skin, ravaged by the sun, scarred along the left jawline, and distorted in places. Lybeck figured that man for having been in a battle or twenty in his life. "I fought for my gilded throne, while Nungal came from the lucky side of the bedsheets, but, that doesn't matter." He turned, raised a goblet to Nungal and sipped his own drink with a gulp. "We are all just game players now, sending other men off to die like cobras and mongooses in a fighting pit, or mongeese, whatever the hell it is, right?"

Arising, Urell said, "My lord, it is good to see you. We are about to head out back to our homes, sirs."

"Yes, is that true?" Nungal put down his cup. "That you cannot do, well, not to where you thought."

"Sir?" Lybeck wondered, then looked at the irregular-faced

Kamala-ur, trying to hide a panic in his soul. He truly feared he'd not live to spend his retirement and perhaps that moment arrived. "What is it?"

Nungal looked at a series of clay tablets and tiny pieces of parchment before him on the table. "There has been frantic testimony from the south that our ally Azrag's group was found dead along with many travelers." He looked up, eyes from Lybeck to Urell. "Somewhat savagely dispatched."

Urell said, "That is unfortunate."

"Azrag himself, too?" Lybeck asked, his voice full of surprise.

Nungal sighed as he nodded. "Ravens carry messages of truths."

"Yes." Kamala-ur inhaled sharp, rasping as he did so. "It damn well is. I love the ravens, they carry such words from afar. Anyway, the story from a survivor of the raid who lay in the dirt said a light-haired warrior killed Azrag and took his mastodon…"

"Mammoth," Nungal corrected.

"Whatever the hell, I get those confused like the mongooses. I'm the fucking king, I'll say what I want. Anyhow, he said a bearded, savage warrior killed the giant, cut off his head and left with the elephant."

"Damn," Urell mumbled.

"Taking the corpse with him," Kamala-ur affirmed and took a drink.

Lybeck asked, "You accept ravens messages and the words of a scared raider as complete truth?"

Kamala-ur's raw words barked out, "He was pissing blood as he talked, so I doubt he thought that story up." One of the women fanning him backed up a little but set her feet again soon. The fatigued skin under the ruler's eyes widened and he glared at the two. "Who in the hell can slay a giant like that?"

"That's why I doubted it," Lybeck replied, hands gripped behind his back. "It seems an unlikely thing."

"Things happen," Kamala-ur sighed, gesturing to one of the girls to refill his goblet. "I have also heard tell that not all of the Kelts in the merc army were accounted for. Is that fact or thing true?"

After a prolonged silence, Urell said, "We've heard a rumor of that, too."

Once he drank again, Kamala-ur asked, "It would be a real episode if some big Keltos fighter slipped away and slew our ally, right? It'd be a bigger gape if he killed him just to get a damned hairy elephant back."

Lybeck pondered the irony of that, how these leaders played with the lives of many on the battlefield over the prize of a mammoth to a Nephilim, but didn't mention it.

Nungal then spoke up to say, "I've dispatched ravens to all settlements and cities, putting a price on the head of this grimy Kelt if he shows his face."

Kamala-ur cleared his throat before saying, "An auburn-haired thug riding a hairy elephant should stand out to most, correct?"

Urell nodded. "Then he will be easy to find."

"But," Nungal said, swirling the wine in his cup. "Not so easy to kill. If he did slay Azrag, as said in these meager dispatches, a few salty bounty hunters will not get him down and dead so easily."

"So, you are nominated." Kamala-ur stood up with a slight groan. Much taller than Lybeck had guessed, the ruler inspired fear by his manner and harsh, scarred body. "You will be given more men and supplies for this endeavor, plus enough gold to attain your goal." He clapped his hands twice and turned back to his drink.

From a hall behind the fanning girls emerged a dozen figures dressed in light battle leathers. Each person looked like copies of each other: Black, lean women clad in leather thongs, and a top that covered but one breast…as each didn't have a right mammary.

"This is Kylene and others from her sisterhood in Kush," Kamala-ur explained without looking up at them lining up.

"That's a place on another continent."

Lybeck had heard of it but didn't say that.

"Before you ask," Nungal said in a teasing voice, "each is of a warrior sect where their right breast is seared off as teen girls."

Urell's eyes widened and he nodded fast as if he understood.

Kamala-ur said, "Makes them better shots with a bow. They are indeed wicked shots, aye Kylene?"

The woman he named stepped forward from her sisters and looked the two over. Her nostrils widened but she didn't speak. Her long locks of hair rattled, beads striking the other jewels fixed to other strains as she moved.

"Kylene's sisterhood are to be delivered to the port of Azar on your way. Each carries a gift for Zazaeil."

Zazaeil. Lybeck hid a strong urge to wince at the demon's name, but Urell's face tightened.

A smirk developed on his face as Kamala-ur stated, "You won't have to see him, as I don't know when he will arrive. They will serve as good support in case you do find that tough-necked savage. You will be paid very well when I get that Kelt's head back in my lap. Remember that."

Urell bowed his head and took a step back.

Kamala-ur added, "I'll also be sending along the Kaldwell twins."

With a slight start, Urell raised his head again.

"I trust you know of the twins?" Kamala-ur questioned him.

"Yes sir, the grandsons of god," Urell's voice returned, very dry. "They will be a welcome addition to the troopers."

Lybeck held his countenance, knowing very well how much Urell lied through his beard then. The twins, Batasta and Binje, were notorious for various reasons, their supposed descent from a Nephilim among them.

When both leaders looked at him for a reaction, Lybeck said, "This seems a great effort for one savage on the run, these great women warriors, more soldiers, and even the mighty

Kaldwells?"

Nungal's face went caustic. "This savage is making us look foolish out there. If word spreads he escaped our grasp and killed a giant, what airs will this put on him? Our station will be bruised badly. You go and bring him or his head back to us so that all know who rules in this region. I cannot be made to look foolish."

Nodding, Lybeck accepted their words.

Kamala-ur asked, "You knew him, right? This Kelt?"

"Yes. Rogan, son of Jarek," Lybeck confessed freely. "He's quite the fighter, a real bastard."

Smiling, Kamala-ur said, "I like him, his meddle speaks to me loud, but he must die. I can't afford to let some swinging dick kid Kelt to brand me as ridiculous. If he had just stolen the mammoth, I'd let Azrag worry about how stupid he looked returning home with just his colossal dick in his hand. Since he slew the giant, it raises brows all over."

Nungal reminded them, "You will be going into a realm where the giants and others of their kind may roam. Have a care as you travel. The twins will be proper help during that trip. This Rogan may feel safe amongst that cover, but once the ravens deliver their messages, he won't find much shelter."

Once the two departed from the presence of the rulers, the women of Kush behind them, Lybeck looked over at Urell. "This isn't what I had in mind for the next damned adventure in my life."

"You'll be paid well."

"One has to be alive to spend it," Lybeck reminded him.

Urell frowned as they returned to where their boots sat. "He's one accursed savage, that's all."

"Batasta and Binje, wonderful."

Eyes closed tight, then open very wide, Urell replied, "Those two melodramatic bastards, that's about all I needed."

"Perhaps the twin sons of a Nephilim can't hurt in our trip." He peeked up as Kylene and the others stopped and watched them.

Urell whispered, "You really want them along?"

"Them or the twins?"

"Either."

"I'd rather have a big tooth pulled fast with no strong liquor aforehand, but we have no real choice."

Urell grunted, and then said, "At least they may throw off any giants we encounter. There really aren't that many in that territory, plus, word is they are heading to Irem to see Marduk."

"Yeah."

"Some family gathering. I don't know, really."

"Let's hope that's all crap."

*****

"He'd be worth more unskinned up," the deep voice filled the room as the man walked about the headless form of Azrag. The huge man who turned up his lamps to better shed light on the body on his long slab didn't excuse himself when he walked past Elisa and Rogan. He gave Thyssen a hard look as the stout man stared from the doorway, but he focused more on the body. The man showed little fear of the others, probably because he stood a foot taller than them and had a body constructed of flesh like cordwood.

"Ludvig," Yana named him as she briefly held the bones on her neck. "I took from him only a few things I need for my magicks."

The white-haired man rubbed his bushy beard and bent down, hands then to his knees, eyeing the body close. "Yes, I know that. The eyes and such things. That's what all the wizards want nowadays."

"I got there first."

Ludvig gazed up from Azrag's stump of a neck and focused on her. "I don't care." He then walked about the body again, looked at the feet.

Thyssen muttered, "All six toes are there."

Ludvig snapped, "If I want to hear a bitch cry, I'll kick the dog, you runt."

Rogan half-smiled at the remark, as Thyssen towered over most men, but not the curly haired Ludvig.

Not to be slighted, Thyssen looked at the floor at Ludvig's feet.

His shaggy eyebrows drawn down, Ludvig asked, "Are you delayed in your mind or just drunk?"

Thyssen wore an innocent look and said, "I was just counting your toes."

"Five, assface," Ludvig replied and walked about the body again. "My parents were just big fuckers." He gestured at Rogan with his right hand. "Did you count your boyfriend's fingers, toes, and balls to make sure they match up? He's no tiny squirt."

Though Thyssen's face turned redder, Rogan shook his head a little and said, "I'm sure you don't get many of these in here."

"I don't recall saying," Ludvig whispered in a flat voice. He faced Yana and said, "I'll give you top rate, woman. He *is* rare, though, but there are quite a few that will miss him now that he's departed. I'll get rid of all of him, well, divide him up so much no search party will be able to tell."

"Thank you, Mr. Ludwig," Yana said, hands from her necklace gripping the handles of her canes.

"If you want any portion of him, his balls, liver, or heart, let me know and I'll pickle them for you for later."

Bodyne clutched her stomach and pushed past Thyssen to get down the hallway.

Ludvig watched her go and turned his face back to Yana. "I hope she makes it to the outside. I'd hate it if she pukes on my rugs."

Yana said, "Again, thank you, sir. I knew I could count on you here for your services at the edge of Azar."

He gave her a nod and looked at the head on a separate slab. "Yeah. I never liked him, Azrag, anyhow. It'll be a pleasure to get rid of him from this world."

Elisa asked, "What if they come after you? What if some idiot that buys a hunk of a giant talks and they come after you?"

"They?" He turned to her and sighed. "It's you all they will want dead, not me. I'm just a business man here. Besides, *they* all bring me a body to get rid of in here now and again. I know too much and where the bodies aren't buried this side of Madron."

"Madron?" Thyssen asked. "City of the Gorgons? You've been there?"

Ludvig's eyes gave a piercing look to the spearman. "I'm alive."

"I see that," Thyssen replied.

"Then I've never fuckin' been there to dance with the Sanrevelle sisters." He then paused and looked to Rogan. "You all run along. I'll deal with Yana more and hold your gold till you depart."

Thyssen's arms dropped to his sides.

Ludwig eyed him again and then went to the long cabinet by the head on the slab. "Safer that way really, as once you are to move on, come back and you will be paid. You all are so damn tough, but I'd hate to think of you getting robbed after you get drunk tonight, I might giggle my fuckin' balls off."

Outside the long dwelling made of bricks, Rogan looked at some of the coins Yana had given him. "Enough to eat up, get drunk and laid on."

Thyssen made a fist on his first payment and said, "We need to get new clothes, no matter what our future holds."

Rogan peered down at his bloody trousers. "Not a bad idea." He walked with Thyssen over by the horses and looked to where Aliene stood by a nearby creek. The giant beast drank from the creek and then sprayed itself with water. Though night had fallen on Azar, several children laughed and watched the elephant in motion. "She's a bright girl. I need a damned proper bath, too."

"Well, look there," a voice cut through the night, causing

both men to twist sharp about. "Look what just walked up? Gold on two legs."

Rogan and Thyssen watched as the two men stepped from the shadows, each armed with a crossbow, strings notched back. Neither made a move as the two closed the distance to a few yards. One of the strangers stood near to as tall as Rogan, but his tunic and kilt couldn't hide his emaciated frame or ruddy skin punctuated with tiny boils. The other, shorter, dressed in a similar fashion, sported a large belly, no boils, but reeked of sour wine.

The taller one asked, "One of you be Rogan, the Kelt?"

Rogan replied, "Never heard of him."

"He's lyin' to us dad," the fatter one said with a quavering voice, his bow shaking a little. "Just shoot him now."

"Shut your mouth, kid," the father retorted, but didn't take his gaze from Rogan. "Not many fair-haired shitkickers with a hairy elephant around these days."

Rogan tilted his head a little. "Why would this Rogan fella you ask about be known that way?"

Both men grinned. Their teeth were dark and jagged. "Fool boy, dunno there is a price on your head?"

"Shoot him, dad, he's dangerous."

"I said shut up, Ephraim." The father motioned at Thyssen. "You back off, mister. We don't have a quarrel with you, unless you want to die with him."

Thyssen did step away from Rogan, using his spear like a walking stick, but he stepped away and toward Ephraim.

The father continued, saying, "Now, you untie that sheath cinch and let that big-assed sword fall from your back. If you try and draw it out, you'll be dead before you can say polish my pecker."

"I never say that when I draw my sword," Rogan said, looking at the other filing out of the dwellings and work house of Ludvig. He noted Bodyne on her all fours near the shrubbery, looking up at them. A look of realization on her face in the night, one that hadn't yet grabbed Elisa as she stretched her arms.

"I said undo that sword," the man insisted. "The order is dead or alive. Dead will be easier for us."

Rogan did unbuckle the strap and the sword drooped, but he held the leather and didn't let it fall. He turned his head and called out, "Aliene, Wodan."

At his words, the mammoth stirred from its labors of rooting in the creek with its trunk and swung about.

As the beast moved, the pair couldn't help but look at Aliene. When Bodyne screamed, their heads twisted the other way and Rogan swung his sheathed blade out and toward the father of the two. When he did this, Thyssen took a single step and stabbed out with his spear at Ephraim.

The chubby youth fired his bow, but the bolt only grazed Thyssen's left shoulder. Ephraim screamed as Thyssen's spear inserted into his girth a few inches.

The father also fired as the sword struck his bow, and his bolt went to the ground. In a few steps, Rogan's right hand pushed the bow down more and then he struck the thin man across the face with a left fist. He felt the bones in the man's cheek move under his blow.

As the father fell back a step, Rogan's clutch on the crossbow tightened. The weapon in his hand as his attacker hit the ground, Rogan gripped it tight by the firing shaft and swung it down. The handle and trigger smashed into the man's head, knocking free his tight kerchief wrap and caving in his forehead.

As the man fell limp, Rogan turned to the screaming Ephraim, who had fallen to his knees. Thyssen stepped forward and swiped, ripping open the younger man's large gut…and then accidentally unraveling the intestines within. Ephraim cried out in terror, grasping a few of the grisly loops as if he could put them back.

Thyssen speared Ephraim in the heart and twisted. The cries stopped after a few shots of crimson jetted in the night.

Elisa laughed and gave contemptuous applause.

Bodyne threw up again.

After they had all purchased new togs and been through a bathhouse, they stood outside lodgings for the night. Rogan and Thyssen eyed the brothel next door as Bodyne, resplendent in a fresh light robe and hood, waved at them, heading up to her room. Yana, clad in a different one-piece garment from her own stores, explained she felt content to sleep in the hammock swinging in their cart.

Elisa, clean but wearing a variation on her boots, leathers, and gloves, stood by the men as they talked.

Thyssen yawned and said, "Price on your head. Go figure."

Rogan shrugged. "Word travels fast." He looked to the night sky. "Damn ravens. What will those assholes think up next?"

"Pretty amazing they sent out a bounty so fast," Thyssen commented.

"After tonight," Rogan said. "I better go it alone. They don't want you, Bodyne, or killer of gnats here, or her mama."

Elisa frowned and a small smile crept on the left side of her face.

Rogan related, "You'll get dead if that stuff like dumbass and junior keeps happening. Best I climb on Aliene and head north up the coast."

Elisa pointed at the giant beast behind the hotel, grazing on a field of weeds and said, "You ought to get rid of that thing. Ludvig would want it for parts maybe. They will spot you for sure on it."

Rogan faked a wound to his chest. "That's barbaric." Thyssen laughed loud as Rogan went on to say, "She'll last longer than a horse in the open territory and she's four times as durable."

"Well," Elisa rolled her eyes, "isn't that just precious? I hope you two will be happy together."

Rogan replied, "Once I get some fun tonight and a bit of food, I'll be gone. You coming along as well?"

Elisa glanced at the whorehouse. "I think not."

Thyssen smiled. "Saving it for someone special?"

Her eyes turned grim as she responded, "You might say that."

"If Rogan heads off for home," Thyssen asked her, "where are you and your mom headed?"

"Where we always were, silly man. South to Irem. I have a goal in mind and my destiny lies there."

Rogan grinned. "Cryptic as holy hell. Ain't nothing but damned giants and bad magick down at Irem."

"Don't be such a prick," Thyssen admonished him with his grin intact. "Might be a good place to hide."

"Not if they figure out it was me that killed Azrag," Rogan reminded him. "I dunno how complex their warrant for me is."

Elisa said, "Too bad you didn't question those idiots before they died."

"Yeah," Thyssen sighed. "A trifle late now."

"Mystery for another day," Rogan declared. He then peered past Elisa at Yana at the rear of their cart. Not using her canes, Yana leaned a hip on the cart and held up an object to the sky. The object in her bony hands glittered in the moonlight. She raised it up and then put it back in her cart.

Thyssen asked Elisa, "What the hell is that?"

"Something from the gods," Elisa replied, cracking a lurid smile.

"Not my god," Rogan said. "Come along, Thyssen. We'll see if your other spear works."

"Hasn't failed me yet."

As the two started to walk down the avenue in the hazy moonlight, a dozen horses rode up and stopped in front of the brothel.

"Damn," Rogan swore. "Hurry, let's not get in behind those guys."

After the figures dismounted, Rogan and Thyssen saw by their sleek frames and faces they weren't men, nor did they appear to be there for the whorehouse. The dozen blocked their path and one of the women stepped forward. Each wore high riding boots, strong linen leggings, leather tunics, plus a curved sword at their left hips.

"Rogan the Kelt?" the deep voiced woman asked him.

"Never heard of him."

"You lie, but we mean you no ill will."

Rogan looked at Thyssen for a moment. "That's twice that hasn't worked."

The creak of Yana's cart door opening echoed as the woman stated, "We are from the wizard Sydow. She means to speak to you."

"Why me?" Rogan wondered. "How could she know of me?"

"The very same reason others do. We receive ravens' messages from King Nungal and hear things on the wind. She will explain her desires for you and yours."

Rogan noted that Elisa and Yana had stepped up behind them. "Better go on and wake up Bodyne."

"No whores?" Thyssen sounded sad.

His eyes taking in the hard expression of the leader of the dozen women, Rogan replied, "Not now at least."

"Curse it," Thyssen spat. "I gotta get rid of you."

"Thanks."

Thyssen addressed the woman, "How much is that bounty on him?"

CHAPTER FOUR
The Wizard

Though Lybeck didn't care for their reputations, he had to hand it to the Kaldwell twins for their capability in a fight. When their party of three dozen soldiers and the women from Kush and the twins rode up in the waning hours of the day on the remains of a wrecked caravan, Batasta and Binje were the first to face adversity.

Though buzzards circled overhead, Lybeck smiled that even they stayed away from what fed on the remains of the dead at the caravan. At the sight of the huge winged creature engorged on the leg of a dead man in the dirt, the soldiers behind Urell and he held up. Their horses shrieked and twisted, unwilling to ride into the area anywhere close to the monster eating the long-dead body.

"Kongamato," Batasta shouted as if the beast would respond to its name. The musclebound Kaldwell twin ran a hand over his bald head and smiled at his twin across from him. Their draft horses, fit to carry men much larger than an average soldier, stepped lively, but didn't fright as much as their cousins.

Binje gripped his reins and then reached back into his saddlebags. "I'm on the right, brother."

With a fast nod, Batasta also pulled something from his buckskin saddlebag and said, "On the left."

Lybeck and Urell were content to hold back with the troops as the twins thundered onto the scene. Both of the thuggish brothers wielded a whip as they rode and approached the beast they named as Kongamato. Admiring their bravery, Lybeck thought that not riding in with a weapon drawn looked more like lunacy than an overabundance of balls.

Resembling an enormous bat, the beast had a reptilian quality about the scaled body and long tri-folding wings. The extended crocodile-like snout was balanced out by a long, bony protuberance extending from the rear of its frightening head.

When Kongamato turned to face the troops, then the twins, a portion of a thigh hung from its maw and Lybeck caught a view of the eyes, striped like a snake, glowing yellow. He felt pressure on his bladder at the sight of such a horror, the clawed, short legs of Kongamato secure…one gripping a wheel of an overturned wagon, while the other held its prey in place by the pelvis. The wings unfolded as it vomited out the leg to screech at the twins.

"Sonofabitch," Harland muttered, one hand tight to his reins, the other secure on the hilt of his blade.

Lybeck noted its claws in the middle of each wing, truly like a bat and reptile crossing. The creature screamed, a howl like metal raking over stone that caused the troops to recede more. The twins, though, didn't slow down in their hurried attack.

Both charged so fast one would think they'd have crashed right into the feeding monster, as Lybeck thought Kongamato believed as well, for the monster stopped and began to extend its wings to escape. The twins, though, pulled up, the huge horses' hooves sliding to a stop as the beast arose off the ground only inches.

The brothers in perfect tandem unreeled their whips, each encircling a limb of Kongamato. Batasta wrapped the right leg of the monster and Binje snared its left wing. With no hesitation, the brothers put the handles of the whips down into their saddles in a slot readily made to secure them. Their horses then turned and took a stride. The whips extended and Kongamato shrieked anew.

A few of the troops gagged and turned away as a cracking sound echoed, followed by a wet, sloppy tearing. The two huge horses' move ripped the leg of Kongamato from its socket, drawing blood. The other wing, though looking fibrous, proved stronger and yanked back, snapping the whip in the middle. The beast flapped, but fell to the ground, long snout jamming in the dirt for a moment.

Batasta turned his horse about, dragging Kongamato a few yards as it leapt from the dirt, trying to fly, but crashing back to the earth.

Binje heeled his mount and the huge horse rode over the top of Kongamato, stomping down its hooves onto the wingspan. After the horse moved off, Binje slipped from the saddle, the spear slotted on his saddle out and twirled about.

With no hesitation, Binje jumped onto the back of Kongamato, boots planted on the ruptured wings, and stabbed his spear down. The weapon drove through the body of Kongamato and into the dirt. Both hands grinding, Binje shoved the weapon further through to pin the beast down.

Batasta swung his leg out from his horse and dismounted, his broadsword off his back. Kongamato snapped at his feet. Batasta danced gracefully, avoided the maw and jumped like a dancer. He landed, boot on the long snout.

He then threw his sword to his brother, which Binje caught like they had rehearsed the move. Batasta dropped down and embraced the long muzzle of the beast and nodded. Binje reared the heavy blade back and dropped it into the neck of Kongamato.

Batasta wrestled the creature's head about so the long bony portion fell out of the way as the heavy blade struck deep in Kongamato's neck. Binje planted a boot on the bone extension and kept hacking with the sword like he cut firewood.

After a few strikes, the head came off and Batasta rolled

away, letting go. The body still struggled against the spear through its middle and the weight of Binje on his back. The motions of the creature soon died as the life of Kongamato poured out on the dirt.

Lybeck and Urell stepped up closer, but the rest of the troopers still held back. The women from Kush didn't move forward, either.

The twins smiled as they looked up from their actions. Batasta exclaimed, "What a magnificent beast!"

"Truly," Binje agreed. "A shame to slay it."

"Agreed," Batasta said, humor fading a bit as he peered down at the twitching body of the Kongamato. "But better it than us."

"Indeed," Binje said. "If we head down the way to Azar, there's a man on the outskirts who will pay us for the pieces."

"Yes, the big man Ludvig." Batasta again eyed Lybeck and Urell. "We've dealt with that man many times."

Dismounted, Urell walked about the ruined wagons, but kept looking at the slain beast. "I know we'll be paid well for this search for the Kelt, but looking to make extra gold really isn't that important."

Binje handed his brother back his sword and said, "Ridding the world of this bad man Rogan is our top priority." He opened his hands out, as if he gave a speech to a crowd. "Look at the dead men the creature didn't eat."

Lybeck's horse stepped about the perimeter of the scene and then walked in closer to them. "I doubt he killed them all. Blood all over in great quantities, that isn't from the beast that just ate the dead."

Urell pointed southeast. "Tracks there from an elephant."

The twins jogged over and checked as well. Batasta wiped his blade on a discarded turban and said, "Horses and a wagon along with it."

Binje turned around and returned to the clearing by an overturned wagon. His body shivered and he went to his knees.

Hands out like spiders, be touched the earth in a large dark patch. After a few yawning breaths, he quivered again.

When Batasta joined him he asked, "What ails, you, brother?"

Lybeck murmured to Urell, "Puddle of congealed blood, looked like."

"I hope," Urell yawned. "It isn't mammoth piss."

While this earned a titter from the troopers, the twins returned rough looks.

Binje said, "It's from a Nephilim."

Taking a knee and touching it as well, Batasta shook a little like his twin. "Yes, this is so. I feel it as well."

Lybeck and Urell exchanged a glance, but Ransim spoke up to say, "They can tell what bled there?"

"Yes," Binje answered, hearing his soft words from a great distance. "The blood of our kindred cries out from the ground."

"If Azrag bled that much," Batasta declared as he stood, gazing at the smears on his fingers. "He's truly dead as we feared. I didn't want to believe it."

As the troops muttering traveled about, Ransim asked Urell, "Sir, what can slay a giant?"

The twins glared at them and Urell answered, "What or who indeed?"

"If this rogue Rogan killed Azrag," Batasta said with a grave voice, "he is truly dangerous."

"Agreed," Binje replied. "He won't get the better of us."

Lybeck said, "Lots of dead men here and not just from a caravan. Some are travelers, one can tell by their clothes, but those men there? They were with Azrag when he came to watch the war. They are his attendants, most fighting men as well."

"Rogan killed them all?" Harland smiled. "Doubtful."

"I didn't say that," Lybeck stated sharply. "I hate to guess…"

Rubbing his hands clean on the tunic of a dead man sitting up against a wagon wheel, Binje grinned. "Oh, go on."

Lybeck pointed the rough road. "This caravan was either

camped down or travelling here when the giant and his men came down the hill, like we have. Just in the wrong place at the wrong time. The giant's men or he himself chose to raid the caravan."

Batasta stood near Lybeck, looking down the road as if he could see the scene himself. "Then where does this Rogan come into it? Perhaps he wasn't here."

Urell shook his head and pointed up the hill they came down. "We tracked him south of the battlefield, down the series of hills and to here. He was wearing boots with pointed tips." He waved at the ground. "You can see there. Shitkicker boots we call them. Damned savages. Others here wore regular sandals."

Binje turned about and pointed to the ground. "Look here, different-sized boots, but similar to the others."

Lybeck said, "Someone else went on with them."

Batasta looked off in the distance. "The elephant went with them."

Urell wondered, "So?"

Batasta still faced the falling night. "Why would it do that? Ever try to get one of those things to move at all? Even one with no hair and small tusks?"

Lybeck related, "I saw Azrag ride it and they'd never met." Again, the troops laughed a bit at his jest.

Binje asserted, "A giant can easily cull a beast to his will, like a man on a horse. A mammoth letting a stranger ride it? Unlikely."

"Unless," Batasta sighed. "The beast knew the rider."

"Rogan," Lybeck cursed. "The damned hairy creature came along with his group from up north. It's an alien to these parts, but the cold places he is from…"

Binje smiled. "Well, at least we know, after a fashion, he is passing this way on going toward Azar."

Urell said, "At least."

"We'll gather up Kongamato, perhaps set up a camp near here for the night," said Batasta. "No use to battle night spirits.

A day's trip to Azar is ahead of us and I feel fortune will smile on us soon."

Lybeck moved away from them and exhaled to Urell.

After he spat, Urell nodded. "Isn't he the optimist?"

"They are the sons of Nephilim, so they say. They reek of confidence to the point of arrogance."

"I wonder if that is true at all." Urell then asked, "They don't have six fingers like the giants and are just a little bigger than us."

Lybeck shrugged and said, "Watering down the kids, after a fashion, I suppose. You see how things are bred out in regular folks, much less giants."

"Yeah, I guess." Urell gazed into the coming night and then the sky. "I hope that flying thing didn't have family or friends nearby."

At his words, all the troopers looked up.

The twins laughed.

Kylene dismounted and scanned the area. "Where is he?"

Binje gave her an indignant look. "Who?"

"The giant. Azrag," she answered.

Batasta mirrored his brother's indignant look.

Kylene spread her arms and let them drop. "He's not here. There's no body."

The twins didn't laugh.

*****

Rogan had slept only a few hours in the night and found himself snoozing in the saddle blanket-harness that fitted well about Aliene. He awoke as the great elephant grumbled and stopped in her steps. Before them lay a shallow creek and beyond that, a savannah of grass blue in color. He rubbed his beard and frowned. The echoes in his mind told him they'd reached the edge of what the wizardess had called the Slough of Despair.

Eyes closed, the words of the wizardess Sydow echoed about in his head. "There's an army coming for you, fifty figures or more, and they will overtake you in time. I understand you don't care for this place and want to leave, to ride back home and be away from us all. I won't task you to stay very long."

"Who in hades are you to task me at all?" Rogan recalled shouting back at the short, slender woman who reclined on many cushions in that brick dwelling. His mind ached as he recalled the labyrinth he went through to meet her, compelled by her acolytes. "You think these dozen bitches could stop me from leaving if I set a mind to it?"

Sydow had smiled. Her teeth were perfectly white. Rogan shivered at the memory. One didn't see that much.

"I mean to help you, and your words seek to injure me."

Fucker wasn't afraid, he remembered. The only thing stopping Rogan from drawing his blade and venting that woman's guts was Sydow's supposed wizardry. Though he saw no evidence of such arcane powers, or even a sense of decorating in the brick structure north of Azar, Rogan played it benign.

"You know an army is after me? How is that? Why do they want me? Did your magicks tell you all that?"

Sydow nodded toward a long window whose shutters stood open. On a perch sat a raven, looking outside into the night. "Messages on the wind, from King Nungal, offering a bounty for your head, even more if it's still attached to your body."

"So, why not take him up on it? Roll your bones, send out your dozen girls to collect me or my head?"

"Because, a man as resourceful as you, Rogan the Kelt, I could use in ways my wives cannot satisfy me."

Wives? A dozen? Rogan had seen more women attendants in the place since they entered, not one man. *Good work if one could get it...*

Rogan gazed across the blue grasses of the plain and reached down to pat Aliene's head. "Drink up, girl. We have a bit to go on this fool's errand."

Aliene dipped her trunk in the water as he reflected on Sydow's words again, heard in the grim night.

"Your friends here all have a desire to be gone from here and escape the blades meant for your back. Perhaps they don't say it, but they think it."

He almost argued they really weren't his friends, but said, "We aren't a company or group. We kinda are running away together. If they wanna leave me anytime, they can, I didn't ask for company when I escaped."

"I understand this, Rogan, and that escape is precisely why Nungal and Kamala-ur want you dead."

That fact made his heart sink. "Kalama-ur?"

"Those old men play games with the lives of their soldiers for silly wagers. I suppose that is the way of the world at large, but I digress. You were supposed to die along with the tribesmen from Keltos and the rest of the band. Living and stealing back the prize, the hairy elephant, much less slaying their ally, Azrag, well, they feel a bit cheated."

"So, they are sending out soldiers to slay me because their little boy games were disrupted by real world crap?"

Sydow nodded again. "That's a simple answer, yes." She turned in her cushions and went slow to her knees. A sudden light throbbed on the floor behind her. Rogan and Thyssen had walked up closer. Though it appeared as a shallow bathing pool behind the cushioned, illuminated blue, the substance that swirled within wouldn't pass for water. The gelatinous material bubbled and the colors shifted numerous times, suddenly becoming lighter and taking on shapes.

"Damn," Thyssen had cursed. "That's a good trick."

"No trick," Sydow told them as they saw figures on horseback riding in the blazing daylight. "Just images from farther away, yesterday, before they arrived at where you slew the great Nephilim."

Hands to his knees, Rogan bent to look closer into the bubbles, "Lybeck."

Sydow said, "Your old commander rides to help corral you."

His grimace deepened as Rogan said, "Urell, too, that ginger prick."

Thyssen spoke up to say, "The Kaldwell twins."

Giving him a short look, Rogan asked, "Who?"

Elisa stepped forward, hands on her hips, and spat at the pool of bubbles. "Twin warriors who claim to be the children of Nephilim." Derision hung in her voice as Thyssen and Rogan raised an eyebrow at each other in unison.

Rogan wondered, "Was Azrag their daddy?"

Her hands curled to fists, Elisa shouted, "A dog is their daddy!" She then turned away and walked back with her mother and Bodyne.

"All for little ol' me," Rogan reflected to Aliene as the beast moved across the creek and headed into the blue grasses. "This place doesn't look so dangerous, huh?"

Aliene said nothing as they moved across the long grasses and a valley dipped down profoundly. Over to his right, Rogan could hear the sea in the distance. He also then spotted the stone outcropping that rose up and crested. In a minute, the land splayed out beyond the blue grasses into a canyon of rocky walls. He eyed the tall outcropping that overlooked the lengthy drop and sighed.

"Stillborn," Sydow had named it in the night. "Ever hear of such a place ever around a campfire?"

Rogan had answered, "I've heard of places like it far from here, wizardess. Best not to talk of them."

"Do you fear ghosts of babies?" Sydow had motioned her hands and the images of the soldiers after him faded and a spectacle of the stone outcropping appeared in the pool. "Stillborn is a place of disposal, like you guess."

Thyssen shook his head as Rogan replied, "They toss imperfect or stillborn babies over the edge to benefit some god or devil. Yeah, I've heard of it. Been done before. I thought ya were so civilized around here?"

"That isn't what is thrown over there," Sydow promised him and looked back at all the women for a moment before she said, "The female offspring of the fallen sons of God are sent there. This is most certainly true."

Rogan glared at her. "What?"

"Ever wonder why one never hears of a woman Nephilim?" Her voice held a lilt of humor. "Only giant men?"

"All right, ya got me there."

"The girls are not extremely tall, handsome giants, but loathsome creatures, what the legends of harpies and whatnot are based on. There is something corrupted in their flesh and the watchers or priests get rid of them there before they are brought to maturity."

"Crazy stories from the campfire," Rogan said, his head shaking and his face twisted in memories.

"A few that do are what the horrors are based on. It is very rare to have one turn out to anything close to beauty in body or face."

Rogan stood back, hands to his waist belt. "So, what are you getting at?"

Sydow sat back, comfortable again. "The bones of such creatures would fetch an incredible price or be very valuable to a mage." She stared at Yana. "Correct?"

The old woman's head bobbed gradually. "She's right. The enchantment from such bones that would be amazing."

"Damn wizards," mumbled Rogan.

"That is why Ludvig probably had a hard-on the size of Nineveh when he saw Azrag, but he played it unflappable."

Rogan turned about and shook his head. Staring at the floor of slick tiles, he said, "I can't believe you are about to ask me to do something stupid like get those bones?"

Sydow smiled. She smiled alone.

His focus on the wizardess once more, Rogan's disbelief shown on his face. "You are jesting me? Jerking my big ol' knob about? Why in the hell haven't you gone there before to do this yer own damned selves? Your girls look tough, rough, and ready to party."

"Oh, I have sent others," Sydow said and looked at the ceiling once.

Thyssen joined Rogan and said, "If it were such an easy task, why wouldn't others gather them up? Any asshole could just walk out there and get them."

"The Nephilim and their priests follow the edicts laid out by their fathers," Sydow related. "The fallen ones and watchers have a bit of sentimentality, understanding their sons will be men of renown, but having a bit of pity on their hideous daughters."

Elisa injected, "Big of them. Why not just burn them?"

Sydow's smile lessened somewhat as she said, "I think they don't really want that. Something about their flesh returning to the earth that the ashes poison the air. They are a bizarre lot, some not right in the head."

"I'm sure." Elisa rolled her eyes. "Then why didn't every scavenger in the bloody territory get after such a valued prize? What did the watchers do? Put a dragon at the mouth of the valley?"

When silence reigned in the room, Yana clutched her necklace and touched her daughter's arm. "Please, stop."

Elisa laughed, gloved hands on her hips. "You can't be serious."

"No, not a dragon," Sydow replied. "A chimera."

Thyssen gave a sharp, single laugh and said, "Is that all?"

"Chimera. Wodan's balls," Rogan spat out. "You want me to kill a fuckin' monster to get the bones of baby girl Nephilims so you can do you accursed magicks better? Speak it plain or you all are gonna meet God today."

"Yes." Sydow smiled yet again. "If you would."

"What if I don't?" Rogan posed. "Killing your brides would be easier than slaying a monster like a Chimera, whatever the hell form such a thing is taking. I'd rather fight the sisters of Sanrevelle at Madron."

"So you think," Sydow yawned and stretched thin arms over her head. "I'm not forcing you to do it, just offering you a choice."

Rogan blinked. "A choice?"

"Life is full of choices. You and your folks could choose to ride into Azar, get a ship, and move on across the sea. I hear the tan-skinned ladies of a distant land are a cream to be tasted. And good fortune to you, if you try. But do you think Lybeck and his men will be denied so easily? Do you think the bounty on you will not catch up with you in time?"

"That's for me to worry on, ma'am. Besides, these folks can go off on their own. They are not wanted. No use them dying for my ass."

Elisa said, "Glad to hear that."

Rogan gave her a venomous look but she just winked back at him. "They are a day behind us, correct?"

Sydow said, "About that."

"If I ride up there and do this thing, they are due to catch up."

"Yes."

"So how does this benefit me at all? What do I get for doing this?"

"The Stillborn, or Slough of Despair, is north of Azar further than us by the sea of blue grasses. It would be on your way if you are heading home."

Rogan frowned.

Sydow studied him close. "Don't want to go home, do you, Rogan?"

They all looked at him as he hesitated to answer. "It's a direction I want to ride, though, maybe so."

"Let your friends go on and sail away or go where they wish. You do this boon for me, and I will ensure their safety. Plus, I will compensate you well in this."

"Gold and jewels aren't dick unless I can spend them," Rogan said in a gravelly voice. "But why would you send me to my death? You have a troll that gets his jollies eating wayward savages?"

Hand to her chin, Sydow pondered his words. "That's an interesting idea, but no. Jewels and gold are rocks. Men are happy to exchange rocks for goods and women. Me? Magick is far stronger than gold. I can find jewels anywhere with my magick. The power I can glean from these bones will make me richer than you can imagine."

"I can imagine a great deal," said Rogan.

"You best not." She reached under her pillows and drew out a couple string-tied pouches. She repeated this action and touched the top of each bag in a sweeping motion. "For you all. Here. Gold coins and jewels, but not so much to be gaudy and draw attention. You can all go wherever you want."

Thyssen fell to his knees, grabbed a bag, and fumbled to open it. His eyes widened as he poured some out.

Sydow said, "You can start your long journey home to Transalpina."

Crazy grin fading, Thyssen asked, "How can you know that?"

"I'm a wizard," she responded with a snort, tossing bags toward Elisa and Yana. "I know things sometimes."

The towering girl picked up the bags for her mother and her. She did open one. Nostrils flaring, she leered at Sydow.

"That will take you unto Marduk at Irem?" Sydow asked the tall girl. "Will it fulfill your desires?"

"It's a start," Elisa replied and gave a bag to her mother.

"You, young lady," Sydow said, shaking a bag at Bodyne. "Will this get you where you wish to go?"

Bodyne took the bag and opened it. Her smile, quick to leave, turned to a snarl. "How can you just give this to us?"

Sydow sighed. "I told you, rocks mean nothing to me. Go on your way. You too, Keltos man, and don't do as I ask. It's all choice."

Her rough hands shaking as she touched the jewels and

gold, Bodyne wept. "I just don't want to be a slave anymore."

Rogan said, "Don't be. Go live like a rich woman. Azar is a good place, safer than most and civilized more than many."

She looked up at him and suddenly threw her arms about Rogan, sobbing.

He held her, but faced the wizardess.

"What is it you know that will make me do this?"

Sydow replied, "What's your desire, right now?"

His forehead felt hot and Rogan wondered if the wizardess walked through his mind. "You know where they are, don't you?"

Bodyne looked up at him glaring at the wizardess. "Who do you mean?"

Seething, Rogan said, "If you have them here...no, you don't."

Sydow said, "You read me well..."

"For a savage?"

"For any man. They are not here, of course, and you will puzzle it out in time, but if you ride off homeward, you will never find them."

"Well, damn, I guess I'll have to go to that valley."

"A wise choice. I know you would rather kill us all and try to find the answer you seek. However, this way is better. We all gain something in this way."

"You will burn someday."

"Perhaps, but not today." Sydow wore a sly grin. "You want to see what lies at the base of the Slough of Despair, don't you?"

"I wonder what your game is, more."

"Life is..."

"Short?" Rogan cut her off, his eyes piercing into hers. "So I hear."

"No, it's long. I've lived a great while. One needs to entertain one's self."

"Not the games I like to play."

"Go to the place of Stillborn and see me afterwards. Take many sacks, my brides will furnish you."

He released Bodyne but she didn't let him go for a long time. "If there is nothing there and I slay a monster for nothing, wizardess, I'll be coming back with more than just my dick in my hand."

"No need to threaten. I don't play games like Nungal and Kalama-ur."

"Yeah? Who is bullshitting who now?"

Sydow licked her pale lips. "I play for keeps."

As Rogan rode Aliene through the morning sunlight down into the valley, he thought he heard rolling thunder in the distance. Seeing the sky cloudless, he could almost hear the voice of his father deriding him on being off on a silly venture as a part of a wizard's game.

"I'll find you, both," Rogan promised his blood and moved on.

CHAPTER FIVE

In For the Kill

"**A** fine specimen, no, Ludvig?"

The huge man bent over the slab where the pieces of the body lay. "I used to have a skull of a Kongamato, years back," Ludvig affirmed, chin dipping low. "I'm glad to get one again." His unkempt white eyebrows raised and he asked the speaker, "Binje, was it?"

"I'm Batasta," the bald man answered and looked at his doppelganger across the slab. "That's Binje."

"I'm not asking you to the fuckin' bathhouse," Ludvig replied as he studied the bones again. "Although I think you all could get the trail dirt off you, for good measure." He then looked at the other two in the room before moving about the slab. "But, I don't really care if you smell like ass."

"I'm Lybeck, that's Urell."

Not looking up, Ludvig countered, "I don't care."

Lybeck stared at Urell for a moment. The red-haired man chewed at the innards of his cheeks and didn't speak. "You are the artisan who pays for flesh and bones?"

"I'm not the chief whore of Azar," Ludvig breathed and

stood up, stretching his back some in discomfort. "That would be Gierich Tanya. Got an ass like a washtub, but can suck the rust off a wagon hitch. If you are into that sort of thing."

Lybeck's ire rose and he stated, "We are not interested in whores this day."

Urell smirked. "The troops and I would disagree."

"However, good sir," Lybeck said hotly, eyes shooting fire at Urell. "We would be very interested in knowing a few things about some people that are rumored to be traveling on through Azar."

"Go elsewhere," Ludvig told him with little emotion, not caring to meet his look. "I deal in bones and flesh, mostly to the ill-starred wizards, witches, and strange fuckers that live in the shadows. I'm sure you can find out more from the masses out there than from a flesh peddler like little ol' me."

Smiling, Binje stepped into the path of Ludvig and looked him square in the eye. "Did your father have six fingers?"

Ludvig took a breath. "I'd bet your mother had four, altogether,"

Binje's smile disappeared and his right hand went very fast to the jeweled sword pommel on his belt.

"Go ahead," Ludvig said. "Skin that cat. Go on and do it. I'll rip out your eyes and skull fuck you before the blade clears the sheath." He then looked at Batasta with the same expression. "And your boyfriend, too."

Urell also held to his own sword's handle, saying, "You'll never make it outside. There are fifty soldiers out there."

Ludvig glared at Binje again. "You guys are real darlings. What makes you think I ever need to go outside?"

Lybeck stressed, "We need information."

"And I said to stick it in your ass," Ludvig retorted, eyes aiming at Lybeck. "I have a murder hole that leads into a labyrinth under this building. If you think you and your fifty jack-offs can get me, skin those blades."

Batasta said, "I've seen the tracks outside. The mammoth

and its rider came in here. The wagons tracks are also here. I can smell the blood of a Nephilim here no matter how you bleach your drains. You might escape us, but what happens when the other giants realize one of their brothers was vivisected by you?"

Ludvig smirked. "I'm all fuckin' afraid. Go on, call Marduk, the head of those giant bastards himself. Call on ol' Zazaeil too and tell on me. I will welcome them inside for a chat and you will still be just as dead, asshead." He took a labored breath. "I'll pay you well for these bones of the Kongamato and you can walk out this afternoon, buy your men all the whores they can eat, and have a fine day. It's up to you."

Binje said, "The savage Kelt…"

Ludvig cut him short, saying, "If he's a Kelt, better think twice 'bout screwin' with him. I'd say."

"And why is that?" Binje demanded.

Still calm, Ludvig ran a big hand down the snout of the dead creature on his slab. "They pray to that Wodan god. Don't fuck with a guy unafraid to die."

Batasta offered, "Everyone is afraid to die."

"Not those crazy bastards," Ludvig said. "They look forward to fighting and fucking forever in their heaven. Not wise to fight a guy with everything to gain in death. I don't even wanna think on how they honor their god."

Fingers dripping sweat from his pommel, Urell asked, "The Kelt with the hairy elephant, he was here with the corpse of Azrag?"

Ludvig exhaled, rolled his eyes, and stepped toward Urell. "Get the shit outta your ears, ginger. I cannot recall."

Binje fumed to his brothers, "He's unarmed and just one man."

Batasta gave his brother a vinegary look. "Binje…"

"He can be made to talk," Binje persisted.

His smirk becoming a grin, Ludvig said leisurely, "Last chance, girls. Get your money and go."

Binje started to draw his blade, but Ludvig turned back to

him, his long arms extending out, boxing the ears of the fighter. Stopping in his motions, but then convulsing when Ludvig planted a boot in his groin, Binje cried out for his brother.

Batasta had his sword half out when Ludvig took a stride and dropped his left hand over the fighter's hand. Ludvig's right hand gripping the ear and jaw of Batasta, he pulled the sword out, lifting his target off his feet.

His face a mask of amazement at the strength of Ludvig, Batasta's stunned look traveled to Lybeck as his body became airborne, thrown across Ludvig's body into the oncoming rush of Urell. While Batasta collided with Urell, Ludvig didn't release the hand over the pommel.

The butt of the sword flew out, two hands on it, and into a curving shot to the face of Binje. The impact landed on his left eye and he cried out again, worse than when he took the groin shot. He tumbled back, falling against the wall and sliding down to his buttocks, but his brother recovered from the impact with Urell. The sword fell from his grip and clattered on the throw-rug over the stone floor.

"You die," Batasta promised and rushed Ludvig.

The big man made no sudden move, save but a quick reach to the slab.

Batasta tackled Ludvig, pinning him to the wall. His moves so hasty, he started to push away and draw out a dagger to strike Ludvig. With no warning, Ludvig smashed the bony protuberance of Kongamato into the side of Batasta's head, smashing his ear and drawing blood.

Batasta dropped his dagger as the creature's skull impacted on his. Ludvig kicked him in the groin, twice. Hard. The fighter dropped to his knees and Ludvig moved about the slab, still holding the skull of Kongamato.

Urell, still trying to set his feet from the impact of Batasta, couldn't brace himself enough as the skull crashed up into his gut, followed by a left jab to his throat by Ludvig. Urell fell and Ludvig faced Lybeck.

Sword out and ready, Lybeck made no sudden move, which allowed Ludvig to move about the slab and laugh. He waved at him as if to say farewell, and dropped from sight. Lybeck rushed to the spot, seeing the trap door in the floor close up after him. He heard metallic bolts draw on stone and then footsteps fade.

"Bastard," Lybeck swore.

In a few minutes, the four stood outside the Ludvig's abode and they all traded curses for the big fellow.

"Damn him," Binje groaned, rubbing his crotch. "We should burn this place to the ground."

Not watching them, but looking at many of their troopers heading back from Azar, Lybeck said, "It's made of stone." He walked to where Harland and Ransim stopped their mounts. "Report?"

"He was here, sir," Ransim said, dropping his arm from the half-salute. "He and a few others with him."

"How can you be sure?"

"He left on a giant hairy elephant. How many can there be like that?"

Lybeck nodded. "True."

Harland said, "He killed a few men here though, locals seeking the bounty on him." He turned and pointed to a pair of smoldering bodies on metal racks in the distance. "He and some big spearman with him."

Urell coughed and sipped from a flask from his belt. "This Rogan shouldn't be tough to track."

Lybeck didn't look his way, but said, "Yeah?"

"He leaves dead men wherever he goes."

"The men are tired after a day on a trail," Lybeck said. "We could use the relax time as well. Let's get them to hit the bathhouses and whorehouses." Amongst the men, they gave out agreeable grunts. "This Rogan had a helluva an appetite for food and women, like all savages from the north. Perhaps they will find out something about him in the depths of the whorehouses."

Urell drank again and glanced back at the twins. "I think

the twins might be bruised for the night."

Batasta walked to them and said, "One power my brother and I do possess is pristine hearing."

After a belch, Urell replied, "I'm impressed."

Batasta said, "My brother and I shall search Azar. You all can get drunk and your fill of the skanky whores."

Lybeck stretched and gazed back at the house of Ludvig. "Damn him."

Binje followed his gaze and then looked to his brother. "What about the one who slipped away?"

"He can die another day," Batasta promised, tenderly dabbing a folded cloth to his ear. "I salute his courage and guts."

Urell drank yet again, adding, "We all can do that shit for sure, but I need a bath and a woman."

Batasta's nostrils flared. "Nungal and Kamala-ur didn't pay us to get sex."

"Shows what you know," Harland corrected him. "They gave good gold in their expenses. They know an army marches on its cock."

"There will be time to empty my mind after Rogan is dead," Binje told him, cracking the knuckles of his huge hands.

"Suit yourself," Urell said. "Keep your prick to the ground, uh, ear to the ground. Never know what you might learn."

Harland muttered to Ransim, "Aren't the girls from Kush supposed to leave us here at Azar?"

Ransim shrugged. "I think so. They don't talk much."

"That lead one, Kylene," Harland eyes widened as he watched her on her horse many yards away, "I want to ride her until she screams."

"Good luck on that adventure," Ransim replied, but Urell gave Harland a virulent look. He then looked to Lybeck. "Onward into town?"

"Yes, let us go," Lybeck said.

Killer of Giants

*****

"They weren't joking about the Chimera creature guarding the Slough of Despair."

Rogan's cloudy mind heard this voice, that tone of a husky woman, ring in his head. His eyes opened and through a bleary haze, he saw sunlight. At first he thought himself underwater, and the ripples to the edge of his vision appeared the same as what he'd beheld while swimming.

Yet, he breathed. That ability not only told him he wasn't underwater but that life still clung to his frame. Why, he pondered would that be such a surprise?

"You better wake up," the woman's voice told him.

Eyes shut again, Rogan's body ached all over like he'd been thrown by a horse. No, he remembered, he hadn't been riding a horse. An elephant. A hairy one…Aliene. What a silly name for a beast like that.

His dreamy state didn't want to lock in on what had happened. Somewhere in his mind, there swam a wish to give into this bleary bliss and fade away. Something else, though, in his chest, that heart, made him burn all over.

The Chimera.

It all rushed back to him, how he'd arrived at the edge of the steep valley and climbed off Aliene. Peering off the slope, he used the long rope the wives of Sydow had given to him and armed up the numerous gunny sacks in preparation to scale down the side. Though he secured the rope about Aliene's torso and wound the end about his own waist, Rogan never had the chance to go down the angled incline and fill up his sacks with baby bones.

From out of the valley the creature sprung up. Rogan cursed, as he hadn't seen it when searching the valley. His mind spun, thinking it down in a cave, concealed from sight, but that didn't matter much.

He stepped back from the edge, letting go of the rope and

causing it to uncoil to the ground by his boots. Drawing his sword from his back, Rogan moved away from Aliene as the Chimera moved over the lip of the valley.

Terror touched him first, but the beast wasn't as big as he'd feared, even if it really existed. From the tales of Chimeras he heard of as a child, he saw why such yarns were spun. Such beasts were to be an amalgamation of a lion, goat, and serpent. The monster probably had a torso the size of a normal horse, but short legs, terminating in hooves; not of a goat but thick like that of a bull.

Hairy like a goat though, the creature did sport two heads, individually, not unlike a lion or great cat, but no mane. Each head sported a pair of goatish horns, but they curled out toward him, ready to strike he guessed. The long, swishing tale for the beast wasn't that of a scaly serpent, nor did it have a snake's rattler, but did have a wicked curve at the tip like a deadly scorpion.

"Come closer," Rogan said, his ire up and power surging in his limbs. Though his sword crossed himself every so often, he also drew out one of his knives.

The creature stomped nearer to him, but showed a bit of caution for him or the mammoth. The Chimera's tail mounted over its back and threated to strike at him over its heads. The tail bobbed as it drew closer, like a long tongue getting ready to flick out and have a taste. Rogan held out his sword every so often as if to parry the shots, but they never connected.

Rogan maneuvered it around, the butt of the beast facing the mammoth. Aliene turned her head, watching through the long tusks, but made no move. He jumped at the Chimera, then back, daring it to attack him.

The second time he did this, the Chimera did make a move. The tail darted out, much farther than before, the point aiming at him. As the tail extended out further than Rogan thought possible, both heads screeched a loud howl and came forward as well.

Rogan's sword thrust forward, performing a corkscrew

move, slicing into the flesh under the sharp curve of the stabbing tail. Not waiting to see if the stinger hung disabled, Rogan planted his left boot and kicked the Chimera's left head with his other boot.

The sword then dropped onto the right skull of the wailing beast. He chopped down, hoping to remove the head at the neck, but in a mêlée things seldom went as they were taught. The sword plummeted fast, didn't hit the neck, but crashed into the Chimera's skull. Rogan's heart felt elated as the heavy blade sank in far.

He laughed, his crazy battle laughter praising his wild father who made the great sword and Wodan for imparting the craft to his sire. He wrenched the blade, almost orgasmic that the skull of the Chimera split, but he didn't dodge the ruined tail as it slapped him across the head. The point didn't enter him, as the stinger hung ruined, but the bitch slap move knocked him back.

His head full of stars, Rogan fell. His right hand released the sword and his foot came back off the other head of the beast as he cartwheeled to the blue grasses. Rolling up to his knees, Rogan shook off the stars in his mind as the screaming creature came after him, hooves stomping at him, and the remaining head's toothy jaws aiming at his right arm.

Rogan dived forward between the heads. He didn't make a move to get his sword back. His right arm curled about the neck of the raging head and he planted the heavy knife into the Chimera's throat.

Again, happy the knife broke the creature's skin, he tried to brace himself and not let go of the headlock hold. Knife out of the Chimera, he quickly stabbed again and again, trying to hit something vital, then let the headlock go.

With both hands, he gripped the knife's handle and pulled down, ripping a deeper chasm in the creature's neck. Once more, the tail struck at Rogan's head. It didn't dislodge him this time or brain him.

The tail, though, coiled about his neck and yanked him

free of his hold on the smaller blade. Knife still bobbing in the Chimera, Rogan flew off and landed on his all fours. He looked at the wounded monster and then up at Aliene, who stood watching out into the valley

"Lotta help you are," he grunted and took out his other knife.

The movements of the Chimera had slowed a great deal. It shuddered, choked, and bled out much.

Rogan hesitated, wanting his sword back, but the bloody jaws of the monster still weren't done yet. The sword looked inviting in that split skull, gray brains oozing from the ruined head, but Rogan dared not grab for it yet.

He rose up and the Chimera made a leap for him, falling a bit short but enough to make Rogan stumble backwards. His unsure steps shuffled, but his fighting instincts propelled him forward. Somewhere in the attack, Rogan's left foot stepped on, then slid off, one of the hooves.

The knife strike he had planned would be so great…if it had worked. His desire to grab one of the horns with his left hand and drive the knife into one of the eyes would've been akin to poetry, but he fell short of the mark. If the horns had been turned up at a straight angle, both would've pierced his guts.

He floundered on over the back of the beast, sliding in the blood that gushed from the back of the neck. The Chimera tried to shrug him off and grip his neck again with the ruined tail, the appendage having lost speed and strength. Rogan rolled crossways on its back, his side hitting the tail.

He flailed his legs and grappled with the long tail, falling off to the grass again. Feeling as if he wrestled a serpent, Rogan pushed off the tail. Facing the Chimera's backside, tail under his left arm, Rogan swung the knife with an uppercut between its back set of legs. Unsure the sex of the monster, Rogan intended to carve out something anyway.

His short blade did descend in the crotch of the Chimera, and it howled with a fresh tenor. The contortion it backlashed him with might have sent a regular man into the air.

"Damn you," Rogan swore, his knife out of the beast and then returning, probing deep and twisting. The tail whipped about, again connecting with Rogan's face. "Wodan's cock," he yelled and sank his teeth into the hair-skin of the tail.

Flipping about like he mounted a horse, he embraced the tail, heaving all his weight against it. The appendage broke against his body then hung limp. Rogan reached back, grabbed the hilt of his sword with both hands, and pulled it free. He set his feet on either side of the creature and swiped his blade down at the tail, cutting the wilted limb off.

Rogan then swung his leg off the back of the Chimera, turned his sword down, and drove the blade home through its midsection. The sword went in but resisted. Rogan gripped the handle both hands together and drove it through to the dirt. Turning the weapon back and forth, in time, he sliced out the side of the monster.

By then, the fight in it had gone. With no gasp it collapsed, legs out, gut flat to the blue grass.

"That's over," Rogan mumbled, taking a few breaths.

When the exact twin of the Chimera leapt over the lip of the canyon and Aliene drew back, Rogan stopped breathing and oscillated his blade out. The sword connected with the right front leg of the Chimera as it landed on its back hooves and reared up like a randy stallion.

The short leg cut loose in a moment, the cut went clean through, and the limb flew over by Aliene, who didn't acknowledge it. The creature stayed on its back legs, roaring in pain or rage.

Rogan roared as well, but only the name of his primal god as he drove his blade up into the underbelly of the Chimera. He stabbed in, curved it around, and then brought it down, ripping loops of guts from the monster as it started to try and go down to three limbs.

Jumping back fast to avoid the monster, Rogan didn't let up his attack, driving forward and slashing right, then left, his sword drawing blood on either horned heads. His backswing down to the left, Rogan reared the blade back and plunged it between the heads, cutting a wedge down the middle of the two necks into the torso.

At first, the blade hung up, but in a single moment pushed on through, touching the blue grass, now soiled by the gushing orange blood of the wounded Chimera.

After a solitary step back and a blade shot above his head to dodge the curved stinger of the tail, Rogan saw a loop of gut at his boots. The Chimera struggled, hurt mortally, but wouldn't give in just yet.

Rogan hooked his boot in the guts and stepped back away, ripping loose more of the intestines as he moved in wanton abandon. When the creature reacted, he again swiped the sword from head to head, then drew back and jammed his weapon into the mouth of the head on the left.

Down the creature's gullet deep, Rogan twisted his sword and held on, kicking at the other head to fend it off. Abruptly, the fight left the Chimera and it flopped down very much like the other.

"Damn them, rotten pricks," Rogan sucked air fast then called out. "Any more of you sonsofbitches down there?"

That's when a stinger three times the size of the other Chimeras slapped his body, sending him rolling on the ground until he came to a halt.

His eyes open again, the blurry waters clouded his vision again. He'd replayed the fights over in his mind. The sky sharpened a little and he heard a set of roars, probably from each mouth of the adult Chimera. Hands empty, no knives or a sword to hold, Rogan breathed and tried to sit up. His body shivered, but didn't rise.

Again, the roar sounded and he cursed in his mind, as his mouth wouldn't comply. He always wanted to face death head-on. Rogan assumed by the call of the Chimera he'd get his legs bitten off first and maybe bleed out. It wasn't the death he figured on, and hoped Wodan wouldn't turn him away from his table in the eternal hall beyond the skies. The image of himself sitting outside the long doors of Valhalla, legless, begging to get in, crossed his unfocused mind at that moment.

As the Chimera's cries came closer, Rogan tried to swallow, but gagged, coughed, and near to vomited, but still couldn't rise. Angry at the monster, his own stupidity, and Wodan for being a real jester, Rogan hoped his demise would go quick.

The sky then went brown, and his mind spun in confusion, but then he realized the sight as Aliene stepping over him. At first, he figured the dumb animal would step on him, crushing the life out of his self before his boots were bitten free.

All right, then I'll be parchment thin outside the doors of Valhalla, whining like a little bitch for scraps. No, he soon understood, Aliene stopped atop of him, the four long legs hemming him in like trees or the bars to a cage. His body did jump at last when Aliene trumpeted, snorted, and dropped her trunk to the ground between her front legs.

Though his mind still went crooked, Rogan managed to raise his head, and then push his elbows up. Between her front legs and trunk, Rogan beheld the adult Chimera. Identical to the offspring, the two-headed monster easily stood twice its children's size. The heads stared at his form under the mammoth, but the creatures big hooves stepped back a little. Both heads soon looked up, trying to face Aliene.

Breathing hard, Rogan near to giggled at what happened. The damn big elephant trumpeted again, the huge set of curled tusks thrusting out, causing its opponent to stride back again. *Opponent?* Did Aliene really intend to fight that thing or just...

His thoughts had no more time to process as the mammoth moved forward, the inordinate strides cutting the distance quicker than the Chimera guessed, for, startled, it didn't retreat fast at first. By the time it did, Aliene's tusks drew across the heads of the beast, breaking off two of the tiny horns of the Chimera.

The pronounced steps of the mammoth stomped down,

clearly injuring the right front leg of the Chimera, and then stopping. Aliene had the beast pinned and again dropped the tusks, this time striking the back of the Chimera.

Rogan sat up, slow, trying to get to his aching buttocks, but his body still rebelled. The screeches of the Chimera went a higher pitch as Aliene took another pace, its back legs crushing the forelegs of the monster.

The elephant reared up, tusks moving side to side, combating the tail as it tried to strike her. Up like a stallion, the elephant's front feet soon plummeted, smashing into the torso of the Chimera.

Both heads choked once, puking out blood and guts between Aliene's back legs. The creature didn't make another sound or action. Aliene took a few more steps, a couple by its back legs crushed the torso of the beast further, but she turned around and trumpeted at Rogan.

Blinking, the female voice returned in his head, saying, "There. Now, get the bones for that wizard."

Rogan cried out and jumped to his feet. The world looked a little brighter and Aliene grazed on some blue grass. She gave him a look, ears flapping away bugs, but no more voices came unto his mind.

"Crazy voices. Were they ever there?" Rogan mumbled, taking careful steps over to her. He pulled a skin of wine from the saddle bag and took a long draw. He looked her in the eye and took another drink. "I better get after this." He stared back toward Azar as if he could see Sydow. "Damned wizards. My sire and sister better be alive."

In time, Rogan emerged from the valley and threw several sacks of bones on the sharp edge. He then climbed out, took off the rope about his waist, and lay down in the grass. He used a sack of the baby bones for a pillow and slept.

When Rogan awoke, he took off his boots and stripped off his bloody breeks. After a drink from his canteen, he took his sword and walked to the bodies of the two smaller Chimeras.

Killer of Giants

Though Aliene gave him a curious look, Rogan sliced through the first body, rooting about in the midsection of the first beast. Hands full of gore, he held up an object to Aliene.

"That look like a heart of a Chimera to you?"

Aliene ignored him as he threw the finding over into the grasses and then proceeded to do the same act on the other body. Once he had both hearts of the Chimeras, he looked at the crushed body of the larger monster. After a sigh, he took the two hearts and one of the many bags of bones he retrieved. He cut open the bag with one of his knives and spread out the bones. He then gathered up some of the dry grasses and made a crude mattress in the dirt. Once this was done, he placed the two hearts on the mat and went back to the saddle bags on Aliene.

The mammoth did turn and watch him as he used his flints and struck sparks into the dry grass. In a few moments, a fire surrounded the hearts. The fire didn't consume them, but it wasn't Rogan's intent. She then watched Rogan howl into the air, and invoke the name of his god...and dance in the circle about the smoking hearts.

Once he'd done this many times, Rogan pissed on the fire, pulled on his boots, and grabbed up the bags. Then, bare-assed, he climbed up on the mammoth with the bags. He smiled up into the sky and relaxed.

CHAPTER SIX

Immaculate Deception

Lybeck washed himself off in a clay pot full of water, using the cloth provided by his host. He cleaned off himself as best he could. "Thank you, kindly," he said to the woman who reclined back on the bed.

She reached over by the candles, taking a cup of wine up to her lips. "No need to thank me, you paid full price." She wiped the ruined lipstick off her mouth with the back of her hand. "I should thank you."

Chuckling, Lybeck replied, "No need to say that at all, I did pay full price after all…Ava, was it?"

"Yes, Ava. Named after the first woman Eve, or Eva, after a fashion." She gave a mild yawn and said, "My sisters were named Awan and Azura after Eve's daughters."

As he wrung out the rag some more, Lybeck didn't bother saying how much he didn't care for that fact.

Ava went on to say, "You are very kind and performed very well, even if I'm an older one here."

"No need to be mean about it ever," he answered, drying off with a towel folded up that lay beside the pot. "You are a wonderful woman, never doubt it."

"Thank you."

"And I don't care for younger women."

"You'd be surprised at how cruel men can be," she told him and stretched her legs out on the bed.

"Oh that wouldn't surprise me."

"And they usually want young women, younger the better for most."

Lybeck shook his head. "I'm not a young man, nor do I share any delusions a younger woman would want me even if I paid for it."

Her grey eyes studied him. "Then you are different."

"I am just me. Once one gets to the age where one is old enough to be a woman's father, it gets odd to be in bed with her, but that's me."

Ava smiled, the lines on her face more pronounced in the lantern's light. "I appreciate you, soldier."

Naked as the day he was born, Lybeck gave a small bow. "I better get dressed and out to where the men are encamped. The younger ones were already setting up a spot even after they went to the houses along the strip here in Azar."

Ava sat up, swinging her legs to the floor with a slight grunt of pain. "See? The young don't last long."

Lybeck pulled up his breeks. "Such is youth."

Heavy footfalls echoed in the room and Lybeck grabbed his sword before his boots. After a pounding on the door, Lybeck shouted back, "Who the hell is that?"

"Binje," the gruff voice returned. "Are you about finished?"

Ava rose up, rubbing her backside, saying, "I think so. One a night is all I can handle at this age."

Lybeck grimaced at her and shouted back, "Yeah, I am. Let me get fully dressed, damn it to hades."

"I'll be out here."

Lybeck sighed, lay his sword on the bed, and then reached for his boots. "I appreciated you, too, Ava."

She hunched her head, beaming, and slid her gown from

the bedpost to her right.

Once dressed and rearmed, Lybeck went into the hallway. There Binje stood, bigger than life and twice as scary. The whores from down the hall peeked at him, but all drew back like scared gophers when Lybeck appeared.

"You couldn't have waited outside with the horses?"

Binje gave him a quizzical look. "From what is said in the streets, and those who watch close, Rogan and some with him went north to the abode of a wizard called Sydow on the outskirts of Azar."

They walked down the hall and to the steps, Lybeck saying, "I can't imagine how you came by such information. You talk too much in a whorehouse and others must, too. Now any fool can find out what you are seeking."

Once outside, Binje took firm hold on his shoulder and turned him about. "I'm a fierce fighter, sir. I fear no whoremonger."

"But a wet-eared puppy about the ways of the world," Lybeck retorted. "Can you understand what I am saying?"

Looking back at the whorehouse, Binje's mouth opened, but then slowly closed. "I shall try and do better." He let go of Lybeck's shoulder. "I can always learn."

The older man straightened up some. "Life is full of lessons."

"I took a dozen of them men with my brother and we went out unto this place of Sydow the wizardess."

Lybeck rolled his eyes. "Not a wise move."

Binje said, "There was no one there."

"Yeah?"

He nodded slow as they climbed on their respective horses. "The locale appeared abandoned, for a long time."

Lybeck replied, "That may be what Sydow wanted you to think."

"What?"

"More lessons. I wouldn't think you and Batasta not unwise to the ways of wizards or their games."

They rode down the street of brothels, and paused before

turning right. Binje shouted, "We shall have this Rogan, one way or another."

Lybeck had stopped, and looked over at a man who exited an establishment. A younger fellow, bearded, rough-looking, stout, he held a spear and stared straight into his eyes. Lybeck moved on with Binje and tried to forget the look that rough man gave him. He couldn't quite shake it.

Binje eyed him and shouted, "What is it?"

"Nothing," Lybeck responded. "I'm just distrustful in my older age."

They rode on out to the boundary of the city and then to an area where the soldiers all encamped. The fifty men and Kushite women had assembled their small tents in even rows. A few larger tents were set off to the edge, away from the neat design.

Binje said, "My brother and I set out our tents over there. The other two bigger ones are for Urell and yourself."

"That's kind of you, but this isn't a proper bivouacked camp."

After a heavy groan, Binje questioned, "Is there any pleasing you?"

"The whore back there did a fine job at that, but it's not a good idea for the men to be so evenly quartered."

"Just for a single night. Tomorrow we'll do it more to your liking," Binje promised with an exaggerated eye roll.

"One night is all it takes."

"We have little to fear in this armpit of the world. Besides, in the morning the Kush girls will go to the docks to be processed."

"Yes?"

"Zazaeil will come for them." Binje grinned. "Does that idea give you pause?"

He ignored him as Batasta emerged from his tent, clad only in his loin cloth. "I trust Binje told you we came up wanting in our search." Batasta pointed at a series of stone buildings away from the edge of the city.

"Sydow's residence?"

"The very same."

Lybeck frowned. "I'd be careful to trust the abode of a wizard or the words in the streets of this place."

Batasta looked to his brother and they both wore an expression showing their weariness of Lybeck.

He rode over to where the horses all stood, tethered in a natural cul-de-sac by a creek. Dismounting, he patted his mount and nodded to the soldier who stood watch there.

"Where's Urell? I see his roan mount by the creek."

Batasta said, "I think he spends time by the creek with that Kylene."

"Really?" Lybeck responded, somewhat surprised.

"Not like that," Batasta shook his head. "I think they are just talking."

"Huh. Where are the others, Harland and Ransim?"

The twin pointed to a tent and Binje mirrored his brother's wide grin.

Lybeck turned his head to the tent, but didn't advance toward it.

The lantern light within showed the shape of Harland getting his trousers on, and the forms of two women as well.

"Ah well," Lybeck said. "One cannot buy class."

Harland emerged from the tent, smiling and waving at them. After him, two women moved through the tent flaps. Lybeck's frown deepened when he saw the two women conjoined at the hip, and struggling to cover up three breasts.

"How's your night?" Harland said to Lybeck.

"Not as challenging as yours."

"Aw, keeps me kicking," Harland declared with a clap of his hands.

Lybeck said, "I hear tell Rogan eluded us?"

"For now." Hands to his hips, Batasta jutted his chin toward the place of Sydow and said, "Word is Rogan and a few with him went there, but all scattered. Looks to be abandoned and I think the tongues in this town are forked more than a serpent's.

I dunno who else is with him for sure, though."

Lybeck joined his gaze. "We only care for Rogan."

Binje suggested, "But if we could find one of his traveling fellows, they could be made to tell us where he went."

Batasta said, "Story on the street was that he rode north of Azar on that hairy beast. They said a few of those with him went into the city, while a wagon with women aboard it headed on south, on the main path."

"South? They headed south?" Lybeck almost laughed. "What in the hell would anyone go south for?"

The twins shrugged as one as Urell waved at the conjoined twins that skipped back toward Azar on the trail.

Lybeck looked south. "Irem and Marduk? That's bad news."

"But Rogan went north," Harland reminded him. "That's where we shall go. He can't outdistance us on that damn elephant."

Lybeck turned, a grim look clouding his face. "But that thing can go a lot longer than a horse, though not as fast."

Harland laughed and waved to the north. "Let him run a while. We'll overtake him in a day. He can't fight us all. This venture will be over and we can pay these women a visit again on our way back to Nungal."

Binje went to his own tent and Harland returned to his spot. From another tent, a skinny boy emerged, covered in sweat, but holding a small purse of jingling coins. The youth blew Lybeck a kiss and then started to jog back toward Azar. From out of that same tent, Ransim's head poked out. He nodded at Lybeck and then returned to his tent.

Batasta walked over to Lybeck and patted him on the back lightly. "Go on then. Get some sleep, sir."

"I'll try," Lybeck told him. "Let's hope for a quiet night."

When Lybeck lay down on his bed roll and put his hands behind his head, he closed his eyes. He thought he heard distant thunder and cursed their luck. His eyes opened when the thunder sounded again, at regular intervals. Lybeck heard no raindrops fall.

Killer of Giants

*****

Rogan stood alongside Sydow when the twins and a dozen soldiers approached the abode of the wizard. The soldiers registered frustration and they rode about the area, all shaking their heads, a few throwing down their torches in anger.

"Why don't they just enter in?" Rogan asked Sydow, his anger and readiness to fight up and about to get raging.

Arms folded across her thin chest, Sydow told him, "They don't see what is in front of them."

"Come again?"

"None of them see the citadel as you do, as it really is." She turned and walked across the room to the place of the small pool behind her reclining cushions. Sydow waved her hands in a slashing motion and the bubbles of the water went blue, then red...then an image of the abode appeared. The shutters hung open, broken, the bricks, decayed, the weeds grew from the sidewalks, and none of the horses or Aliene appeared tethered outside.

"That's just pure madness," Rogan said hotly, head shaking a little. His eyes met those of the brides assembled behind him, and they all held hands to their lips, suppressing laughter, he guessed.

"Just how weak minds choose to see it," Sydow explained in a sarcastic voice. "The big men, the twins? Something bothers them, but they cannot grasp it. They are more sensitive than the rest."

Watching the images, he grunted knowingly. "Children of Nephilim."

Sydow smiled. "I think you need to terminate that thought."

Rogan's eyes narrowed at her. "Look, if you are hiding anything more from me, you need to let me know now. I nearly got my ass eaten looking for those bags of baby girl Nephilim bones, so where is my father and sister?"

"Feel better after that bath and the new pants we gave you?"

"Water was salty, but yeah, thanks," Rogan replied.

One of the women giggled and said, "You smell so pretty now."

"That's what I was going after," deadpanned Rogan.

Sydow's repression changed to one of happiness. "I do so thank you. Slaying the Chimeras, that is a great thing."

"I had a little help."

"The Chimeras are of legend and no one will discover their deaths for a long time. I am very grateful for the bones. They will power my magicks for a long time."

Rogan recalled being in that peculiar pit of bones, looking up to where Aliene stood. The long rope bound to his waist and up to her, Rogan figured he could climb up the walls if he had to, but the sight of various caves didn't fill him with happiness.

Surely, he'd thought, that's where the Chimeras lived. Were there more? Why did they congregate there? Had a different wizard, demon, or god bound the beasts to that valley to keep others away from the bones? Unsure of the answers to his wonderings, he'd scooped the sacks full of bones as fast as his big hands could.

"But those bastards, how many of them are out there, the soldiers?"

"Over fifty," Sydow said, her long nails drumming on her forearms.

"That's quite a few for one guy."

"They must really want you."

"Well, you can keep them from seeing you, but they are going to spot my big ass on that elephant in a days' time, no matter what direction I travel."

Sydow's look appeared almost too friendly to Rogan. "The answer will come to you. I don't suggest you go north towards your own homeland. That isn't where your errant blood-kin have went."

"I never said I wanted to go home."

"I care not for your reasons, but let that be as it is. I suggest a different trail for you to follow."

Rogan gazed at the bags full of gold and jewels that were his payment. "I'm through doing tasks for you."

"This task will be one for yourself, and for all mankind."

"Fuck mankind. I hate people. That are swine."

Nodding, Sydow gave some agreement. "I won't argue that. However, your friend Elisa and her mother have set a course to the south, to fabled Irem, to go to the grand meeting of world leaders and giants."

"To Marduk for real?" Rogan sighed. "The king of the Nephilim? Why the hell are they going there?"

"To slay him," Sydow confirmed. "Don't smile too much. She can do it, the girl, if she positions herself correctly."

"A dwarf could, if he crawled up Marduk's asshole. What is your point? Why do I care for all of this?"

"Representatives from all over the known world are going to Irem. Not every community, but a great many are sending parties to Irem."

"For what?" Rogan asked. "To what end? Marduk is the leader of the giants, but there aren't that many of them."

"A great deal," Sydow said. "But not all will attend. Not all world leaders or chiefs will attend, but they fear the retribution if they do not go."

"So what is his angle? To declare he's king of the world?"

"I think many believe that is what will happen." she clapped her hands and two of the brides brought them red wine in large cups.

"What will?"

"Marduk isn't a grand ruler and imperious as many think he is."

"Always heard he was."

"Not anymore." Sydow drank deep and shook his head. "Zazaeil, the demon in human flesh that is with him, has grown fatalistic. He might he calling them all forth to a party to end them all."

Rogan sighed and drank. "Good. Fewer politicians than before. Sounds like a winning deal. Where are my father and sister?"

Sydow waved at the pool and the bubbles erased the images there. An image of daylight appeared, and a group of men on horses, followed by several more men walking, hands tied behind their backs.

Rogan turned and near to spat his wine out. "Goddamn."

"Jarek, your father," Sydow said.

"I know who he is, damn you."

"Don't be wishing damning on me, Rogan. I'm giving you a clue, a means to save your father from a slaughter."

Rogan took a knee and looked closer. "What in hades happened?"

"By silly chance," Sydow informed him. "Forces of Azrag and other Nephilim from up near his territory sang a song of distraction. He was taken with your sister to Irem. There, they can fight in Marduk's big army, serve him as guards, be a slave, or meat for the mill of flesh at the Foundry."

"He's a mean bastard," Rogan replied. "He won't die easy."

"But against the giants…"

Rogan stood and yelled, "What difference would I make? One more Kelt going to his death? He held back and didn't join us in the venture against Nungal. They were to go on home, damn it."

"And you all died. Perhaps he was wise."

His ire dropping, Rogan mumbled, "Perhaps."

"I'm giving you a chance to save him."

"Fuck him." Rogan walked over to the bags of jewels. "What makes you think I want him saved?"

"You lie to me and yourself. You and he have differences, but you don't wish him a death like that."

Rogan gazed back at the pool. "How do you know so much of us?"

"I'm a wizard, right?"

Suddenly, Rogan's eyes widened and he glared at Sydow. "Gale!"

Sydow's face beamed. "Ah, it has occurred to you at last."

"My sister was with him." Rogan's eyes narrowed. "Gale is but twelve winters old." He faced the pool. "Where is she? Does she live?"

Once Sydow pointed at the pool, the images shifted from Jarek in the column of the captured to a long train of wagons. The pool showed that one wagon held ten girls of pre-teen age, one wore a face of anger, peering out the back. Her face, dirty and pale, hemmed by auburn locks, betrayed her as Rogan's blood.

"I'm surprised she doesn't jump out," Rogan said.

"She has," Sydow responded. "Her ankles are chained together."

Rogan smirked. "That's her."

Nodding, Sydow said, "Word is Marduk loves a spirited girl for his harem."

Smile gone, Rogan raged at her, "Are you mad? She's a child."

Sydow shrugged. "Perhaps she'll be sold to a sultan for a harem, I cannot be sure. Marduk is a giant. He slays with his member regular women, but, in time, she might grow to be his bride."

Rogan glared at the pool.

"Now, does she deserve that?"

"Bastards, rotten bastards," Rogan muttered. "What do you get from this? Me saving my father and her? Are you filling out a list of good deeds? That dog won't go to his puke. What is your angle?"

"Save your father and baby sister," Sydow said and exhaled. "If you see that big girl out to slay Marduk, you might want to help her."

"Killing a Chimera is one thing. Slaying the king of the giants is another."

"You slew Azrag."

"I jumped off an elephant. I had the element of surprise on

my hand. I have other things to worry on, like those fifty soldiers. But now I'm glad I killed the prick if he double-crossed my father and sister."

"The elephant is helpful," Sydow agreed. "She might help you again. Not with Marduk, but with other matters."

Rogan opened the bag of treasure. "I'll take some, but this is too much to carry on such a crazy trip."

Sydow put her cup down by the bag and patted Rogan's forearm. "You will come back for the rest."

"This place better look really good when I pass through."

Sydow smiled. "Avoid Madron if you can."

Rogan replied, "I stay away from campfire tale places if I can."

She grabbed Rogan by the wrist. "I'm sorry to have kept you from what you really desire this night."

Peering into her eyes, Rogan thought about how she would sense such a thing about him, his desires, his inner passion, and a desire for a release. He thought himself dumb for even considering how she understood that, after all she was a wizardess.

"I'll manage," he replied and started to walk toward the doors of the temple.

Sydow didn't release him and his steps staggered for a moment. She reached into his mane of auburn hair with her other hand and practically climbed up to be able to put her lips firm on his.

Not fighting her kiss, he let it happen, and then it felt a chance to pull away came too late. Her tongue, not really warm or wet, touched him, and suddenly Rogan's ears popped and all went still in his body. Before he could pull away or take in a breath, Rogan felt more hands on him.

It seemed impossible that so many hands caressed him and then that so many mouths touched his frame. Across his skin, he felt the brides of Sydow kiss and nibble at him, mostly at his nipples and then to his private areas. Caressed, touched, and then wantonly yanked, Rogan felt himself explode in an ecstatic episode that rivaled any paid-for experience in whoredom. His breaths grew stronger, but his body hadn't moved much.

"Come to us, Rogan," Sydow's throaty voice echoed in his mind, though not through his ears.

He felt the heat on his balls and then the incredible sensation on his manhood, like two mouths adored him. He felt fingernails grip his buttocks and even sink in a bit, causing enough pain to get his attention, but not enough to dissuade him from getting a delight.

"Come for us, Rogan," the voice in his ears echoed,

The thrills rippled across his body and rested down to his cock. In a moment, he felt himself explode in orgasm, and even his breath sucked in and out as he caught up with the perception.

And then it was over, and he stood outside the temple complex, alone. The mammoth eyed him at a distance and he looked down to see he still wore his pants. After a few more breaths, Rogan wondered if he came in his breeks, or if any of it ever happened. If anything, they delivered on his pleasure. He recalled the smile of Sydow and it made his entire body shudder repeatedly.

The smile of that wizard hung in Rogan's mind as he sat astride Aliene in the dead of night. They had moved in silence until coming to rest as the valley crested up before the dip downward. If anyone looked at them from afar, they'd not spot them in the moonlight with ease. He heard no shouts, whistles, or cries of their presence, so he smiled.

"Wodan smiles on us, girl," Rogan told Aliene. "Better than him crapping on us in our moment of need."

His eyes tapering, then widening, adjusted as the moonlight showed him the valley's floor a short way away.

"There they are, girl," Rogan said, staring into the night beyond where the army camped. "No matter where I go, they will follow."

Aliene breathed heavy a few times, but didn't utter another sound.

"Life is a real outhouse, huh?"

Again, Aliene rendered no opinion.

"Wodan," Rogan whispered and then let his head tilt back. His eyes shut at first, he opened them to look into an endless sky. "Be with me."

The sky stayed still. Wodan didn't reply.

His head level, Rogan looked across the valley.

"Let's do this, girl."

Aliene rumbled deep in her guts, then her trunk cleared out as she snorted.

Rogan thought if she were a horse, she'd be dancing. He couldn't stop smiling at first, but then gritted his teeth.

He snapped the harness and heeled her gentle. They started to move on forward. They walked for a good clip, but as they approached the perfectly laid-out camp, Aliene started to pick up her pace.

He heeled her on and the mammoth pushed forward at a rapid pace. Rogan knew she could go fast, as he'd seen it on trips to this besotted sector of the world, but the way they covered ground at that moment made his heart leap. He didn't know if any horse could cover ground like that so fast, and certainly, would never be as deadly. She stomped on as if her legs had a grudge against the earth.

Aliene broke into the open, going across a shallow creek down from where their horses were wandering. The mounts reared and ran at the thunder of Aliene as she charged at the tents of the soldiers.

Rogan didn't understand why soldiers sleep so close together, but these soldiers made their task much easier.

Aliene rumbled into the camp, a growl from her maw. Rogan didn't bother to yell for Wodan or entreat his help. He could feel his god under the feet of the elephant, with every spine and ribcage that crushed.

Wodan felt pleased.

CHAPTER SEVEN

Trashed

While the irregular thunder rolled in Lybeck's ears, his tired thoughts lit on actually confronting Rogan. He himself wanted nothing to do with fighting such a warrior. With the soldiers along and the twins, Lybeck hoped such a task wouldn't fall on him. Lybeck knew Jarek, the father of Rogan, and he wouldn't have wanted to fight that old man.

He sat up as the thunder he heard couldn't be weather related, as it had a specific rhythm. His heart throbbing, fear rose in his mind and dropped to his bladder as the thudding thunder carried on. As if death came for him in the night in a drumming thunder, Lybeck near to passed water as the loud crushing sounds came close to him.

Clear from his near slumber, Lybeck almost made it to his feet when the crashing sound and earth-trembling wave passed by him. When he grabbed for his boots, he fell flat on his face, his ears full of cries and thunderous noise. Lybeck crawled outside, seeing the chaos and destruction wrought.

Though the moon hadn't reached a full state yet, it cast enough light to show what transpired. The fifty soldiers, all camping in tents set out in neat rows, faired bad. The rows of tents resembled small loaves of bread, rolled out into perfect rectangular bundles, but then ruined in their uniformity by angry children stomping on the baking table.

After a shake of his head, this image vanished, and his eyes confirmed his terror. The huge man had ridden a white mammoth through the camp.

More terror birthed in him, for the hirsute elephant stopped at the edge of the camp and turned about. He didn't just ride away. It wasn't over.

Lybeck seized his boots and weapons before running away from the camp. He had little time to perform this as the rider directed the mammoth to take another pass through the camp. Legs pumping as he moved out of the site, Lybeck's eyes closed, remembering the disfigured tents and ruined bodies as the elephant moved through.

BOOM, BOOM, BOOM…

He stopped, turned, and saw a repeat of the horror in real time. Lybeck saw founts of blood shoot up in the moonlight, streaking the hairy snow-white legs of the beast. Like a horse stabbing down into a muddy river, the ejecta of the soldiers' bodies squirted up and made wellsprings in the campfire lights from the mammoth's path. One voice cried out, startled awake, a portion of him crushed, but the back feet of the elephant cut off the cry brusquely.

"Urell," Lybeck called out, unsure if he could hear his cry in the din. Amidst the cries of what soldiers crawled out in terror, the roar of the elephant, and the howl of the rider of the beast, chaos reigned. "His god," Lybeck snarled, trying not to spit as he talked to no one. "He's calling on his god. The sonofabitch."

He looked over at the pickets who must've half-slumbered at the entrance of their invader. They gaped at the scene, holding crossbows. They never released a bolt and their mouths shut as they swallowed.

"Fire, you assholes," Lybeck screamed at the pickets. "Shoot him, shoot him down fucking now!"

After the second pass around the camp, the rider...
ROGAN...waved his huge blade and kicked at his mount again.
He directed the beast about as easy as anyone could a dancing
horse. Lybeck thought that near to impossible to his eyes, and yet,
the beast responded. Rogan headed the elephant toward the tents
away from the others already crushed, toward where the twins,
Urell, and he had bedded down.

Though the pickets did fire at Rogan, he didn't seem to act
as if he'd been injured. The creature trampled on over their larger
tents and in a straight line. As the invader aimed south, a picket
did stand in their way. His crossbow aimed high, he tried to shoot
Rogan off his mount.

The auburn-haired Kelt went low, hugging the mammoth,
so Lybeck guessed the bolts missed. He gave the picket credit for
courage, if no brains, and points for reloading so fast. Nonetheless,
the soldier couldn't dodge the rampaging beast, unable to elude
the swathe cut by its long tusks.

The elephant scooped up the soldier, who still clung to his
crossbow. The beast moved its head from side to side as it ran,
shaking the soldier like a dog does a prized bone, but the man
didn't dislodge. Lybeck wondered if the trunk came up as the
soldier soon did fly up between the tusks and near to over the
mammoth's head...only to be met by the sword of Rogan, and
lose his head at the root.

When the animal paused and turned, a few of the pickets
came forward to try and get a better shot. Lybeck didn't run
to help them and felt glad he ignored this initial desire. Rogan
jumped off the elephant, sword over his back, then chopping
down on the first picket near him.

The force of the blade drove through the soldier's head,
slicing it clean in half, then cleft down the neck and lodged deep
in his chest. Lybeck expected Rogan to cut the man in half to the
crotch. Hell, he wagered Rogan thought that would happen, too.
The big youth didn't hesitate, but quickly returned to his mount,
jumping up on the elephant as it swung about.

Lybeck thought he'd see Rogan fly off the way the mammoth moved so abrupt, but the Kelt held on and righted himself in position, atop again.

Chaos reigned in the camp when many of the soldiers did arise. Lybeck saw bodies in the night run to and fro, not knowing where a safe place lay. They didn't take up arms to fight back, each seemed to just want to escape what alarm arrived in the night. As reality dawned on a few of them, they did look about for a weapon, but were quick to just run away.

Save for a few.

One of the Kushite women popped out of the debris like a rabbit from a hole. A mirror image of this warrior woman arose, but tripped and fell as her sister ran toward the assaulting elephant. The woman reached to the ground and her hand came up with a short sword. Lybeck doubted the weapon one of her own, but the way she swung it in preparation to fight looked like that didn't matter much.

Since the hairy creature didn't run at a great clip, and seemed intent on swinging about to cause more destruction, the Kushite woman had no trouble attacking them head on. He thought her attack madness, but saw what she had in mind all the same. The woman leapt at the face of the mammoth, gripping the left tusk with her free hand and soon balancing on it with her bare feet. Scrunching at the knees, the Kushite prepared to launch herself up at Rogan for a death strike.

Even Lybeck knew better than to stand on a living thing to launch an assault. However, the woman planned her attack without this idea as a base plan. As she went to jump, the mammoth's great head thrust up, sending the Kushite up off the tusk and into the air.

Her planned death strike on Rogan swung into empty air, but his great blade swiped out and connected with the woman's face. The sword tip sliced into her face, removing her jaw. The strike sent the jaw spinning around her face, her teeth and tongue in the back of her mane of hair for a moment as she hung in the air. She then fell down, the head of the mammoth butting her back, pushing her in front of the hairy elephant. The wounded Kushite fell, screaming until the beast flattened her into silence.

Lybeck expected him to turn around and go for another pass through the derelict camp, but the attacker knew when to go. The elephant rumbled on out to the south, moving fast and almost jogging as it went.

Running back into the camp, Lybeck saw the twins crawling on their all fours and Urell trying to get his trousers on.

Urell stared after the invader, saying, "That sonofabitch." His eyed widened in the moonlight as he yelled at the crawling Kushite woman, saying, "Kylene!"

"Rotten bastard," Batasta swore, his brother helping him up by the forearm. He pointed over at the horses and started to command, "Mount up and get after him…" He stopped when he realized the spooked horses had wandered away and that there weren't many to pay attention to his orders.

Binje's arms swung about, his mouth hanging open as if he could embrace the camp and put it back together again. He, like Lybeck, watched Urell scramble over to the one called Kylene. They woman had stopped over the body of the slain Kushite warrior. Urell embraced her shoulders for a moment, but let her go quickly, giving her room to wail and growl at the empty night.

Lybeck pitied the soldiers, many who were good fighters, perhaps longtime servers, to die in such a mangled way. *Poor bastards,* he thought, *they woke up beyond night and might never know why.*

Urell looked away from the wailing woman to stare at Lybeck and then across the devastated camp. "The gods piss on us this accursed night."

"Gods," Lybeck spat. "Speak to me not of gods. Surely, that Kelt is in league with devils."

Batasta scanned the demolished camp. "His god must be God." His voice came out steady but in a low tone. The contrast came when he yelled, "How did this happen?"

Binje stood in front of his brother. "Let's figure out what we have left."

As the twins shouted at the pickets coming into the camp, Lybeck stood beside a rising Urell and watched Rogan disappear into the night.

Urell offered Lybeck his flask.

The container touching his stomach, Lybeck didn't look down as he grabbed it, uncorked it, and took a swig.

Urell said, "This just got more difficult."

"I doubt Nungal or Kamala-ur saw this coming," Lybeck replied, drinking once more before handing the flask back.

Urell gazed across the encampment. "Most that were struck are dead, a few maimed..." As he spoke, Binje speared a survivor that kept crying out, his mangled arm slapping at the twin's thigh. "...nasty business, war."

Lybeck's face turned red with anger. "This isn't war. This is all bullshit. Doing the bidding of those rich pricks and their men were slaughtered...for what?"

"Keep your voice down," Urell hissed, eying the twins and the pickets going through the camp.

"Another bunch of men killed because of them, no more important in scope than the fake war on Nungal for their betting jollies."

Urell turned in front of him, blocking his view of the others. "We are being paid to kill that bastard that got away. We need to do our job."

"That bastard just slaughtered a small army single-handed."

"He had help," Urell reminded him. "I salute his ingenuity. He couldn't fight us all and we would've caught up to him in a day."

Lybeck twisted, ripping himself away from the scene. "There isn't enough booze to mute this madness."

Urell said, "We have to figure out what we have left."

Kylene's screams turned to words, saying, "I'll kill him myself. I will slay that Rogan, the rotten bastard himself with my own hands." Her eyes glowered at them all, full of tears and not caring if that was so. "I swear unto Amon this will be so."

Ransim and Harland walked up to stand with the men and look down at her. As the two men exchanged glances, Kylene leapt up and drove her knee into Ransim's crotch.

She kneed him again, saying the word, "Kasaque!" Over and over. "Her name was Kasaque!" Ransim grabbed his fruits with both hands and dropped to his knees. Harland stepped away, turning to one side to guard himself. "You rotten pricks! So busy buggering boys or screwing freaks! You couldn't get out to fight that thing or kill that savage?"

"Stop all of this!" Batasta walked over to them. "What a nightmare. There are only twenty of us left, counting you four, my brother, and I."

"Thirty dead," Lybeck stated as his hands flexed, wanting a weapon to fill his fingers. "Damn it all."

Batasta raged, "We shall get him still. I'd go after him still if it were just Binje and I. Let us gather this up and get ready for the morrow."

Urell said, "Better craft a good raven's note to Nungal."

Touching his elbow lightly, Lybeck led Urell away from the group without making it obvious he wanted to speak to him. "What were those girls still doing here anyway? I thought they were to be given to Zazaeil at Azar?"

"The demon Zazaeil, living in flesh, didn't want a few of them." Urell, such a hard man, shivered as he looked at the sky and thought of what he knew. "The devil Zazaeil saw a few of them had no babies within, and thus, didn't want them."

"Damn," Lybeck muttered. "They couldn't have been far along and he could tell?"

"So, they are here and the girl met her fate this night under the hand of Rogan." Urell breathed and then said, "He must die."

Turning away, Lybeck looked south, no longer able to hear the steps of the mammoth. He heard it thunder a few times way far off, and cussed with color over all of it.

*****

Rogan didn't know how long Aliene could carry on the fast pace she used leaving the camp. In the past, Rogan hadn't seen one of the mammoths put to the test for limits. However, once they'd been south of the camp for what he guessed a mile, her steps started to slow. She kept up a brisk walk for a few more miles before stopping and seeking out one of the creeks far off the path around Azar.

He slipped off her to relieve himself and get a drink. Rogan kept looking back, but no one pursued. Cursing himself, his father's words rang in his ears to never look back. He oft thought that a manly boast, but considered it did take time. Then again, they were usually on horseback and not on one of these beasts.

Aliene stopped drinking and turned about, facing south.

Rogan climbed atop her again and they rode on, walking in the night, but covering territory well. They went across many paths well-travelled by wagons or horses, cutting corners and heading down small slopes dangerous to some. Aliene gave no troubles and moved on at a steady pace, as if she understood where they headed.

"Wodan's asscrack," Rogan said aloud to nobody. "I don't know where the hell I'm headed now."

Though he had jerky and hard tac in his bags, his stomach ached for something of substance. Riding parallel to civilization, Rogan understood that what he really craved wasn't far away. Again, gazing over his shoulder, he wondered how long those fools would take to set off after him again. He recalled their horses running into the night like mad. He figured they would want to bury or account for their dead in some fashion. Recovering their mounts and getting ready to go after him still, he figured he had some time.

"Can't hide riding on you too well, can I?" Rogan said to Aliene, who gave no response. "We shall see what we can find."

Not knowing the layout of Azar well, he could surmise the city hugged in a crescent about the edge of the sea.

Rogan blinked hard and coughed, not realizing he'd been asleep atop the mammoth for some time. Startled awake by the huge animal stopping, Rogan gripped the handles of both knives as some terror lit in his chest. His eyes scanned where Aliene halted and his body relaxed. At first, he thought himself dreaming as they stood behind a series of buildings on the outskirts of Azar. A few torches lit the area where a couple large tubs recessed back from the rear of one building. Out of one of these tubs climbed a nude woman, reaching out for a towel to dry herself, unconcerned with the giant creature and the man atop her staring at her.

"Good evening," Rogan said quietly.

"It'll be morning soon," she replied, still drying herself, not hiding her nakedness.

His eyes drank in her body, guessing her age much older than himself, but still a fine-looking woman. Her small breasts sagged some, but they didn't have far to go anyhow. With her leg on the side of the tub, her saw her ample rump looked as fine as any younger woman.

Her eyes on his, she asked, "In town long, outlander?"

"You know I'm from afar?"

"I'm not stupid."

"Never said you were."

She smiled and her teeth weren't the best he'd ever seen. Then again, Rogan didn't plan to marry her.

He slid off Aliene and reached into the side pouch on his belt. Though the light from the waning moon and the torches ran dim, the tiny jewels in his hand sparkled.

Her eyes flared. "That's a fortune, just to have old me?"

He gave a mild shrug. "They're just rocks. I'll find more."

She wiped her abdomen down and between her legs. His eyes studied her there but saw nothing in the darkness. Her grin widened as he handed her the jewels.

"What?"

"You are such a child, still looking for what you know is there out of instinct. An older man would have his breeks down and working it, trying to get hard."

Rogan then smiled. "I'm hard already."

She winked and put the towel over the edge of the tub. "Such is youth." She then gripped the jewels in her right hand and waved him closer with her left. As she reached out to start to undo the front of his pants, she lay the jewels on a tray beside the tub.

He helped her open his pants and then shoved them down to his knees.

Her hand gripped the long shaft of his manhood and she looked up into his face. As she pumped at him slowly, he leaned down a little, reaching out with his right hand. As his fingers probed her sex, she gasped a little.

"Tender touch for a savage."

Eye to eye with her, his mane of hair touching her wet locks, Rogan whispered, "I'm not a complete animal."

He turned her about, guiding her shoulders down. Rogan then gripped her hips and lifted her up to stand on the steps beside the tub. He still had to squat a little to line up the act, but made the best of it. He guided the head of his member to her, worked it at her for a while, to the point she shuddered. Still, he didn't enter her right away, content to play a bit with her. Again, she shook and fought down a cry.

"You didn't have to make me come," she said, then gasped as he entered her, giving her a few inches at first and then slowly working into her more and more.

Rogan said nothing as he clutched her hip and shoulder, not holding her tight enough to hurt her, but clasping plenty to keep her from falling off the tub.

As he moved into her over and over, Aliene dipped her trunk in the tub. She inhaled a great measure of water and then squirted it over her right leg. Rogan continued on the woman as

Aliene again refilled her trunk and washed off another leg.

The mammoth's actions didn't deter Rogan a bit as he sped up in his motions, his grip on the woman tightening. At last he grunted deep and thrust harder many times until his pace slackened.

His breath a bit faster, Rogan stepped back from her and grabbed her towel. He dipped it in the tub and then wiped over his manhood. He then had the humorous image of Aliene bathing them in water as they did the act, but knew it wouldn't have stopped him.

She turned, trembling as if she read his thoughts, and said, "If that thing would've squirted us, I'd have peed."

Both laughed and Rogan pulled up his pants. "Fare you well…"

"Ava," she replied. "I'm Ava."

"Like in the creation story?"

"Kind of."

Rogan gave her a small bow fitting for royalty and turned away. Back atop Aliene, he guided her away and back to the outer edges of Azar.

He clung riding to the outer reaches, careful to avoid the plain that led to the area of Ludvig's ranch. Rogan saw the torches and dim glow of lanterns that signified civilized abodes. As he went along, dreaming of roasted meat and perhaps another woman to go with the meal, Rogan saw a few flickering lights on the edge of the city. He could smell the sea, but the tiny fires intrigued him.

Though only a few piles of stones, Rogan saw metal rods across them and noted the flames seething out like a beating heart. On the rack of metal rods lay the ruined bodies of animals, goats he guessed by the horned remains. He saw a thin figure walking about the stones in the night. When Aliene strolled up, the figure turned, putting back the hood to show long strands of gray hair.

"Evening," Rogan said as Aliene stopped.

Her eyes twinkled in the firelight as she said, "It'll be morning soon."

"Your goats smell fine."

Her long face titled as she looked the huge elephant over and then stared at him. "You must be hungry to think that."

"I'll pay you for some."

"The goats aren't mine," she answered.

Rogan guessed, "They belong to the gods now?"

"A slight appeasement," she explained.

"I was never one for belief in animal sacrifice to make the gods up there happy," Rogan said and started to climb down from Aliene. "Would you have one to make for me that the gods don't want?"

"A god will come for these," she gestured at the smoldering goats. "If I were you, I'd keep going on that monster."

Rogan sighed. "I'm really hungry, woman."

"You will soon be hungry and dead."

"Are dead goats worth dying over?"

"Some might think so," she shrugged a little, "but you are a big man with a big animal. I cannot stop your will."

"Damned religious maniacs," Rogan muttered. "Waste of flesh for gods." He walked closer to the nearest sizzling goat and sniffed.

"You aren't really going to eat that, are you?"

Rogan picked up a mitt the woman had used to adjust the hot rods and folded it over the edge of the metal poles. "It looks plenty done, but it'll do." He pulled the rods down and smiled at the smoking meat.

Her arms folded under her robe, the woman said, "I suppose it doesn't matter, really." She gazed off into the waning night. "My husband has eaten his full and this is what the night gods demand."

Rogan leaned the rods of the stones and cut out a hunk of meat with one of his knives. After he started to chew some of the meat, he said, "Tell your husband thanks."

She sighed a little. "He won't be pleased if he awakes."

"Yeah?" Rogan wondered as he glanced about, still wolfing down the meat. "Your husband a god?"

"Close. He's a cyclops."

Rogan nodded with no emotion. "And Wodan's wife juggles my balls. Many cheers unto you."

"You should go. He'll be displeased and probably beat me."

"Guess ya shouldn't have married a damned cyclops." Rogan swallowed and bit into the goat more.

"The black cyclops of Azar."

"I'm all aflutter with fear." Rogan snorted, spat out some fat, and asked, "Could ya tell me anything about the roads to Irem down south?"

"Why do you want to go there?"

"I don't recall saying."

She blinked and looked back to her abode. "Follow the coastline mostly and you will find Irem. That is the smarter way to go instead of the open lands. Avoid Madron. Mind you, there are a few things in your way before you reach Irem."

"Like more black cyclops?"

"Your humor is not appreciated."

Rogan fumbled in the pouch that hung from back of his waist belt. He retrieved out several shiny stones and threw them at her feet. "All right. Anywhere near the coast I could get a map or a guide?"

"The sailors at the southern ports ought to be able to direct you. Don't mistake them for the pirates, for they are many hereabouts. One or the other, they will know. A man like you can get information one way or another, I'd bet."

"Hope so."

"The sacrifice to the black cyclops awaits in the stocks by the docks." She pointed in the distance to the east. "The sailors who offer up that sacrifice, much better than a goat, they can tell you all you need to know if they don't choose to kill you."

"Yer scaring the crap out of me," Rogan said with

guilelessness. He then ate a great deal and threw what he didn't back up onto the metal grate. He wiped his mouth on the mitten and dropped it to the ground.

Indignation in her tone, she asked, "Is there anything else you need?"

"Not that you can provide, but thanks."

She looked at her home and wrung her hands. "He's stirring. He's drunk. He will want his sacrifice at the dock."

Rogan shrugged. "Good for him. I ate his damned goat up. He'll wanna kill me dead for just that?"

"Piss on the goats," she shouted. "His sacrifice is something I cannot give him. Be gone fast or he will take it from you."

"I'm not afraid of monsters," Rogan said, looking at the stone dwelling and reaching back to draw the sword from his back. The blade slid out slow and he brought it to bear as the door opened to the brick home.

From tales about the fires of youth, Rogan expected a great deal from the cyclops. The figure that emerged stood taller than him, but not by much. The cyclops didn't wield a club, mace or sword, but held a skin of wine in one hand and a portion of bread in the other. He staggered down the hill toward them, but walked on regular feet, not hooves. His lower portion weren't goat loins, but hairless legs suited for any man. What swung between his legs, though, impressed Rogan and would belong better on a horse.

"Wodan, you are a prick," Rogan cursed his god's humor.

The closer he stumbled to them, Rogan discovered the persona had one eye, but that was because the other one appeared melted or ruined to his flesh, like a wound closed with a branding iron. The single eye wasn't in the middle of his face, but over to the right. His skin did glisten obsidian in the moonlight. When the eye focused on Rogan, the head snapped back, throwing back his long, beaded locks of hair like a cat o'nine tails.

Not moving his stance, Rogan waited, but the woman progressed back.

Killer of Giants

"You have sealed your doom," she snarled. "He shall slay you and then go take his sacrifice of the stocks by the sea."

His curiosity high on what that meant, Rogan paused still as the cyclops dropped the wine skin and charged. The steps of the cyclops were shoddy, as the drink hung heavy on him. Rogan baited him in and easily swung, dodging the big man.

Rogan dropped his sword, grabbed the cyclops by the back shoulders, and swung his right boot up between his legs. His boot connected with a pair of testicles larger than apples. Cyclops or no, the being choked out a cry, stumbled forward more, and then fell to his knees. Both hands on his groin, the cyclops wailed, He then convulsed and ejected a huge stream of vomit.

"Thus ends the Cyclops of Azar," Rogan stated, picking up his sword.

"No," the woman screamed wild, running to the cyclops and embracing his head. "Don't do it."

Rogan stepped up behind the cyclops, sword at his side, and kicked him full on in the balls again. This time, the cyclops fell over, whimpering, holding his crotch, trying not to choke on his vomit.

Saying nothing, Rogan returned his blade to his sheath and went over to Aliene. He gazed at the woman, stroking the long locks of her cyclops as he struggled on the ground. The woman kissed the cyclops over and over.

Rogan climbed up on Aliene, took a deep breath, and didn't look back as they headed toward the docks.

CHAPTER EIGHT

Warning

Urell cursed as he stood up in the sunlight from the edge of the creek bank. Working his head from side to side, he stopped in his motions, glaring at Lybeck who stood a few yards away.

"Get a taste of blood, did you?" Lybeck asked, wiping his face dry with a towel and then drying his neck under his beard.

A shiver went through Urell and he smacked his lips, spat, and then scrubbed his face with his own towel. "Dammit, did one of them crawl to the creek?"

Lybeck gave a mild shrug. "The twins hauled one out a while back when you were doing your morning ritual."

Urell looked over at the twins in the high grass and said, "Funny you call it that, Lybeck. Our morning ritual is dropping crap and wiping, and theirs is that stupid sacrifice to their forefather."

His face turning south, Lybeck said, "I don't care what religion a man has or what god he chooses to delude himself with. The twin's usual morning thing of cutting and burning a rat, ground squirrel, or rabbit doesn't matter to me. However, this morning, they are having a greater sacrifice."

Doing a double-take at Lybeck and then facing the twins in

the wildflowers, Urell asked, "What in the hell? You said they..."

"Hauled one of the ones we thought dead out of the creek, yes."

Blinking many times, his voice grave, Urell hissed, "Damn those wretches. They need something alive."

"Rogan and that damn elephant mutilated so many soldiers, the twins have a larger sacrifice today."

"Bastards," Urell mumbled.

"Coulda been either one of us if the Kelt chose to ride a different direction. Think on that for a moment."

"Fuckin' twins," Urell gripped the pommel of the blade strapped to his waist. "The other soldiers, Harland and Ransim, let them have one of their wounded number?"

"Look around," Lybeck advised, his left arm sweeping about the camp. "They are out getting the horses back."

"Fuckers." Urell stomped over to the high grass area where the heads of the twins rose above the long stems.

Lybeck followed along at a more casual gait, but arrived in time to see what made Urell gasp and retreat a step.

The twins didn't react to Urell's intake of air. They had bound the hands and feet of the wounded solider, but that appeared silly to Lybeck. The soldier, whose name he couldn't recall, appeared to have a pulverized pelvis and broken thighs. How the poor young man lived as long as he did amazed him. His life ended in front of them as Batasta slit his throat and Binje ripped the youth's ribs open with his small hatchet. In a moment, Binje held the beating heart of the soldier out into the daylight as it broke over the land. The twins chanted something Lybeck couldn't quite get, and he felt glad when it ended that it was over.

But it wasn't over.

Lybeck saw so many men pray or sacrifice, and then go about their day, he wagered this would be that, like in those cases. Nonetheless, light shone on all of them, but it didn't flow from the rising sun over the horizon. In the opposite direction, a golden light shone bright, but not enough to splay over the countryside.

The unique light bathed the brothers, and, in turn, made Lybeck and Urell cast long shadows. Lybeck and Urell turned to face from whence the light came from, and, in turn, backed up. The twins, though, both fell to their knees and broke into great smiles.

"Grandfather," Batasta exclaimed to the floating cloud of light moving toward them just above the grasses. The small cloud churned into a gelatin like substance, mixing about in the air, and then taking on a humanoid shape.

"Synuria," Binje said in reverence, his face dropping near to the earth for a moment before looking up in ecstasy. "You have come unto us."

The shape in the air floated over the land, taking on more features, but nothing too remarkable to Lybeck. He would've been more impressed if the figure sported long spikes, claws, and razor-tipped wings. This figure appeared plain, lengthy geared, rounded at the edges, like a child molding a doll out of earthen clay. The face even took on the appearance of a series of folds, bearing no real, stable humanoid features.

The being stopped over the dead soldier, who shuddered and expanded like a great breath had entered the body all over. In a few moments, the soldier relaxed and fell to pieces like old leaves falling to the ground. A red mist arose and drew unto the being that was Synuria.

"My boys," the figure grated out in a voice that made Lybeck and Urell stumbled back and fall to the ground at once. "You are deceived."

"Tell us, Grandfather," Batasta implored him, still on his knees.

Synuria faced Batasta. "Those of the dwelling beyond, those of Sydow, deceive you. They are there and have brought about your near destruction."

Binje begged, "Tell us how to crush the spells of these evildoers."

Synuria tilted his head toward the other Kaldwell twin and said, "The Kelt rebel has slain the Chimeras and looted the Slough of Despair of bones."

"The bastard," Batasta growled.

Lybeck elbowed Urell. "Slough of Despair? Is that a real place?"

Urell said, "Heard of it in tales, I don't know." He gripped Lybeck's arm. "Who the hell is that? What the hell is that?"

The being said to the twins, "With the bones from the Slough, Sydow will gain even more arcane abilities, but that is not my actual concern. She flummoxes you with her own abilities, now."

"That bitch," Binje spat.

"She has sent the rebel Kelt on an errand to the south," Synuria said in a nonchalant voice that still made Lybeck scared enough to piss. "Sydow plays games, but forgets who else can move pieces on a board of chance. Her power has made her careless. Her power has made her arrogant."

Batasta asked, "What shall we do, Grandfather?"

Lybeck and Urell locked eyes. Both mouthed the word *grandfather*. They'd heard it before, but the same thought sank into them at the same time.

"I will open your eyes," Synuria promised them. "Go forth and attain the bags of bones the Kelt gave unto Sydow. They are the remains of your many displaced cousins, your sisters, from the Slough of Despair."

Both twins bowed their heads quick and then looked to their grandfather again, both smiling.

Synuria said, "I grant you this boon for the heart of this soldier. His soul will keep me company for a while."

Binje asked, "What shall we use the bones for?"

The being turned his face toward Binje. "Whatever you like. Sydow's games disrupted by me and your future plans insured better, that is all one can ask."

Batasta nodded. "Where is the Kelt bound for? What is his

true enough errand for Sydow?"

Synuria shuddered, the image fading a little. "Not enough heart here for that, my boys. Fare you well."

The image over the dead soldier glowed brighter, and then started to glitter all over before disappearing altogether.

A sound like thunder rippling away echoed in their ears as the twins stood tall. They faced Lybeck and Urell, rubbing their eyes at the same time. They blinked, squared up against each other, and broke into hearty laughter. They then turned to the north and shouted out in unison. Loud.

Lybeck whispered, "Is Nungal paying us enough for this?"

His head slowly shaking from side to side, Urell said, "They see something. Their senses are sharp."

The two sprinted forward a few yards, then broke off their advance and jogged over to where they all had made a new makeshift camp in the night. They started to pull on their undershirts, chainmail vests, and then leggings.

Also returning to the camp, Lybeck said in a low voice, "They look like kids bundling up to play in the snow."

No sooner had a group of the soldiers returned with some of the horses, the twins ran to the arrivals. They barked out orders and even started to saddle up their own mounts.

Urell sighed and then walked with Lybeck to retrieve their own horses. "I think the boys are off on their own errand. They forget our purpose."

"They think they are so great and chosen, they follow their own noses."

"They do talk to demons," Urell named the image they saw.

Lybeck gazed back at where the remains of the dead soldier lay. "Yeah. Grandfather, indeed."

"If those twins are from a Nephilim, their grandfather had to be one."

His face screwed up with anger, Lybeck answered, "I figured it out, yes."

"Something one doesn't see every day."

"But Synuria wasn't at their service, mind you. That thing played games with them, but they were like giddy kids getting candy or cheap coins."

Urell grabbed up his own saddle and watched the twins getting ready. "Sydow. Huh. They go to fight a wizard."

"Yes, their grandfather endowed them with a gift, opened their eyes, hell, wiped their asses for all we could tell. Now, they head off to do the bidding of that demon. He was very coy, getting them to go after Sydow for him."

"Bones from the Slough of Despair," Urell affirmed and shuddered. "The stuff of camp tales and nightmares."

"Where the female Nephilim are cast aside," Lybeck said. "The thing said Rogan slew the Chimeras there. If he did that, well, I'd feel better if we had the thirty men back."

Urell stared over at the bodies, bound and wrapped up in rows. "We'll tell the names to the families or representatives back in Communal. I sent a few of them into Azar to fetch propellant that will aide in the pyres."

"You going with those twins to Sydow or will you stay here?"

"Screw them in the rear," Urell remarked bitterly. "I'm a soldier. I'll watch out for my soldiers."

Lybeck knew him more of a mercenary and retired soldier, but figured Urell wanted no part of the wizard of Azar.

The twins mounted up and turned to them. "Lybeck, are you with us?"

A bolt of fear went through him, but Lybeck found himself mounting up. He looked down at Urell.

"Good to know ya," Urell said and winked.

Lybeck fought down the bile brimming in the top of his guts and gripped the reins tight.

Killer of Giants

*****

The sun came near to breaking over the sea as Aliene and Rogan neared the docks. He studied the structures in the distance, greater places built out into the sea where some vessels drew close. Other greater ships lay anchored further out in the water, their smaller crafts sent forth and moored in the docks. Several log structures peppered the land near the docks and he questioned the wisdom of building such things near sea water. He didn't have long to contemplate that thought when he heard his name shrieked.

His shock of auburn hair twisted, confused who could even know his moniker at such a distant locale. In a moment, he smiled, recognizing the small woman who ran across the weeds toward him.

"Rogan," Bodyne screamed out again, her left hand holding up her long frock so she could run.

In the next second, Rogan saw why she wailed as two thin men appeared not twenty yards behind her. Each carried a short sword and neither wore any pants.

Bodyne closed the gap between them fast and Rogan slid from atop Aliene. The enormous creature turned, tusks and trunk up at the sight of the running naked men.

She didn't say anything more, but fell against Rogan's legs. His left hand touched her hair softly, while his right hand drew out the blade from his back.

The two skinny men, clearer to Rogan then as sunburnt men full of gaudy tattoos, beheld him and Aliene at last. One stopped, the other stumbled and near to fell before he also ceased running.

Rogan patted Bodyne's head and stepped forward.

The first man held up his left hand and let his sword arm drop. "Ho, traveler! What are you doing?"

No words came from Rogan as he reared back with his blade and struck.

The man did raise his small blade in a defensive move, but Rogan's father knew his craft…and the large sword passed through its shorter cousin and the man as well. So skinny and frail the man stood that Rogan's sword cut him across in half, off at the top of his neck, across his chest, and out the right side. As his body fell and his lungs flared out like baby birds seeking sustenance, Rogan stomped toward the other who stumbled.

The second man turned and started to run.

Rogan reared back and threw his sword. It spun toward the runner awkward, but only struck the man across the back, drawing no blood. The move was enough to drop the man. In a few moments, Rogan jumped on the man's back with both boots. Air left the man abrupt and he gagged, but Rogan didn't hesitate. He picked up the man's own small blade and inserted it through his back, sure he nailed the heart.

While the man died, as the blood gushed and then he broke wind, Rogan retrieved his sword from the grass and returned to Bodyne. She'd pushed herself into hugging one of Aliene's legs for cover.

"You need to choose your friends better," Rogan informed her.

"Pirates, sea scum," Bodyne said and spat in their direction. "You wouldn't believe what I've been through." She then looked at her hands and Aliene closer. "Goddess! She has blood and guts on her legs."

"It's been a rough night for us too."

Rogan lifted her to her feet as she proceeded to tell him all about her bad luck in the city, being captured by pirates as she tried to just get a room.

"They just wanted me to cook for them," she said with a pouting face. "They never even found all of my loot money."

Rogan looked back at the bodies. "What was all this about? No pants? They didn't like breakfast?"

She gave him a twisted grin. "No. They have been out all night, drunk, and decided to rape the cook. They were too stupid drunk to get it up so I kicked one in the balls and ran for it like mad."

"There's a third one?"

"He won't be running for a while." Suddenly, her eyes widened and she grabbed both of his sinewy forearms. "Rogan! You must save them!"

"Who?" he sighed. "I'm not some hero in a tavern yarn, remember? I just want to get away from here."

"No, no, Thyssen and the dwarf princess, Shazia."

After an incredulous look of his own, Rogan asked, "Are you drunk?"

Again, she gripped his forearms. "They are in the stocks by the docks. They are to be sacrificed to the cyclops."

His head moving side to side in disgust, Rogan turned to Aliene and then knelt. "Get on my back."

"What?" Bodyne said, eyes blinking fast.

"I can't pull you up on her. Get on my back. Come on."

Bodyne stood behind him, and then wrapped both of her arms about his neck. As he started to stand, her legs went about his thick torso. He climbed up the side of Aliene and swung his leg over. Bodyne settled behind him on the great elephant, but slipped her arms down about his midsection, tight.

"Hold on," he ordered as Aliene started to move forward.

Her grip already tight, Bodyne replied, "I won't let go."

"Damn Thyssen," Rogan said and cursed again. "Damn you all. Why I should give a damn about any of you is a jest from Wodan."

"Don't blame your god for our bad luck."

"I'm pissed at my god for my bad luck, sweetheart."

"I'm not your sweetheart."

Rogan grunted a little as Aliene moved on. "Maybe ya like the company of the limp-dicked pirates?"

She fell silent as the mammoth rumbled forward.

As the sun began to break over the earth, Rogan spotted the figures in stocks facing the sunrise. There were three people tethered there in the stocks, not far from the docks. Their approach did garner the attention of a few men clad in loose-fitting breeks and turbans, but at the sight of Aliene, they retreated back into the buildings nearby.

They stopped by the series of stocks and Rogan looked down at those imprisoned there. All three were secured by the wood planks by the head and wrists, their bodies bent over, asses aiming east: Thyssen, a female dwarf with curly black hair, and something not quite human...mostly in the form of a man but sporting reptilian skin in green scales.

Rogan leaned over to see the face and hands of this one creature, and his teeth clenched tight. The hands with four-fingered claws and the head almost appeared to be that of a toad crossed wicked with that of a snake, as the eyes were stripped, but protruding large...and the mouth round and open, but sporting four long fangs.

Bodyne whispered, "One of the viper men of lore, Rogan. Just kill it or leave it for the cyclops."

"Huh," said Rogan as he began to climb down, leaving Bodyne on Aliene. "Wonder how they got that thing in the stocks?"

The viper man hissed loud, and then clicked loud tones, but Rogan couldn't understand if it was a language.

Thyssen laughed, "It was tough from what I saw, but forget that thing. Damn am I glad to see you."

Walking around behind them, he saw they all had their trousers dropped. Rogan looked to the east and saw a tall figure approaching, staggering as it walked.

"So," he wondered. "You are put here for the cyclops?"

"Yeah," Thyssen muttered. "Let us go. I don't really wanna die, but I really don't wanna be rogered to death by a one-eyed beast."

Rogan opened his mouth but Shazia shouted, "Shut your damned hole, ya cunt. Let that one-eyed prick do his worst to me!" As she yelled, her hips wiggled and her dangling, stockinged feet clenched.

"Princess?" Rogan asked, gazing up at Bodyne.

"That's what she calls herself," Bodyne replied.

The words were barely out before Shazia shouted, "My goddamned name means princess, ya rotten cunt."

Rogan drew out one of his daggers and asked, "I wonder what the name for bitch is around these parts?"

As he broke Thyssen's lock, Shazia looked over at him and grinned, saying in a sweet voice, "I hear tell it is *Rogan*."

Free from his stock, Thyssen chuckled again and pulled up his pants.

Rogan knelt, looked into the face of the dwarf, and asked, "Now, princess, why should I free you?"

"Piss off then," she remarked, looking away from him, stretching out her plump legs. "I've had worse than what's coming up behind me."

Rogan saw the black cyclops on his way, his long, horse-like appendage waving in the shadows, and he said, "You might want to rethink that."

The cyclops paused, twenty yards away, he reached down, massaged his testicles, and stared at Rogan.

"So," Rogan mumbled. "He remembers me."

Thyssen looked from Rogan to the dock cabins. "Such a guy you are, Rogan. You make friends everywhere?"

"Yeah."

"Those pricks have my spear," Thyssen related, looking to the docks.

Rogan frowned at him. "I make a habit of saving your ass, it seems."

"Very funny."

"Remember that if I ever need it, or go to hell if not." He inserted his knife by the lock of the middle stock and flexed it out. The lock popped and the princess fell to the ground, her dark socks in the dirt flat.

"Damn your asshole to the worms," she swore, rubbing her

backside, turning on her knees to face the cyclops. Her snarling expression faded to a blank stare. "Lilith wept, look at that thing."

Thyssen whispered, "She mean the cyclops or his thing?"

Rogan moved over to the viper man and then knelt as Shazia adjusted her tunic. He stared into the face of the hissing beast and said, "Are ya gonna kill me if I set you free? If I don't, are ya smart enough to get what will happen to you?"

The creature's sizzling tones broke into pieces and the words, "Just…kill…me…" popped out.

Shaking his head, Rogan jammed his knife in again and broke the lock.

Thyssen and Shazia shouted in terror as the viper man fell out onto his all fours like a cat. The thing stood up, didn't bother to pick up the loin cloth that fell from its ankles, and faced Rogan. It then turned to face the cyclops. It then confronted Rogan again.

Rogan said, "I reckon you're pissed at those assheads up the way that captured you and put you here, huh?"

The viper man's face turned to the cabins where the pirates had retreated.

Thyssen said, "Damn the gods, he understands you."

"He comprehends just fine," Rogan assured him. "Your choice. I give you life again. Cyclops or the pirates."

The viper man screeched, leapt up over Thyssen and bounded toward the cabins, its hind legs bent back and propelling it like a frog. Hopping yards at a time until it went out of sight at the docks.

Rogan drew his sword off his back and said to Thyssen, "We'll see about your spear once sugar-face there clears out the pirates."

Thyssen opened his mouth, but didn't speak as the screams of the dying pirates down the dock rang out.

The cyclops tilted his head, hearing the bloodletting.

Rogan stepped around the stocks. "Come on, ya bastard, or go back where ya came from. Yer ol' lady is callin' you."

The cyclops didn't take a step. Rogan assumed his feeble mind at war with itself over what move to make. The one eye focused on Rogan's sword, then at Shazia and Thyssen. He then looked at the mammoth and exhaled loud.

"Well?" Rogan asked, stridently.

The cyclops stared at him for a few moments before he reached down, grabbed his long, swinging member, and turned around.

As the cyclops walked away from them, Thyssen took a weighty breath and said, "I feel bad for his wife."

"I don't," Rogan admitted and spun toward the docks.

Still, the screams and gurgling continued down the way from there.

Rogan stepped about the stocks, heading toward the docks, but Shazia stepped in front of him fast.

Hands on her ample hips, she snapped, "Hey, stop there now. Do you know who I am, big pecker?"

"A pain in my ass," Rogan replied, pausing only for a second. "Kiss it hard, little one, as I go by."

After Rogan had moved past her, Shazia screamed, "I'd bite your balls off first, sandy-haired prick."

"Get in line," Rogan said and started to the dock, Thyssen following, and soon, Aliene began to bring up the rear.

At the first long cabin, they found the bodies of three pirates violated, ribcages tore open, throats ripped asunder. The viper man had moved on to the next dock cabin and clearly slayed its inhabitants by the sounds they heard. They heard the last man beg, scream, and choke on the name of his god or mother before falling silent.

Rogan didn't rush on to see more, but he did wonder, "How did they ever catch that damned thing?"

"It drinks," Thyssen said with a wave, "heavily." He then went into the cabin and clapped his hands. "Hot damn, my spear!"

"Good, good," Rogan said, looking out on the waters at the

larger ships anchored. "Lots of other pirates out there down the way. We better get to moving."

Bodyne pointed at a spot out of their vision but clear to her from atop Aliene. "There is a corral behind the cabins. We will needs horses."

Thyssen called from inside, "They have lots of supplies in here, jerked meat, hard tack, good traveling food."

"This is a good thing. Any wine or the water of life?" Rogan asked, tongue running across his dry lips.

"Yeah, we should be set."

"We," Rogan muttered in disgust. "At least I didn't have to worry about that tough-assed Elisa in a real fight. Wish she was still here."

"I bet you do," Thyssen grinned.

"She didn't get caught, by Wodan!" He then peered down at Shazia, who grimaced up at him. "And I suppose you think you are coming along?"

"Well, where the fuck are ya goin' to?" she asked.

"A land of giants, you wouldn't like it there."

"Piss in your helm, jackass."

Rogan half-smiled. "Then again, everywhere is a land of giants for you."

As Shazia let loose more profanity, Rogan helped Thyssen clear out some skins of wine, flasks of whiskey, and more food. The small one kept cussing.

Thyssen muttered, "The mouth on that one…"

"Yeah, a real princess."

While Thyssen went out to look at the corral, Bodyne asked Rogan, "Where are we going to now?"

Rogan looked south and answered, "Hell, eventually, I suspect."

CHAPTER NINE
Disturbing the Priest

The sun had fully rose over the horizon as the Kaldwell twins dismounted and walked into the dilapidated dwelling of the wizardess Sydow. To Lybeck, they appeared as remnants but the twins kept using their swords, prying open things in the empty air and saying they were overcoming obstacles, breaking charms, and opening doors. *Madness*, he thought. Lybeck wished Urell had come along, or any of the soldiers than himself, as at least they weren't batshit crazy as the twins sure looked to him then.

The madness soon spread, though, for about the time the sun washed through the crumbled window frames of stone did the reality in Lybeck's eyes change. He blinked several times and rubbed his eyes to see the view before him ripple like a disturbed pool.

As the waves rolled out, the structure of the ruins took on a better form. None of the blocks looked weathered or broken, but precise and at perfect angles. He also saw solid plank doors that the twins had broken locks off. His head throbbed, understanding the two fighters really had broken a spell meant to conceal something.

"Come along, Lybeck," Batasta called out, smiling in

excitement.

"Damned fool kid," Lybeck mumbled, thinking the youth unwise for smiling happy as they broke into the home of a wizard. But, again, he shared in their lunacy, for he drew his sword and followed along.

Once through the wooden doors, the dim sunshine showed a long chamber with various torches, candles, and braziers, all dark. He walked to one of the convex shapes by the candles and thought it appeared to be an altar. In the basin on the oblong altar of stone sat jewels: They might have been diamonds, rubies, and sapphires. The concept of filling his pockets and riding off away from this entire adventure crossed his mind…many times.

"Come on," the voice of one of the twins yelled past the next barrier, one crossed by just tearing down a woven tapestry.

Still, he persisted in the mad escapade, figuring if the twins got themselves killed, he might be able to run out. That hope felt light in his heart as the heavier reality sang a song of doom for him.

"Down here," one of them yelled at Lybeck, and he saw the speaker waving down a series of stone steps.

With caution, Lybeck moved down the stone steps, barely able to see in the dim light cast by fires down in the lower chamber. Once on the next level, Lybeck saw several torches near to going out that cast light on the scene.

"These ones won't hurt us," the twin he thought Binje said, pointing at the figures strapped and nailed to the six wooden crossbeams on either side of the room. Twelve men had been secured in place, and all slumped against their bonds, limbs nailed in place. Each man had been castrated with no skill by the look of their injuries, and bled out.

Lybeck's chest fluttered at the vicious method of death and thought of such an agony. His groin and thighs ached bad as he passed by these poor souls, luckily dead then and beyond further pain.

"Damn them!" Batasta emerged from beyond his sight in

another room. "Come along. You have to see this."

Lybeck spoke up to say, "I think this is enough. Let's get out of here."

With a single guffaw, Batasta shouted, "The best is yet to come. Here, you are a strong man, no?"

Lybeck's shaky feet took him across the room, past the limp, hanging bodies to the opening of the next chamber. More light poured through this opening as many candles burned and even a fireplace flamed.

"What is this new insanity, boys?" Lybeck found himself laughing himself at the other room.

Twelve cushioned couches were spaced in the long room, six along each side of the walls. On each reclined a woman, her upper torso covered in a sheet of linen, but her thighs and legs up in the air, curled, a pillow under their buttocks. Each woman had an attendant, a woman of considerable advanced age, giving them a drink or mopping their heads.

"A bunch of women with their asses and legs in the air?" Lybeck named the scene. "What does this have to do with what we just saw?"

The twins had stepped to the middle of the room, but no one said a word. Binje said, "Do they see us?"

Batasta replied, "The nursing women eye us but I can't say about the others."

When a novel voice sounded out beyond the room, Lybeck's bladder pounded near his balls hard.

"Be gone from here, right now, and I might let you live.," the husky voice called out.

"Show yourself, wizardess," Batasta shouted, his sword at the ready. "I don't fear you, Sydow."

A soft giggle rippled through Lybeck's ears and he certainly did fear her.

"Go away, little boys," her voice slithered in their ears. "Your demon friend has liberated your mind to my powers, but that doesn't mean you can best me."

Binje said, "We don't care to best you, we just want Rogan."

"Rogan?" the voice curdled and a new glow from a large room beyond where they stood surged bright. They all saw the slender form of Sydow appear in the wraithlike glow. "Rogan is not here."

"Where is he bound?" Batasta roared. "Damn your eyes."

"Why would I know?"

"Our demon grandfather has told us you sent him on a course," Batasta said.

Sydow cackled with laughter.

Trying to keep from pissing himself, Lybeck shifted from boot to boot.

"Run along, little boys," she told the hulking warriors. "None of what transpires here concerns you."

The twins exchanged a look, but Batasta spoke up to say, "You will tell us where Rogan is bound for."

"Why would I know? Why would I tell you if I did know?"

"Because," Binje said, his brother moving off the middle path in unison with his twin, swords rising at the same level near two of the women. "While I think you would be able to fend us off with your magicks, these women aren't witches or wizards."

Batasta's blade near to bounced off the raised knees of the woman nearest him. "But these women can die and they will if you don't tell us."

Sydow's long face lost its humor. "Get away from my brides," she said quickly, then near to bit her tongue.

The twins locked eyes for a moment and then looked back to Sydow. "Brides? You joke us, truly."

"What do you care what I call them?" Sydow replied with a heated tone.

Binje admitted, "We really don't care. One hears many strange things in this world. Just tell us where Rogan is bound for."

"You seek him…why?" Sydow questioned them. "Out of obligation or some strange loyalty?"

Batasta answered, "That is our business. We don't ask you yours, just to tell us where you have sent him."

"I sent him nowhere. The Kelt does nothing for me. Your grandfather is a liar, like his father before him."

Binje's lips peeled back. "You lie to us, accursed witch. You might have sent him on his true way, but you have your own reasons. Why did he do you a service and where is he bound for now?"

Batasta stepped away from his victim, though his brother stayed in place. He didn't approach Sydow but looked past her.

"What goes on there? Those old women beyond you grind in bowls like an apothecary? What are those bags?" His eyes widened and he faced his brother. "Synuria said Rogan brought out the bones from the Slough of Despair." His look cracked around toward Sydow. "The bones of the castaway Nephilim girls?"

The left side of Sydow's mouth tightened. "You are nowhere near as stupid as your muscles make you look. Very good."

Batasta gazed back into the room beyond and then at the women on his side. "What devilry is this?"

"I thought you didn't care?" Sydow chuckled, stretched her arms out wide, and then suddenly swiped them together. A great rush of wind traveled through the room, making Batasta stumble a few steps and near to knocking his brother over.

Lybeck maintained his stance and kept his bladder in check, but both acts were a struggle. Terror filled his senses as wind inside a sealed place couldn't happen.

The twins, though, just maintained their stances.

Sydow said, "You fake boys, so full of bluster and courage rooted in lies. You have no idea what the true bloodlines of the gods mean or what I have gone through to create my own family of goddesses."

Batasta and his brother took a step nearer to each other, but not toward her.

Binje said to his twin, "What is it?"

"Some wizardry I cannot understand, but I don't need to comprehend it all to hazard a guess."

Sydow roared with laughter. "Oh, do guess, you farcical dolt."

Nonplussed, Batasta said, "Your hags in there grind out the bones of the Nephilim girls Rogan retrieved for you. We all know what power the bones of a Nephilim have for you wizards and how much anyone will pay for them. For a girl one? Who can tell their magicks as they all die young save for a few that live to turn men to stone?"

Her laughter still making her belly heave, Sydow mocked him with applause.

Batasta went on to say, "If I had to guess right now, you had those poor bastards out there prisoner, cut off their balls, and worked their man seed all in with the cursed bone meal of the Nephilim girls."

Her hands to her face as if astonished, but still japing them, Sydow asked, "Goodness! And then?"

The twins looked at the girls, legs in the air. Batasta said, "You put the mix in these servants of yours. They put their asses and hips up to let the mix run close to the soul so a child can be made."

Again, she clapped her hands. "Oh wonderful! You are a sharp one. If I had cookies, I'd give you some."

The twins glanced back at Lybeck and then to her again. Binje asked, "But why? What filthy magick is this?"

His brother shook his head, his face scrunching up, giving him a tart look.

Her eyes intense, darting from one to the other, Sydow replied, "Your brother's curiosity betrays his mind and the one who shares with him."

Batasta said, "He cares more about people than me. He's a few minutes younger than I. It's youth."

She said, "I will create a new race of daughters of the night, the children of Lilith will sweep across the lands in the night."

"Lilith?" Binje said, "I can't believe Rogan served such a purpose or anyone who loved a night howler."

Sydow replied, "He didn't know everything and only served us for pretty rocks. Men base their petty lives on warm slits and pretty rocks, perhaps both."

"Who cares?" Batasta growled low as she spoke, his shoulders squared at her as his brother took a few steps closer to him. "Where is he going to now? I am honor bound to get him back for my king."

Turning in a circle as she laughed at him, Sydow threw out, "Your honor? So lovely a concept, fake grandson of god." Her humor evaporated and Sydow's lips curled back from her teeth like that of a tiger. "He is as deluded as you with his personal code. He goes to save his father and sister, far south at the grotto of Marduk. He rides into a great horror for his own pitiful honor and love of a bloodline."

Eyebrow raised, Batasta hissed, "Does he now?"

"He's a Kelt fool. He should have headed north back to his homeland. We all have our weakness."

His guile dropping, his sword drooping a bit, Batasta nodded deliberately. "Thank you. I have deliberated what his motivation would be in truth. As you say, we all have our weakness." He turned away and faced Lybeck, his left arm out, almost as if to shake his hand from across the long room.

Confused, Lybeck tried to puzzle that move, but for a moment, until Binje made a sudden move at Sydow, but only a single step. The move fell so abrupt, Lybeck thought the wizardess' magicks stopped the big youth. No, the move played out like poetry, as his left arm interlocked with Batasta's and they spun in a fast dance…and Batasta went flying through the air at Sydow.

Sydow screamed, hands up, an emerald glow flying from her hands and encompassing the big man as he flew at her, sword at the ready to kill.

Suspended in the air for a moment, Batasta then dropped

to the floor. The echo of his sword slamming on the floor rang out as his brother charged at Sydow.

Binje's blade, held back to deliver the overhanded deathblow, never arrived. A second blast of green light struck Binje from the wizardess. He nearly reached her, but froze, raised in the air. Binje, though, twisted in air and Sydow's arms shuddered, struggling to hold him a moment before she slammed him to the floor.

A moment was all Batasta needed to roll over, his sword swinging up from the floor, slicing both of Sydow's hands off.

She bellowed, eyes wide, glaring at the bloody, effusive stumps on her arms. She had just the time to go eye to eye with Batasta as he got to his knees and swung the blade again, slicing her in half at the waist. Sydow tumbled down, her torso splattering on the stone floor as Binje rolled over, blade swinging down, cleaving her head from her shoulders.

Lybeck gagged and stepped forward, stunned at what he witnessed. His eyes and mind doubted the speed of the twins.

He watched Batasta rise up fast, jog over, and then jump into the air. His boots both landed on Sydow's head at the same time and her surprised expression disappeared forever. Batasta jumped on the head a few times until the skull pulped to a glob.

Binje set about cutting each arm off the torso that remained upright. He then kicked her in the back and this portion of Sydow fell over swift. The twins eyed the legs and pelvis of Sydow that still stood.

The twins grinned at each other and reached out with their left arms and said in unison, "Make a wish."

Lybeck turned away and threw up, unwilling to watch the twins rip Sydow's lower portion in two pieces, but he could heard the cricking, wretched sound. Lybeck reckoned he would hear that forever.

"The south then," one of them said. "To the Grotto of Marduk."

"We were there as kids," the other replied.

"I recall, but we were so young."

Lybeck wiped his mouth and staggered to the doorway. He dared not look back, but in his peripheral vison, he saw the twins but they didn't look at him.

"This needs to stop, here at the root," one of them said.

"I agree. We shall dedicate these lives and those conceived unto the appetite of Synuria, grandfather of us."

"In his boundless wisdom, he sent us here to stop this immoral mischief, to help feed himself as well."

The other giggled like a child. "A cunning but prudent move."

Lybeck peeked back as the two raised their bloody blades over the prostrate women nearest to them.

"For you, grandfather, with love," the other said as the swords dropped.

Lybeck ran. He made it to the other side of the room with the castrated men before he had to pull out his member and pass water. He no longer could hold it, but wished he could've made it outside. As soon as he had choked enough urine out of himself, he ran from the wet sounds and echoes of the dying women…and the song the twins sang as they slew the twelve wives of Sydow.

*****

After Thyssen secured mounts and supplies, the group set off south, but hugging the coastline, not travelling the road oft taken. To Rogan's anger, Shazia also came along, riding along by Bodyne and Thynnes.

"Why in the hell does she need to come along?" Rogan had sworn at the time of leaving. "I won't save her twice."

"I know the territory, donkey," she told him. "I'll make sure you don't fall in a gorge on our way to Irem."

Rogan replied, "I'd like to think I can see good enough up

here to avoid such things on Aliene."

Shazia shot back, "Good luck. With my help, though, you can avoid the wicked city of Madron."

At that name, Bodyne shuddered and Thyssen took a sip from a flask.

Eyebrows low, Rogan eyed Thyssen. "What is spooking you all? You look like ya just got the evil eye."

"Madron is worse," Shazia promised. "You all know what is said to live there."

Thyssen nodded fast and drank more.

Bodyne said, "Yes, I know who lives there."

After a slew of curses Rogan demanded, "Tell me, you pricks, or I'll ride off and leave you alone."

"Madron is the home of the daughter of Zazaeil," Shazia said in a sweet voice. "A living, breathing female Nephilim."

"I thought those were all throw-away?" Rogan asked with a tired voice.

Thyssen shook his head and said, "I've heard that story since I was a kid, some monster bitch that can turn ya to stone."

"That's such bullshit," Rogan declared. "We have all heard such stories. They make that shit up to scare kids and fools. Which are you all? Besides, how ugly could she be?"

Shazia snorted and laughed. "Not her looks at all, you stupid ass. She's beautiful as the moon I hear tell."

"I wonder who could tell," Rogan didn't ask anyone.

They all stared at him as they rode. Thyssen asked, "What?"

"If ya turn to stone by looking at her, how the hell would anyone know if she's beautiful or ugly?"

"That's not how it's done, shitheel," Shazia smiled, a look near to as creepy to Rogan as her evil face.

"Well," Rogan said. "To be on the safe side, we'll try to avoid Madron."

They rode on for several miles, keeping near a creek so that Aliene could rehydrate at times. This benefited the horses as well. On one such stop, Thyssen asked "How far can that thing go in a day?"

Rogan faked a hurt look and replied, "*Aliene* can go further than a horse, I would bet. She has to eat and drink a lot, but no trouble."

"All right," Thyssen sighed and refilled his water canteen.

Rogan asked, "You going to tell me how ya managed to get in those stocks?"

"Oh, I screwed the wrong woman."

Pondering that, Rogan admitted, "I can see that."

"Yeah," Thyssen yawned. "It happens. I was stupid spending and drunk."

"You need to get home. Never made it to the boats, huh?"

"Nope." Thyssen winked at him. "I figured I'd relax and celebrate first."

"Maybe you can get a boat at Madron or Irem."

Again, Shazia snorted, laughing

Rogan said, "Maybe you can trade the princess there for something, like a sack of potatoes."

"Screw off, assface," Shazia shot back.

"Okay, some rotten potatoes?"

After Shazia stopped cussing, Thyssen said to Rogen, "Your father and sister, huh?"

"I didn't ask you fuckers to come along."

Shazia informed him, "I'm not going to fight in some war."

Frowning, Rogan asked Thyssen, "Did you hear something?"

Thyssen said, "I do wanna get home and back to my father's troops."

"I thought you didn't want to be a soldier forever?"

"All this rotten living is changing my mind. At least if I were a soldier or an officer, I'd have some order and a place to lay my head without danger of being rogered by a monster. Plus, my land back home is pretty good."

"And ya left all that?"

"Young, drunk, and stupid," Thyssen shrugged, "ya grow up after ya been in chains for a year or so."

Rogan nodded. "I would guess."

"Ever been a slave?"

"No. Been in chains a few times. That isn't for me so I understand."

Shazia chimed in, "I was forced to serve in a harem for a few days."

After a long exhale, Rogan took a breath and said to Thyssen, "I don't know if I can save my father and sister or if they are already dead. I have to try, though."

"I understand."

Rogan looked at him sideways. "After that, I might just get on that boat with you and just ride away."

Shazia giggled, "Make sure the elephant goes, too. Good sailor I bet she is. Damn, that is a funny idea."

"That's it." Rogan stared ahead and said, "I'll feed that rotten little twat to the first monster I see."

"It'll choke on me," she promised.

"At least we'll be down a monster, then," Rogan admitted.

Shazia shouted up to Rogan, "Hey, shit for brains, don't ya wanna know why I'm such a sweet girl?"

Rogan peered down from the mammoth and said, "I want to see you dead, little one, so no, I don't want to hear it and I'll come down there and shove you up Aliene's ass in a moment so I don't have to hear your mouth."

Shazia smiled at first, then her manner dropped and she grew silent.

After many hours and miles on the trail, Rogan squinted in the distance. "That's the wagon up there, isn't it?"

Thyssen asked, "What is what?"

"You'll see it in a moment."

After a few minutes, Thyssen shielded his eyes from the early afternoon light and said, "By the gods, I think it is."

"Who?" Bodyne wondered.

Rogan replied, "Elisa and her mother. Their wagon is up ahead."

When Shazia asked who that was, Bodyne explained.

Thyssen said, "It'll be good to see them."

"Wonder why they are off the beaten path in a wagon?" Rogan pondered.

Thyssen stared up at him until he looked back his way. "Elisa's tough and her mama is a wizard."

"And Azrag 'bout got them before we saved them."

"Remember," Thyssen told him. "Elisa was pissed you saved her."

"Wanted to kill Azrag herself," Rogan recalled, smiling. "Let's hope something worse hasn't got to them this time."

It took them about twenty minutes, but they arrived at the wagon, seeing no horses remained attached to it, nor was there any sign of life about.

Rogan climbed down and searched it with Thyssen. "Their stuff is gone."

"Even that damned rock the old gal kept so secret, the one from the stars," Thyssen said ruefully. "Gone."

Bodyne tried to explain this to Shazia who waved her waves, dismissing it all. "What stupid thoughts. A fallen star? Really?"

"It's just a rock," Rogan responded. "Just that it fell from the sky, or at least that's the story. Don't know how one would prove that unless ya saw it fall and picked it up."

"I hear those are hot," Thyssen said.

Rogan shook his head in disgust. "What's the point? It's just a rock."

Bodyne said, "Some places say they are from the gods, great gifts, and others worship them as idols."

The tall weeds about the carriage area rattled and sizzled, causing Thynnes and Rogan to draw weapons.

Shazia even showed fear in her face. "What in the hell was that?"

Rogan's eyes darted about, and he said, "Sounds like a rattling snake but all the hell about us."

"Get by the elephant," Thyssen shouted. "Whatever they

are, it will have a tougher time with the beast."

"She's Aliene, ya prick," Rogan said without looking his way.

Bodyne and Shazia retreated under the hairy legs of Aliene while Rogan and Thyssen stayed back to back at her left side.

Aliene turned in a moment, her head and trunk higher, and she trumpeted loud.

The hissing in the tall grasses increased.

Rogan's eyes tried to focus on the areas about them and said quietly, "We're surrounded."

Then one head rose up, followed by another, and then a half-dozen more stranger shapes, but all too familiar soon.

"Viper men," Thyssen said. "We're fucked."

Rogan readied his sword. "They can die as easy as a regular man."

"Good, glad you think so," Thyssen told him. "These is what ya get for sparing that freak back there."

The viper men stood taller, no longer concealing or hiding their motives. However, they didn't rush the elephant or the men. One of them stepped forward, no different than the rest, and came nearer to the party.

Thyssen whispered, "You have to be shitting me."

Rogan answered back, "What did you say about my act of kindness?"

The viper man turned to his brethren and hissed, his mouth clicking, and the others didn't advance. The creature came closer to Rogan, its striped eyes focusing on his.

"Seth," the word croaked from the mouth of the viper man. The clawed hands of the creature settled on its chest. "Seth."

"Rogan," he replied to the viper man, but it nodded already, aware of the name.

Seth then pointed his claws away from the area and nodded more.

"We shall go," Rogan promised.

Seth shook his head violently. "Madron," Seth croaked.

"Took them…to Madron."

"Who has?" Rogan asked. "The old woman and the tall girl?"

"And the god…in the box," Seth answered.

Thyssen gaped at Rogan. "The what?"

"The rock." Rogan grimaced at him. "The rock in the metal box." He faced Seth again. "Who did?"

"They did," Seth explained, pointing over the rise in the ground away from the creek they had followed. "Brothers…of Marduk."

"Crap," Thyssen cursed. "They can't be good."

Rogan asked, "Big suckers, are they? Giants?"

Seth looked at his brothers and then back at Rogan. "Monsters. Animals." Seth hesitated. "Two very bad…ones. They serve…the sister in Madron."

Thyssen cleared his throat. "Well, that Elisa wanted to be known as the killer of giants, remember?"

"Maybe a couple bastard monsters got the best of her."

"Maybe," Thyssen said. "What did the monsters look like?"

Seth put his claws up on either side of his face. "Two faces… one is…that way."

Rogan nodded. "The other?"

"Snake…bad snake…" Seth tried to say. "Not like…us… monster."

Rogan glared at Shazia who was about to speak. "Shut your mouth." He turned back to Seth. "Can you show us this place?"

"Can show…won't die…for you."

"Not askin' ya to share a bath, dammit," Rogan retorted.

Thyssen grabbed his left elbow. "Watch your ass."

"I am." Rogan said to Seth, "Show us."

Seth turned to his brethren and they all went low in the grasses again, hissing, but the grasses clearing aimed a path away from the wagon.

Shazia said, "So much for avoiding Madron, aye?"

"Shut up."

"Aren't you curious what you will face?"

Rogan looked down at her. "For the one of us most likely to die in this, ya sure got a big mouth."

"I don't want to die," Shazia admitted.

"You are on borrowed time," Rogan told her. "Tell me something useful about this daughter of Zazaeil or whoever she is. Tell me how to fight her, the name or the way to kill her, and I might not just feed you to the monsters he described."

Shazia grinned. "I'll tell you what I know, but I'll enjoy watching you die."

"There are many waiting on the other side of eternity for me, probably jacking themselves in anticipation of my death. Ya don't scare me and neither does a couple monsters."

They set out to follow the tribe of lizard men and Shazia started to speak.

CHAPTER TEN
Hand of Doom

Urell stood on the beginning of the dock, gazing out at the vessels anchored in the sea. Lybeck saw Urell wiping the blood from his hands and throwing the rag onto the dock. Looking down at his blood-spattered trousers, Lybeck thought he'd seen enough death for one day before they arrived at the docks around midday.

"Filthy scum," Urell said, making obscene hand gestures at the ships out beyond. "Fools, a bunch of wormy dogs, no match for our trained soldiers. They should've stayed on their nasty ships."

Lybeck didn't argue, but looked over from the bodies of dead pirates to the stocks near the docks, where the black cyclops stood imprisoned. The being stood up straight, his long member inserted and secured through the head hole of the stocks, and reinforced with rope, as the soldiers and Binje Kaldwell questioned him.

Lybeck then looked to the cabins where Batasta Kaldwell spoke to the local sheriff from Azar, showing his credentials from Nungal and Kamala-ur, and explaining that the pirates had attacked them. Hands on his hips, the sheriff of Azar appeared properly pissed that a few dozen dead bodies of men Lybeck deemed as pirates were strewn about the cabin and dock area.

"What an asshole. Sheriff won't be getting anymore kickbacks from this lot," Lybeck said steadily, recalling the frenzied fight they brought to the soldiers as they arrived. "But Rogan was here first."

Urell waved at the cyclops, the soldiers stretching the arms of the one-eyed man, and said, "He's easy enough to track, though. Too bad he stirred up this hornet's nest before leaving."

Lybeck walked over by Urell and gazed south. "He's gone on half a day ahead of us, I'd say."

"We'll catch up to him soon."

"He's really going to the Grotto of Marduk in Madron?" Lybeck mused, rubbing both his eyes as if that would help him see Rogan in the distance. "The south will bring no answers or hiding place."

"It's the bottom of the world," Urell reminded him as he watched Kylene wash her hands with water poured out of a canteen by one of the other Kushites. "After a lot of open territory, it's Madron and Irem, then, nothing. Besides, what you said Sydow told you all says where he is going."

"Phah," Lybeck spat. "I can't believe Rogan is that much an idealist to go to save his kinfolks on the word of a few wizards. If he really is heading that way, I'd sooner we grabbed him before Irem or Madron."

Urell nodded fast. "I agree. I'd rather not deal with those freaking giants or Marduk either."

"They have no beef with us, and have good relations with Nungal and Kamala-ur."

"Exactly."

"If they would find out we are in any way knowing about the death of Azrag, that might not go well."

"Rogan slew Azrag."

"Because we let him out of our grasp and still have not found him."

Urell swore and then said, "Inhuman fuckers. I wish…"

Lybeck eyed him. "Agreed. Best hold your tongue or you might lose it."

"The Kaldwell twins have some sway," Urell remarked and gobbed at the sea, missing. "They will massage down the situation."

After he glanced down the dock, Lybeck added, "I doubt if they will get anything useful out of the black cyclops, other than amusement or his death."

Urell took a sip of his flask and then froze. "Out there," he mumbled, the whiskey drooling from his lips.

Lybeck followed his gaze out beyond the pirate ships and saw a much larger vessel slide in by the pirate ships. The bigger ship, though impressive, wasn't what froze Urell, Lybeck guessed. Out in the sea bobbed a large round object, that soon broke the surface and took on a clearer shape of a humanoid head.

"Boys," Urell called out and then repeated himself, louder.

The twins abandoned their tasks and walked over to where Lybeck and Urell watched what emerged from the sea. Kylene and the Kushites joined them, but started to whisper in their own tongue.

A foot at a time, the figure came out of the water. Long wet hair and a long beard framed a face that belonged on a stone relief or in a temple. The giant moved in a steady manner, walking out of the ocean beside the dock. He let his hand rest on the dock once, as if to show how insignificant the object served him. Clad in just a kilt to his knees, the giant stood on the shore, stretched, and began to saunter toward them.

Urell wiped the whiskey from his mouth and shot Lybeck a look.

Lybeck surmised this giant an even taller one than Azrag, who had stood near to two feet taller than the strapping Kelt, Rogan.

When the giant stopped near them, Lybeck saw that his feet and hands bore only five digits each. Eyes up to the face of the being but for a moment, Lybeck quickly looked down at the ground. His heart raced as his mind grasped what came to stand before them. While many muttered, he comprehended that this was no Nephilim.

Batasta spoke and named the being, saying, "Zazaeil, good tidings."

At this name, several soldiers took a further step back and a few dropped to their knees. The Kushites stood firm, their look turning grim.

"Yes." Zazaeil's black eyes scanned the area beyond the group of soldiers and didn't peer down on them. "Where is my brother?"

Binje blinked and asked, "Your brother?"

The gaze full of menace dropped to focus on Binje Kaldwell. "My cousin, my step-sister twice removed, what is it to you, little Kaldwell, how I address the absolute absence of the great Azrag?"

Lybeck clasped his hands together, trying to fight down the nerves he felt certain all experienced at the ire in Zazaeil's voice. How the twins stood up straight and faced the giant outright earned points for guts with Lybeck.

Zazaeil said, "Our seers have felt him die." He then focused on Batasta. "The ravens tell a story of his fall. Your leaders have told us via the ravens that they have agents abroad in search of an outlaw key in his demise."

Batasta spoke up to say, "That is us."

"You have no outlaw in your possession?"

"He's proven elusive, but we are on his trail."

Zazaeil's massive head nodded marginally. "Good fortune to you, Kaldwell. The death of one of our kindred is never a good story. Did this outlaw truly slay Azrag?"

"That is a theory," Batasta admitted.

"My transport was passing this way and we stopped on the far side of Azar to resupply for wine on our way to Irem, and for me to dine on the Kushites that traveled with you here," Zazaeil related, his huge chest expanding as he took a bored breath.

"Word of all this came to us, then of this scrimmage with the pirates and the Kaldwells. Intrigued by the tales, I decided to see for myself. Fortune smiles on me that we even met this easily."

Binje said, "We will find this indescribable outlaw and haul him back to Nungal, alive or dead."

Again, Zazaeil studied the land in the distance, his nostrils expanding. "See that you do. If this brigand slew one of our kindred, I might better the offer of Nungal for his head." He yawned and turned away, his long legs stretching, his kilt shifting, the head of his long member peeking out the edge of the wet fabric. "Or not. I have greater events on my plate than the death of a rambling giant." He paused, eyed the Kushites, and asked, "Good afternoon, women. Are you with child yet?"

Kylene and the others said nothing, but Lybeck saw how they seethed at the sight of the great giant.

Batasta called out, "Good fortunes in the coming ceremony at Irem."

Zazaeil stopped at the edge of the sea.

Everyone on land held their breath.

The giant turned to look at the twins and smiled. "Good fortune, is a kind wish, but wishing one to have fine luck is a real jest. There is no luck, just irony in life. Strength creates good fortune. Luck is for gamblers, fools, and rambling men. That thought of luck by virtue of chance or karma is for fools. A strong man makes his good fortune. I go now to brand my good fortune greater."

Once the giant had walked back into the sea, the soldiers stood and half of them turned to urinate.

Lybeck and Urell walked to the twins.

"Well," Binje said after cracking the knuckles on his hands. "That was different."

Harland and Ransim walked up from the dock, then stopped to giggle at the urinating soldiers. "Glad he's gone," Harland stated.

Batasta faced away from the coast, pointing to something

they couldn't see over the ridge. "We shall take the main road to Irem, if that is where he is truly bound."

Lybeck turned in that direction. "Rogan is a Kelt. They live by the blood vendetta. They will do terrible things if their blood is wronged. He seeks to save his father and sister."

Binje joined them and said, "That's a lot of trouble and bloodshed he's doing over a little of his own blood."

Turning to the scene where they had just slain all the pirates, Lybeck swiped his left arm out and said, "Aren't we shedding a lot of blood and going through a lot of trouble for just one man?" He then looked to Batasta. "What would you do if your brother were imperiled in such a way? Would you give up?"

"No," Batasta stated, ice water in his veins as he leered at Lybeck. "I'd kill the world to save my brother."

Binje nodded in agreement. "Me as well."

Lybeck shrugged. "Rogan is a savage to you all, but his kindred are all he has." He turned to the south. "He'll kill himself to see those who harmed his kin dead."

Harland coughed and said, "That's crazy."

"I didn't say it was right," Lybeck admonished him with an acrimonious look. "I just said he'd do it."

After a few steps, Urell knelt and looked at the prints left by Zazaeil. "I thought he had five toes."

Batasta smirked. "So?"

"He's a giant, that one, Zazaeil."

Binje asked, "Your point?"

Urell frowned. "The six fingers and toes, you know? And he said 'our kindred' about Azrag."

The twins contemplated at the sea. "He's not a true child of the sons of god. Zazaeil is one of them, the sons of god himself, hiding from the host above in human flesh, unlike our grandfather."

"How in the hell does that work?" Urell asked. "One of the fallen ones of the Creator god? Wears flesh?"

Batasta and Binje's heads turned together. "It's complicated."

Lybeck sighed and said, "He's a devil on two legs, Zazaeil, worse than a crazy giant, far stronger." He turned and looked at the soldiers, all wide-eyed. "Tell your grandchildren you saw one, if you live through this."

The sheriff of Azar stepped up and raged at the twins anew, saying, "This is all insane. We do good business with all. You have slain all of these men that are our allies."

Batasta faced the sheriff. "The ships of your associates are still out there and we have taken none of their stock. Go get it from their ships. If you have complaints still, take them up with Nungal and Kalama-ur. We are headed on to fabled Irem. Perhaps you want us to talk to our great cousins and send some giants to indulge themselves in your city of Azar? You don't want that? No?"

The sheriff shook his head.

"Then shut your ass."

*****

His back pinned to the cobblestone floor of Madron's town square, Rogan brought his sword up across his face. When the two sisters of Sanrevelle's open mouths bit on the blade, he thanked Wodan for giving his father superior skill in his craft.

Rogan didn't know if the incisors about that heavy blade oozed venom or spit, but his mind raged with gladness that the weapon held. The weight of the body on him held him down, but he wrapped his legs about the torso of the sisters.

Yes, they had one body, three legs that terminated in feet better suited for a camel, but a body that split in the middle, forming two wicked sisters. Though not hideous to look at in the face, the double set of breasts would distract any man. Their faces, while topped with mounds of shiny black hair, sported mouths that opened at impossible angles. He could not worry on the physiognomy of their jaws, but just fought to avoid their impressive teeth.

His weight shifted, trying to shove the sisters off him, but this move failed. Their arms slapped at him, trying to move his hold on his sword. Their jagged fingernails scraped at his forearms, drawing blood, and inspiring him to heave his weight against them more. Still, he couldn't dislodge them.

In all this, he cussed Shazia in his mind. She had told of this beast before they entered the barren streets of fabled Madron, but hadn't said how to defeat her. Rogan, off Aliene, had went through the first streets trying to locate Elisa and Yana. He figured his time would be limited, as though he locked the blade in their mouths, once they drew back, they'd surely bite a hunk out of his body.

Almost on cue, the sister on the right opened her mouth much wider. Rogan's body boiled, waiting for the next move, but her mouth didn't roar, nor did she threaten him. The jaws gagged when a few rivulets of blood dropped from her lips and nose.

He felt the pressure of Sanrevelle's body start to give some, then the other sister opened her mouth widespread and stared down between them. Not missing his chance, Rogan pushed back again. This time, the twins moved off him and he saw why. A spearhead protruded from between the pointed breasts of the sister on the right.

Though clear of Rogan, the sisters turned and kicked back with their third leg, striking Thyssen in the groin as he tried to wrench back on his spear. He released his weapon and crumbled to the stone street, hands to his crotch, legs twitching. The sisters turned back, the spear still through one of them.

Up to one knee, Rogan swung his sword out awkward and sliced off the left sister's arm at the elbow. This sister of Sanrevelle wailed and roared as the other tried to push the spear out of her chest.

However, the sister on the right began to fail in her movements. Her head bobbed, eyes rolled back, and the arm fell limp.

Rogan returned to his feet and swung his blade again, trying to remove the head of the sister on the left, but the blade stuck in her neck an inch and stayed that deep. He cursed, not anticipating her flesh being that tough.

He drew the sword back, stomped down on the camel foot nearest him, and swung again, this time in an overhanded arc. He'd gripped the sword with both hands and brought the weapon down with everything he possessed in his arms. The blade split down into the sister's scalp and sank deep between Sanrevelle's eyes, dividing her face. She blinked at him once on either side of the blade, and then the beast fell to the streets of Madron.

Rogan heaved his sword back and breathed deep, watching the other sister convulse and give a final death shudder, slapping the street.

A sharp clapping sound echoed in the street, starting up where the death slap stopped. He looked up in the moonlight to see Shazia applauding. She said, "I was rooting for the Sanrevelle twins, but that was impressive."

Bodyne swiped the top of Shazia's head when she stepped out of the shadows. She went to Thyssen and tried to help him up. He still held his crotch and shook his head.

"I'll be all right," Thyssen mumbled. "Maybe."

"She might did us all a favor," said Rogan as he wiped his blade on the hair of the sister on the right, who gave out a rasping breath as he touched her. "Destroying your balls would help you not infect humanity with any more dumbasses like you."

Thyssen stood and shook each leg. "That's the thanks I get?"

Rogan looked down at Thyssen's legs. "I'm waiting to see if your nuts roll out."

Taking a profound breath himself, Thyssen replied, "They feel ready to."

"Maybe the princess will kiss them and make them better."

"Piss off," Shazia spat out.

Disregarding her, Rogan said, "Get your spear. You'll need it."

As he stepped near the dying creature, Thyssen said, "I don't know if I like Elisa and her mother this much." He gripped the shaft of his spear. "Where in the hell does something like this come from? The sons of god screwing camels?"

Rogan shook his head. "Who can say?"

Shazia cackled and said, "They come from the stars, from places beyond our imagination."

"Figures she could say some crap like that," Rogan sighed. "Shut up with all that foolishness. Every time someone can't explain something, it has to be the gods or things from the stars. What if it just is?"

Shazia giggled. "Ever see something like this in all the Earth?"

"Nope," Rogan conceded. "But I haven't been across all the Earth."

Thyssen drew the spear out by levering his foot on the sister's shoulder. "Didn't Seth say the other monster was a snake, worse than them?"

Rogan gazed out of the city the way they came in as if to look for the viper men that abandoned them at the edge of the town. "Yeah, fills ya with joy, huh?"

Bodyne looked around the city. "Who built this place? I've never seen bricks cast exactly like this in all of Shynar."

"Dunno," Rogan said. "They did a helluva job, though. It looks all perfect, the stones in the street, the buildings and all."

Thyssen offered, "It's fucked up, though."

They all looked at him. Bodyne asked, "What?"

"Nobody is here. No bodies, bones, or anything. Where did everybody go? Why make such a good city and then abandon it?"

Bodyne replied, "Devils took everyone away, that's the story."

Shazia snorted and offered, "Not men from the stars?"

After more curses, Rogan walked to the other side of the city square and said, "I wonder if those things are a few of them folks."

Killer of Giants

They walked up behind Rogan and saw what he referred to: Several figures, humanoid shapes, in various places around a neighboring courtyard.

Thyssen squinted at them and said, "Statues. Weird shapes."

They stepped closer to the courtyard and Rogan wondered, "Who would carve such things? They are all in various crazy states."

Bodyne put her right hand to her mouth. "They are awful, broken, and in the rictus of death."

Thyssen knelt by one and said, "All of them guys, all men, and this fella looks pretty happy."

Shazia laughed again. Her sniggers rippled about the masonry above them as she walked about the various stone figures. "Look at them. All sexed up and nowhere to go."

"Yeah," Rogan nodded. "Look, they are all having sex"

Thyssen pointed to each figure. "Their peckers are gone."

"Maybe someone broke them off," Rogan said and looked at Shazia.

She rubbed her eyes and blinked knowingly. "You have an idea, huh?"

"Make it real for me," Rogan replied.

"They are not statues," Shazia said. "They are victims of the daughter of the demon, all turned to stone in the act of copulation."

Thyssen shook his head and stood up straight. "You mean they saw the gorgon and turned to stone while screwing?"

She frowned. "You are thick, big man. They screwed her and turned to stone. All that seeing the gorgon is dung in a handbag. That is the curse of a female Nephilim. They screw you and you turn to stone."

Rogan smirked and stepped on through the figures. "Well, I'll do my best to count the fingers and toes of the next woman I lay down with." He gripped the hilt of his blade tighter as he stepped through the various stone figures.

Thyssen walked a few steps behind Rogan, saying, "Wouldn't

ya wonder why this woman wanted to screw ya amongst all these other figures in such a state?"

"They look aged, weathered like the rain has melted them some," Rogan noted. "It must be some woman to cull their worries and be taken here."

"Or," Thyssen threw out, "these figures were hauled out here."

Bodyne asked, "Like a collection?"

"Bizarre," Thyssen said, eying them close as they all walked past.

"Weirder than the twin bitches in one body?" Rogan called back. "This place is weird all over."

Bodyne hissed, "Listen! The crying!"

They all stopped walking and each person strained to hear what she spoke about.

"A woman weeps," Rogan said in a steady voice. He stepped away from the rest of them and walked into an open area past the courtyard. His sword poised to strike, he moved ahead and around a bend to his right.

"Rogan," Bodyne called out. "Look out..."

Shazia cackled. "Let him get his dick wet." She called on, "Go on, you bad boy. Get an eternal stiffy."

Ignoring her, Rogan moved down the narrowing stone walls. He gazed up to see the sky shrinking overhead. Before he reached the end of the avenue, he spotted a slumped-over figure against the left wall. When he stopped near the figure, Rogan cleared his throat.

The robed shape turned to look up at him. "Rogan?"

"Yana, that you?" Rogan named her and took a knee, touching her back with his left hand.

She fell against his chest, her right arm curled about his waist, her right hand clutching her necklace of bones and jewels. "Help her."

Guessing who she meant, Rogan asked, "Where is Elisa?"

"Beyond," she pointed at the oval opening to a multi-pillared rectangular building before them, "there."

Rogan stood, but Yana clutched his calf.

"She battles them," Yana wept. "I could ward them off me with my magicks, but Elisa…"

Casually patting her head twice, Rogan progressed out of her grip. He stepped toward the oval doorway into the pillared building. Though a dark passage presented itself at first, he saw a clearer place lit well by the fading light beyond. Cool air rushed over him as his boots took him through the passage.

"Stop her," a male voice wailed into Rogan's ears.

Just before he reached the end of the route, a short man faltered into the opening and fell down. Tears wiped on Rogan's knees and blood smeared on his boots before he fell to his back. Rogan saw the small man sported a few slash marks, as if grazed by a blade on his belly.

Rogan knelt and faced the gasping man. Eyes wide, the man gaped at Rogan, then looked back at the opening.

"Who?"

The man screamed, "The giant girl, slays my mistress!"

Rogan stepped through the opening and saw the long chamber, filled with small wooden kneeling benches all tossed out of order, a few smoldering square altars by the corners, and two large figures.

One of them soon lost mass, for Elisa's blade fell on the other large woman, over and over. Rogan didn't call out for her to stop, he only moved up slow as Elisa dismembered the figure, jetting blood in every direction.

"Die, you rotten bitch," Elisa shouted in glory, each word grunted hard as the sword fell down. "Die!"

Rogan stayed out of the spray of blood and way of the weapon, but could see the battle won by Elisa, who kept fine tuning her victory by slicing wounds in her victim.

Elisa's face turned to glare at Rogan.

"Don't mind me," Rogan said. "Just passing through."

Elisa took a few breaths, then grinned as her gloved hands

gripped the handle hard, letting it drop over and over.

The figure she dismembered looked to be a bigger woman than Elisa, and had sported a knife and crossbow before Elisa cut off her hands, thus no more defense was offered. Rogan counted the fingers on the hand on the floor nearest him. Six fingers.

After a few more minutes, she stopped hacking at her. Rogan wondered if she wore out or arrived at the idea that her task ended.

"Is that Zazaeil's daughter?" Rogan asked her.

Elisa sucked in breaths and stepped back. "I've slain her." She looked at him and smiled weakly. "I am the killer of giants."

"Those poor stone bastards in the courtyard?"

Nostrils wrinkled. "Her handiwork. Her servants came for mother and me."

"I saw Yana. Where are the servants?"

Elisa's grin widened. "All dead by my hand. Pitiful scum thinking they were strong men at war. No challenge."

"At least not as strong as you."

Her grin disappeared. "Where is that little prick? Where's Lucas?"

"The bloody guy? I saw one in the hallway. Is he one of them?"

Her head shook once. "Lucas is worse."

Rogan and Elisa went to the passage and found no one. She said, "We have to stop him." She ran down the hall before him.

"What is his story?" Rogan wondered as they moved down the passage.

"Lucas seeks after the wrong god," Elisa had a chance to say as she stepped out of the oval door in time for Lucas to hit her in the midsection.

He swung what looked to Rogan like a rock, but whatever it was, Lucas doubled over Elisa, then swiftly turned about and smashed the rock on her hunched-over back. As the big woman went down, Lucas turned to Rogan and planted his feet.

"You're finished, squirt," Rogan smirked and readied his

blade to swing.

The small man wore no look of terror as before. His eyes ogled Rogan, in that split second, causing the hulking Kelt to pause. The pupils of Lucas' eyes drew back like a stone falling into infinity.

Rogan moved forward to strike and Lucas shrank back, his scarred skin taking on an appearance as if a thousand ants ran across it. Rogan's sword swing missed and his follow-up strike deflected off the stone the man held.

There wasn't much to the second shot, as Rogan watched Lucas start to change. In a few moments, the ants Rogan thought he saw were ripples and newborn spikes as Lucas' skin popped up into a leathery matrix.

Rogan didn't wait to see what Lucas would become. He used his left hand and pushed the rock down and thrust his sword straight into Lucas' chest. As much force as he used and from his weight, Rogan blinked that the blade didn't go straight on through. The sword tip entered into Lucas, but stopped a few inches inside.

Unsure if he hit bone or some product of the person's transformation held him up, Rogan howled the name of his god and drove the sword on. The blade went in with difficulty. He felt it scrape on something within Lucas, ribs or a spine, but he didn't question it. All about the blade, Lucas grew in mass, like a mouse turning into a rat, or rather, in this case, a frog into an alligator.

The voice of his father Jarek rang in his ears, of being taught to run a man through. If he hit an obstruction, saw like he worked on tree limbs. Rogan did so, working the blade up and down and sawing it lower through what became Lucas' abdomen.

"Damn you, Seth," Rogan cursed the viper man. "You were right." The sword popped through the alligator-snakish man Lucas turned into with an abrupt thud. Rogan stumbled forward, near to embracing the creature.

The hissing face of the monster Lucas turned into came

near to snapping at Rogan with a long snout of pointed teeth, but he shoved him away. In the move, he let go of his sword. Lucas stepped back, grabbed the pommel, and started to work at pulling it free of his leathery skinned midsection.

Elisa then smashed the rock Lucas had dropped into the back of the monster's head.

Lucas wavered on his clawed feet until she repeated the move, this time in an overhand shot. The creature fell down, gutting himself worse on Rogan's sword as he dropped.

She straddled him, saying, "You want to see your god?" She raised the rock and brought it down to his skull. "Here he is." Over and over she smashed the monster until it went limp and the skull ran of pulp on the stones. She breathed hard, looking up at Rogan. "What? Don't get prissy that I went too far."

Rogan shook his head once. "I just want my sword back."

CHAPTER ELEVEN

Turn to Stone

Lybeck rode with Urell near the head of their column just behind the twins. He looked over his shoulder to see the grim face of Kylene and her remaining Kushite warriors bunched up in front of the regular soldiers. His eyes locked a tad too long with those of Harland and Ransim, who headed up the regulars. *Assholes, always laughing about something.* Lybeck turned away and searched the rough road ahead that led to Irem.

Urell said, "High grasses along this road, they give me the evils."

While the Kaldwell twins exchanged a glance at these words, Lybeck just observed the tall grasses, yellow in the season, and then looked to the many birds overhead.

"Well?" Urell pushed on. "It doesn't bother you?"

"What will happen will happen," Lybeck dismissed him. "I shan't spend time on this Earth afraid after nothing."

The twins stopped the group and they all dismounted to rest. Binje spoke up to his brother to say, "Evening will come soon. We won't make Irem tonight."

"You want to camp in all this?" Batasta returned, a meaty arm waved at the tall grasses. "The gods know and piss on what lurks beyond."

Binje suggested, "We could make Madron, though, before dark."

His brother shook his head. "The idea of bivouacking in that accursed place makes me want to sleep in the tall grasses and pray for deliverance."

"Perhaps," Binje started to say but fell silent.

Kylene snorted, which came to surprise the soldiers. "What?" she spat out with a sharp tone. "You like your women as culled cows? Their tits ripe and full of milk? You are so scared of what might lie in the weeds or beyond our field of vision?"

Harland smirked and elbowed in the direction of Ransim, but both soldiers soon wore forced stoic faces as Kylene continued.

"You fear other men, either with stronger arms or tougher wills? You utterly fear men with bigger cocks and better abilities on the bedmat? That is why you kill others, to cover your simple inadequacies. You have no idea what true horror, or a domineering male persona, can be, do you?"

Batasta said, "What do you get at? We need to get moving. What silly thing do you wish to paint our minds with?"

"It is silly because I am not a man? Could you endure what all of my sisterhood have gone through? Can you dare to be one of us?"

Binje stepped up to face her, looking down into Kylene's face. "What is it you want to reveal about this?"

"You manly swine," Kylene barked back at him. "All of you are the same down deep, even if you care to give a damn. All of you are happy if your balls are empty. You are no different than Zazaeil, the demon on two legs. The one who wears human flesh because his wings were torn from his back."

Batasta glanced at his brother and then glared at her. "What did Zazaeil do to your sisters and you?"

"Not to me," Kylene fired back. "I wasn't qualified as one who carried a gift from Kamala-ur. Many of my sisters were."

Lybeck mumbled to the soldiers, "Where are they?" His

words weren't meant to be passed on to the others, but Kylene heard him anyway.

Eyes flaring at him, she raged, "They carried the seed and child of Kalama-ur. This was the gift to Zazaeil, the demon in human flesh. Yes, he put his filthy head between their legs, extended his forked tongue, and ate the gift out of their wombs."

Urell's face ran chalk white and he stepped away from the others, walking in a circle. He then bent, hands to his knees.

Eyes tapering, Batasta asked her, "You and your sisters carried babes conceived from King Kamala-ur as a gift to this fallen son?"

Lips curling from her teeth, Kylene said, "Not all of us held such a babe in our bellies. All claimed to be with the gift of Kamala-ur."

Harland chuckled and said, "Then a few of you were either lying or hoping got the best when sent to Zazaeil."

Kylene turned and tried to kick Harland in the balls, but he jumped back. She then said, "The best? Bah. We were slaves to Kalama-ur, sent on this errand with no real full knowledge of what would happen, save for that what grew within us would be done away with. We were promised it would bring us no harm."

Binje sighed. "What madness."

Kylene's ire dropped and a tear ran from her left eye. "It seemed so damned simple, a small life, a real blessing we'd be paid greatly for. However, when the method came to extract them from us, the demon's tongue scrounging it from us, well, that didn't seem pleasant when it happened."

"Horrible," Urell stated, standing again.

"So okay," Harland replied. "You are as tough as the rest of us. I guess you are along for the ride until we hit Irem."

Kylene replied, "Awfully big of you. Just remember what we have endured when you try to think of yourselves as such big men."

His toothy grin broad, he said, "I'm all a shaking at your sacrifice, sugar tits." He paused and added, "Maybe I shoulda said tit?"

Her look ripped from his gaze, Kylene returned to her few sisters left.

They all returned to their mounts and set about their trip. The twins exchanged looks and then focused their eyes forward.

Batasta sighed loud. "You would rather those fools are allowed to ride up to Madron and do as they requested?"

Binje glanced back at Harland and said, "The arrogant prick wanted to ride on ahead fast with a few soldiers and search it out."

"Huh," Batasta snorted. "Harland has a puerile death wish. Arrogant fuck. We should've let him go."

Binje whispered, "We should."

"Wha?"

"Let him go. What could be the harm? If he gets turned to stone or inside out by the local beasts, we won't have to hear his mouth any longer."

Batasta fell silent and Lybeck thought him pondering this in earnest. "But if he succeeds, his tongue will fork worse than a cobra's."

Harland laughed and called out, "What are you girls discussing?"

Binje muttered, "I'm willing to take that risk."

The twins stopped and turned their horses about to face the rest. The column stopped as Batasta began to speak.

"Harland, are you still up for that investigation into Madron you proposed at the dock?"

A grin spreading on his thin face, Harland asked, "Change of heart, sugar?"

Batasta didn't react to his words, but Binje did frown. Batasta said, "Something like that. Take a few soldiers and check it out. Report back or wait for us. We can make Madron by nightfall. Report back, though."

As Binje turned his mount back around, he said, "If you can."

Before Harland retorted, Kylene said, "We shall go with them."

As Batasta opened his mouth, Harland snapped, "No, I don't need a wet nurse."

Her eyes narrowed at Harland, Kylene said, "You need more than that. How you've managed to wipe your ass this long in life amazes me."

His wicked grin returned, Harland said to her, "How bout I show you how clean it is?"

"Children," Batasta sighed. "Kylene, stay with us. Harland and Ransim, take two men you choose and ride on ahead."

Glee spread on Harland's face. He looked to a soldier that rode near him and said, "If we kick them hard, we'll make it before dark falls in full."

The soldier nodded, swallowing loud, and followed as the others joined Harland.

Lybeck shook his head a little. "That poor soldier almost pissed himself at the idea of searching Madron in the dark."

Kylene turned her horse about, bottom lip jutting a little, but soon a smile appeared on her face. "They won't be coming back."

Binje scanned the tall weeds as the party left them. "Keep your eyes alert, or we won't be making Irem ever."

The six that rode off had been gone but a half-hour when the column stopped again. Batasta reined his mount about and his brother cocked his head.

"The sky is clear," Batasta said. "And yet, it sounds like rain."

Binje also scanned the sky and then looked across the fields of long grasses. "The sound comes from there."

Lybeck drew his sword. "From all around us."

"Dismount, all of you," Batasta ordered. "Get in a ring."

All climbed down from their horses and formed a ring together, away from the mounts. All drew weapons as the hissing sound grew louder.

Urell stood elbow to elbow with Lybeck, saying, "We are all

kinds of fucked."

"Steady on," Lybeck responded.

Binje shouted, "Here they come."

No more warnings were needed as the viper-men emerged into the open. Like an anthill disturbed, the viper-men flowed from the grasses, all running low to the ground, mouths agape to show their fangs.

"Have at you pricks," Batasta roared, slashing out with his sword, striking one in the face and dodging another with his shield. His brother, back to back with him, fended off many the same way.

Lybeck and Urell weren't back-to-back, but they waded in hard, impossible to miss a target as there were so many. They smashed and chopped, being pushed back at first, but then driving out into the wave.

The viper-men were so many, but slight of build. A few of the soldiers perished, taken down by the initial wave, but in a minute, they had cut down dozens of the attackers.

Kylene shouted orders at her fellow warriors, elbowing one of the viper-men in the chest as her boots kicked another in the face. She waded into their number, unafraid, and slew so many before Lybeck saw her get taller...or at least that is how it appeared to him.

Her back arched and Kylene stretched up...mouth open wide. Lybeck saw two viper-men at her, one with long fangs sunk into her left thigh and the other biting deep into her buttocks. Her body froze and she gagged, stuck in place, too stunned to even drop her blade on her attackers.

"Gods," she cried out, body shaking. "It hurts..."

Lybeck angled himself off Urell and clobbered a viper-man with his sword's pommel to get near her.

Kylene's high voice went guttural low as she started to bend in the middle and convulse. She vomited a long spew of blood and bile as Lybeck swung his sword about and removed her head at the neck.

Kylene out of her misery, Lybeck chopped at the two vipers at her lower section, crushing one in the mid-section and beheading the other. The one he hit in the chest drew its fangs off Kylene, screeching until Lybeck swung his blade again.

"No," Urell shouted as he fought and watched Lybeck's actions. With wild actions, Urell fought and slew like Lybeck figured he couldn't. Urell ran through many viper-men, heading in his direction.

Unsure if Urell planned to attack him or not, Lybeck kept an eye on him as he fought. Empty of enemies, both men took deep breaths as Urell stared at Kylene's head on the ground. He then glared at Lybeck.

"She was dead already," Lybeck told him. "I sent her on her way."

Shaking his head fast, Urell turned about in search of more targets, but saw the only ones around were being taken out by the Kaldwell twins. The twins still fought as one, as they must've done many times before. At last, they were done, but still scanning the grasses for more attackers.

Binje said, "Why did they attack us?"

"They are snakes," Batasta snapped. "They don't need a reason."

Binje persisted, saying, "Is this place sacred? Others pass here unmolested."

"Well," Batasta replied, "We didn't leave any alive to question."

Lybeck stated, "We lost a half-dozen good soldiers."

On his knees, petting Kylene's hair, Urell said, "And good women."

Binje grimaced, and looked at Urell. "She was a true warrior. She understood the risks of such a trip. We will honor her."

Urell stood and looked into the sky, then to Lybeck. "I'm going to sound like Lybeck soon, saying is that bastard Kelt worth these lives?"

Lybeck realized Urell sported amorous feelings for Kylene,

but this struck closer to home at her demise.

Batasta went nose to nose with Urell, saying, "You can quit any time you want, ginger-man."

Urell sneered, "I'll see that Kelt dead by my own hand."

"Good," Batasta smirked. "Bury your feelings and focus."

"She was a good woman, damn you."

Binje joined his brother saying, "Plenty more of those."

After the twins returned to their mounts, Urell eyed Lybeck and said, "Dickheads. I'd see them dead, too."

Lybeck near to gasped, figuring the twins heard him with their heightened senses. If they did, the two never reacted or seemed to care.

Binje said, "We will attend the dead and stay here or nearby. There is no reason trying to make Madron this night."

Urell looked down at Kylene's head. "I wonder how those jackasses will fare?"

*****

"Why did you have to kill her?"

Rogan's head still reeled, but he could pick up Elisa's words through the muck he swam through in his brain. His attempt to lift his head worked only long enough to see the moonlight stream in through the curved window of the stone grotto. Again, Rogan hung his aching head, and he heard Elisa yell.

"You're a beast. Why did you have to do that to her?"

His bleary mind focused on just which event she referred to. Alas, he understood what earned the strong blow from Elisa to the back of his head. Rogan took a few breaths before he spoke, though.

"She was a monster."

Her screams and calamitous curses faded out, moving out of his ears like they whirled down a tunnel gushing water. However, the voice of Thyssen seeped in from a different route. Thyssen's voice cupped with his own, and he understood it a recollection, not an event happening in the grotto in Madron.

"I see Elisa and her Ma got their thing back," Thynnes had said to Rogan, not long after the tall woman finished bashing in the skull the creature with it.

"That's what the gorgon here wanted?"

"It's what those pricks Marduk and Zazaeil want as well."

"Phah, bullshit," Rogan had dismissed Thyssen as they drank from skins of wine to properly reload their selves.

Indignant, Thyssen retorted, "What? You think *they* want more ass?"

"Who doesn't want more ass?"

"They can get ass anywhere and don't turn it down, but they collect stuff and have egos bigger than men."

Rogan spat and then said to Thyssen, "I know they are petty bastards, bored with life here, wanting to rule in heaven, so they shit on us."

"Yeah. They want stuff, like the ivory mammoth, one more silly thing their brothers cannot have. That rock? Fallen from the sky? From another place out there in the other world or stars?"

"Backwash from the Outer Gods?"

"They would want it if not to just collect it, but may know what it really is."

Rogan remembered in the vision the wine ran sour, but he hungered for it again as his retention recalled asking, "What is it do you think?"

Shrugging, Thyssen replied, "I dunno. It's a rock."

"Damned philosopher, you are. You suck at it, though."

"Piss off. But why go and risk their lives over such a thing? What is it they are after there with the giants?"

"Maybe ya need to ask Elisa and quit screwing my ear."

"I did ask her," Thyssen said with a frown visible in the waning hours of day back then. "She said to go screw myself and that it's her own business."

Rogan pondered that. "I reckon it is."

"Wonder what the big secret is?"

"Piss on your curiosity."

Thyssen walked in a circle and said, "She wants to be the killer of giants?"

"That's what she says."

"Maybe she wants to get close enough to that Marduk or that rotten devil Zazaeil. Why? To kill them?"

Rogan had laughed at the idea. "Huh. Her life won't be worth spit if she managed to kill either one."

"I don't think she cares. Something weird about her."

"Yeah."

"Elisa seems to have a motive she won't reveal. Her mother would know."

"Do ya think she will share?"

Thyssen took a drink. "Prolly not, they seem to be on a mission, a hard undertaking. It's a real puzzle."

"We all have our own reasons to go to Irem, though. You want a ride home, I want to free my lost kindred. Bodyne, hell, she has nowhere to go but along with us. That Shazia? Who the hell knows, she's freakin' nuts." Rogan took a swig of wine and suggested, "cuddle up to Elisa's mama. She might tell you."

Thyssen drank more as well, then replied, "I'll mention your name. That'll get her all creamy."

A disgusted look on his hairy face, Rogan shot back, "Damn the gods, Thyssen, I am drinkin' here."

"She was prolly a handsome woman, once."

"Someday we'll be old too."

"Fuck that," Thyssen declared. "I'd rather die in battle."

Rogan shook his head. "I wanna die screwing. Really, I do."

"Yeah?"

"I wanna come and go at the same time. When they burn my body, no one will cry, but their envy will light up the night with my ashes."

Both men had laughed. It was the last laugh they shared before both men were clubbed by unseen weapons out of the night. Rogan recalled thinking how stupid he had been to joke on dying in the act of sex, when death rose up and greeted him by the edge of the grotto.

Falling to the stone courtyard, the world askew in the night, Rogan expected a cold death blow to follow…a spearhead, a blade, but none arrived.

"Come on, sissy boys," he'd heard the cackling voice of Shazia. At first, he thought she taunted them, glad in their demise…but suddenly his idea faded.

"Be gone, rotten troll," a gruff voice shouted.

"I'm a dwarf princess, sissy boy," Shazia giggled. "You are such a manly man? Come take my prize."

Another male voice said, "Harland, the others are battling that big woman. She's a terror."

"Ransim, I figured they could take her as we went after the two big fighters."

"Harland?" Shazia sang out in the corners of Rogan's groggy mind. "Are you man enough to take it?"

The voice from one called Ransim had said, "Look, sir, there at the little freak on that altar."

Harland said, "Yes, presenting like an animal in heat. She's downright squirrely. Just ignore her, man."

Shazia cooed, "What's the matter, twatty boys? Threatened by a dwarf touching herself?" She cackled again as the men cursed her. "Your swords are your manhood. I bet they are not even daggers out in the air."

"Rotten freak," Harland had cursed her and his footfalls echoed in the grotto. "I'll show you a dagger."

Shazia still laughed as Rogan turned over. Eyes blinking, he saw the back side of the one he guessed Ransim. He faced away from them toward the altar, where a taller man, Harland Rogan presumed, dropped his trousers.

Angry, Ransim said, "We don't have time for this."

Harlan laughed, "I've always got time for this."

His hands sliding to his belt, Rogan gripped the hilt of one of his daggers as he heard Shazia say, "Come on, big man. Put it in me."

"Take it, you freak," Harland grunted.

Rogan felt Thyssen shift near his boots as the tilting world stabilized a little. The Kelt pulled his dagger free of the holster and slowly got to his knees as Harland slammed himself into Shazia on the altar.

As Harland grunted and Shazia laughed more, Rogan got to his knees. He reached out, grabbed Ransim by the thick waist belt and stabbed forward, cutting the hamstring in the soldier's right thigh.

When Ransim cried out in distress, he tumbled on back into Rogan's arms. Catching him like a dancer at a big party, Rogan whipped his arm about his neck and then slashed across Ransim's throat, hushing his cries in blood.

Rolling the body off him, Rogan let the man thrash as he died, gripping at his throat, trying to fix the wound. Rogan made it to his feet, preparing to go behind Harland and do the same slaying action as the man raped Shazia.

Rogan's actions stopped as he saw Harland's body start to shake all over like the tail of a deadly snake. Never had he seen any man tremble so much at once, nor make the chittering sounds Harland made.

"Don't Rogan," Thyssen gasped from the floor, eyes wide at what the Kelt witnessed. "Damn, don't touch him."

Abruptly, Harland's heaving pelvic thrusts stopped, but his body still shook wild. In an instant, though, this action ceased, and he stood still.

They heard an extended wheeze escape his mouth and an irregular sound rippled in the grotto, one Shazia's merriment couldn't suppress. The inimitable sound ran akin to rocks grinding on each other, but for a few instants, and then was no more.

When Thyssen joined Rogan at the altar, they saw that Harland was no more, either. Though they hadn't gotten a clear look at their attacker when first struck down, there he stood… well, he'd stand there forever, as his form had turned to stone.

They looked down at Shazia, who lay on the altar, legs spread, and her middle finger poking at her pubic ridge. She winked at them. She had six fingers.

"You boys want seconds?" she asked in an innocent voice before belching loud and then laughing deep again.

That's when Rogan drew his sword from his back and chopped her in half.

Though a long exhale escaped from her mouth and a quizzical look stayed on Shazia's face as she died, Rogan didn't stop his actions. Thyssen stepped back, turning to look at others who entered the grotto. Rogan let fall his sword, repetitively, like he cut wood for a fire with a heavy axe. His blows were measured, and sometimes ferocious, but didn't miss the dwarf a single time.

He recalled the cries of Elisa at his vicious actions and then felt the blow to his head. Rogan twirled again, struck down once more from behind. As he'd fallen, he cursed Thyssen in his mind. Yes, his friend should've stopped her cold, but perhaps he too stood shocked at Rogan's uncouth actions.

His head clearing and reality fixed more in the present, Rogan looked up at Elisa, who did look to insert a sword in him, but Thyssen held her arm.

"She was a monster," Rogan croaked again, then looked to the bloody altar. "Damned gorgon."

"You are the monster," Elisa yelled and heaved her arm from Thyssen's grip. "Who were you to take her little life?"

"Blow it out yer ass, sister," Rogan rumbled low and sat up. "That's why they throw them things away at birth, the unwanted Nephilim. Look at that prick there? Stone-dead motherfucker in every sense of it."

Thyssen nodded and said, "He kinda had that coming."

Getting back to his feet with a hand from Thyssen, Rogan said, "I dunno if anyone has that coming, but I'm not sorry he's dead."

Rogan stepped to Harland and grabbed him by the elbow. He pulled on the stone figure a little and then shoved the shape with all his might. Harland's stone form fell and broke into several large pieces before them, causing another gasp from all who looked inside the grotto.

Elisa sheathed her sword and cracked her knuckles through her gloves. "That was mature."

Rogan eyed her but a second and looked at the pieces of Harland. "I can't kill him, but I didn't like his face." He then stomped on Harland's head until it went to dust. Rogan then said, "I hope you took care of the rest of the soldiers?"

He heard a sound not unlike Bodyne gagging before she asked, "How am I supposed to sleep after that?"

Retrieving his sword, Rogan rubbed the back of his skull and said, "Like the dead, ma'am." He then looked at the altar and the remains of the two invaders. "Like the dead."

CHAPTER TWELVE

I Won't Cry For You

Lybeck's eyes popped open as Urell dropped onto the prairie near him. His ass in the grasses, the red-haired soldier sucked on his flask and looked at the sky.

"Slept well?" Urell grunted and lay back on the matted down grasses.

Adjusting a little on his bedroll over the grasses, Lybeck replied, "No, not actually. Not so much."

"You were snoring when I walked up."

"Sounds unlikely." Lybeck shot him a forbidding look. "I must've slipped in there deep for a spell."

After a sniffle and spit, Urell grumbled, "Don't mention spells. I've had about enough of all this magick and otherworldly things."

"Huh?"

"Those two unpleasant jackoffs are out there, trying to talk to their demon whatever-the-fuck he is."

"Every morning they do it," Lybeck sighed and looked around. "Not quite dawn though." After a big breath, he said, "Maybe that devil trickster will give them great revelations on what awaits us."

"Yeah, yeah."

Lybeck turned his head toward him. "I'm surprised at you, Urell. Losing your faith in this grand operation?"

Eyes up at the sky, Urell replied, "I didn't think this would carry on so much, I thought we'd be back in the whorehouses by now. I thought we'd have had Rogan in a day and been done with it all."

"I had hoped."

Urell glared at him. "But you knew that big Keltic sonofabitch might just elude us for real, huh?"

"I suspected," Lybeck replied. "I don't feel so good about confronting him now. Our numbers are way on down. The women are done, really. We haven't heard word from Harland or Ransim."

"Pricks. I hope they die."

"I'd feel better taking down that big Kelt with a small army at the ready. Our forces are depleted badly."

Again, Urell stared up at the sky. "He doesn't frighten me."

"He should," Lybeck said.

"Yeah?"

"Yes," Lybeck then confessed, "He frightens me."

A long silence hung between them for a few minutes before Urell said, "All the women are dead."

"I hadn't noticed."

"I thought one was alive, but I didn't see her walking around." Urell then sat up, his face a picture of fury. "If those twin pricks used her as a sacrifice for their bullshit…"

Lybeck responded, "I'm sure a living soul is better than any river rat they can scrounge." He then sat up as Urell stood. "You best unfuck that attitude toward the twins. You dreaming of besting Rogan one on one is a solitary dream, but taking down those twins single-handedly, you are rather delusional."

Urell's face moved slow from side to side as the laughter of the twins filtered to them, just as the sun broke over the fields.

"Rogan is near," came the loud voice of one of the twins.

"We have seen it and our plan ahead of us," came the other voice. "We shall make Madron before noon!"

Up to his feet, Lybeck said, "That's such great news. I'm hungry."

Urell said, "We combined rations from the supplies leftover of the dead. We better fill our bellies."

"Those twins will be aching to get going, so I really doubt we have time to cook anything."

"My appetite isn't for food, but we better eat anyway."

Lybeck's mind tried to shut out the lingering stench of the dead they wrapped and stacked in the fields the night before. With no wood or adequate propellant, they couldn't burn all the bodies. Since burying them wasn't an option, they would do as his father told him when they lost a few men on a campaign in his teens.

"Head out and don't look back. The earth will claim them soon enough."

That thought brought no less horror then for Lybeck than it did when he pondered it as a youth. The idea that bugs, plants, and wolves would soon consume those who they'd just supped with didn't make for a happy stomach.

"Still," he said to no one as he munched the hard tack and dug in his saddle bag for some jerky. "Still alive."

Urell didn't look his way but also ate near his horse. "Yeah, aren't we lucky? Going to be a long day."

Chin jutting at the twins, Lybeck said, "Those fuckers are certainly raring to get going. They look so happy like they just got laid."

"They are pretty fearless."

"Stupid to not have any fear," Lybeck said, head giving a single shake. "Rush into anything like idiots."

"Their audacity has served them well," Urell noted. "So far."

Trying to mentally dismiss Urell's ire and desire toward the Kaldwells, Lybeck climbed into the saddle.

Urell, though, went to the weeds and bound up his bedroll.

After securing it to his mount, Urell returned to the weeds. He picked up something, hid it in front of himself, and walked out into the higher grasses. In a few moments he returned and climbed up on his horse. He nodded, facing towards Madron.

Lybeck heeled his horse, shoving down in his mind deep the image of a dead girl's vomit on Urell's lips and beard.

They reached Madron in only a few hours. The twins rode in first with great boldness. Their curses echoed in the eerie streets of Madron to Lybeck and Urell, telling the tale that their prey had gone already.

"Figured that," Urell mumbled. "Damn it all."

Their horses treading slow on the streets of Madron, they stopped and dismounted as they heard the twins thunderous with laughter. After a swapped glance, they drew their swords and headed through the narrow openings and exposed buildings.

"Carnage is an easy map to follow," Lybeck commented as both men navigated through pieces of the dead men that had went with Harland and Ransim.

"Meat grinder, that Rogan is," Urell said, his voice full of caution as he went toward where the twins still laughed.

"Who can say it was just him?"

Urell's frown deepened. "I know he has others with him."

"You aren't going to tell me Rogan is the only killer in that group from the bodies we've seen so far." Lybeck eyed him as they crept along. "Let that sink in while you dream of fighting him single-handedly."

"That's what you and the twins are for," Urell told him with a smirk. "But I'd feel better if our numbers were better."

Lybeck nudged the errand head in the street with the edge of his boot. "That soldier, he was a fine warrior, but it did him no good."

"His mother will pray for him, as many days as she lives," said Urell. "Her and many more others."

"Does your mama pray?"

"My mom is dead. Has been since I was a kid."

Lybeck almost told him his own mother still lived to an amazing age, but didn't want to pursue the talk. "There they are."

They halted, seeing another dead body. Urell gagged a little, then asked, "What in the world is that thing, or things?"

"Monsters. Dead ones, thank the heavens."

"Creatures joined at the sides," Urell observed the bodies, "I need a drink. I don't know if my flasks have enough refills for this trip."

Lybeck turned away from the bodies, saying, "That crazy Harland screwed something akin to this, well, it was human."

"You think he tried to screw that thing?"

"Doubtful. I think there'd be pieces of him around here if he did. He's horny and inane, but not completely stupid."

Batasta and Binje's laughter had subsided as the two walked out of the stone grotto, one of them went over by a wall, passed water, and still didn't cease laughing.

Urell stepped in first and looked down. "Ransim was a great fighter, too, but look at him. There he lays, throat slit like a bitch."

"Damn," Lybeck sighed and then looked over by the altar. "What is that on the altar by the broken statue?"

Urell walked over and gazed down. "Gods, something cut to pieces. A small thing, but not a child." He then studied the headless stone figure by the altar and then his face turned back toward Lybeck.

"Over here, I think..." Lybeck's voice trailed off as he spun the stone head on the floor over with his boot.

Urell's smile spread wide and he started to laugh.

The urge to cackle gripped Lybeck, but he fought it down. The feeling ran like a crazed desire in him, and that felt disturbing...almost as disquieting as what they found. Would it be out of finding actual humor in the fact that the stone figure proved to be Harland, or the giddy insanity of his mind trying to deal with such a reality.

True enough, Harland had his prickish ways, and Lybeck

never cared for him, but this reality came tough to accept. One might joke over too much ale or wine about a monster getting an enemy or rival in death, but seeing Harland turned to stone didn't bring any good feelings to Lybeck.

Urell had no trouble diving into real humor, slapping the rocky, broken, stone rump of Harland with the flat of his sword as if to spank him.

"Just quit," Lybeck rasped and started to turn away,

"I'm not quite done yet." Urell teetered on the edge of choking on his laughs as he pulled his blade back and dropped it on the other side of Harland. The move knocked the stone penis off the figure.

Lybeck walked out of the grotto and kept taking fast steps until he reached his horse. He held onto the saddle but didn't sheath his sword yet.

The twins walked about the area, still smiling, but their loud humor had recessed somewhat.

Batasta ceased giggling and said, "It looks like the group slew whatever monsters prowled around in here."

Lybeck looked back toward the grotto. "That's crazy."

Binje looked from side to side and said, "See what happens when you let one of our sisters live?"

Eyes closed, Lybeck returned his blade to the scabbard. He watched the twins speak low to each other and climbed back into the saddle as Urell emerged from the grotto.

Batasta spoke louder to say, "The bodies and mounts of the men are stripped of anything already."

With a nod, Binje said, "Yes, they butchered and half-assed roasted one of their horses. That meat must've been pretty raw."

Urell spat, "Swine."

"When you are very hungry," Batasta stated, "sometimes all real manners can go by the wayside."

After he mounted up, Urell turned and said, "There's the four of us and about a half-dozen soldiers left."

Binje's smiling face didn't falter as he said, "On to Irem!"

Killer of Giants

Rogan and Thyssen stood beside their horses, looking further south. The three women were on the other side of the buckboard wagon. All about them were endless valleys of high yellowish grasses, but hills rose in the distance, peppered with jagged rocks wanting to be great mountains.

Thyssen rooted in his saddle bags as Rogan mounted up. He asked, "Rogan, are they done pissing yet?"

Not looking toward the women, Rogan replied, "You gonna go see?"

"No thanks."

"Then eat that crap you stole from the raiders and shut up."

Thyssen munched the jerky and offered some to Rogan, who waved it off.

"No thanks, jackass. Probably poison."

"Hah," Thyssen dismissed him and went on eating. "They'd leave poisoned rations in their own bags?"

"I wouldn't trust them."

"They didn't know they'd end up dead," Thyssen reminded him. "You Kelts are so damned untrusting."

"Know your own, trust your own," Rogan muttered as Elisa helped her mother back into the crude swing hammock they'd made for her in the rear of the buckboard. "Yana can't even ride a fuckin' horse."

"Yeah."

Rogan said with a quiet voice, "Wonder why she's all the way out here in the middle of Asshole, Shynar if she can't?"

"What do ya mean?"

"I mean, damn, why haul your crippled ass across the world? Seems like a helluva thing to do."

"She's with her daughter."

"Yes, but something doesn't wash about all that." Rogan shook his head a little and turned to watched big Elisa mount up. Bodyne then climbed up to drive the buckboard. "I know we are all in this trip together now."

Thyssen said, "We'll be in Irem soon. Ever give any thought to how you're gonna find yer ol' man and sister?"

"Yes, I'm about to." As they started to move down the crude road, Rogan's horse went over by the cart. He asked Yana, "You know this place Irem?"

Her gray eyes met his. "You presume much, Kelt."

"I'm not stupid. Whatever the business you and Elisa have is none of my concern. However, I'm only going to find my father and sister. You would know the most likely place for them to be, right?"

Yana nodded slowly. "Your father is a warrior?"

"Quite. Even if getting on in years, he's a true fighter." Rogan stared off across the grasses, seeing the parade of men he'd seen his father kill or strike down.

"If he is seen as worth it, Marduk's people will want him for troops, or a guard perhaps. Would he fight for Marduk, even to feign it?"

"Jarek is a wily sod," Rogan agreed. "He might to see a path to escape. He's a killer, but no fool. If he fakes being a slave, he does it to kill again."

"Killers? Haha. Marduk is the killer you should worry on. Lives mean nothing to that Marduk. One fighter can be eaten for flesh as easy as a coward, no matter how many fools he has killed before he reaches Marduk's door."

"I see."

"Deceiving Marduk's people will earn him death or true slavery, no matter his grit. If he is as strong as you, they can use him in the mills, chained up for work. If he makes them angry or refuses to serve the demi-gods, all will go bad no matter his strength. Or, they will kill him. Flesh is flesh, strong or not."

Rogan looked straight ahead, no words coming out.

"Your sister, well, is she fair?"

Rogan shrugged. "I never thought of Gale as fair. I guess

her hair is sort of fair compared to others around here."

"Is she an attractive lass?" Yana sighed. "I'm just asking if she isn't repulsive. These pigs won't like an ugly girl."

Thyssen exhaled a laugh and Rogan volleyed him an obscene gesture. "She's a tough girl, but not unattractive, I suppose. She's young, not even a teen yet."

"That won't matter." Yana shook her head. "If she has muscles like a horse, she could be used as a slave. However, if she can be cleaned up and made up proper, she might be grist for the mill of their loins."

"For what?"

Yana rolled her eyes to heaven. "They, the royals or sons of god, will use her for sex, willing or not."

Rogan said, "Kind of small for a giant…"

Yana cut him off. "They will screw her to death then. For Marduk it is sport, not about sex or pleasure, really. Lives mean nothing to them."

Rogan stared at Elisa, who listened to them as she rode along, but said nothing. He then asked Yana, "How will I find them? What place will they be at?"

"I doubt they will let you just take them, either one, but I will show you. There is a great fork in the road when one gets outside of Irem. One way to hades, the other to paradise, that is the joke. You see, I'm going to where they would be getting Gale ready for her duty to whoever wants to consume her. My daughter and I have business there for real, as you and that asshead like to say."

"I don't care what your business is. I just want my kindred."

Yana said, "I know where to go. We must journey fast. The forces behind us will catch up before long."

Rogan looked behind them on the road toward Madron. "I've thought of that, too bad we just don't have at them and be done with them."

Yana's eyes rolled back in her head for a few moments and then she said, "There are ten of them. Eight soldiers and the

Kaldwell twins. The twins themselves would be quite a battle for Elisa, you, and that asshead with the spear."

Thyssen corrected her, "That's Sir Asshead to you, ma'am."

Ignoring him, Yana said, "The twins are powerful and beyond skilled. The soldiers would make it too much. We need to stay ahead of them."

"It's me they want, though," Rogan stated. "They will follow me in my path, whatever I take. You all go unto this place where Gale might be, where they will prep her for whatever. You said you had business there?"

Elisa looked over at last and smirked. "Yes we do, jackass. They are going to make me a princess."

Eyes on the road, Thyssen bit his lip.

Elisa snapped, "No jokes?"

Thyssen loosened up to say, "Too many."

"Piss off," Elisa replied, smiling.

Yana gave Rogan a deep look. "You plan to go off to find your father, and the great mill of Dis? I will show you the path unto Hell."

"Those behind will follow me there. That's all right."

"You will never return from there, Keltic warrior. You will suffer the same fate as your father."

Rogan thought on her words. "If I know my father, he has done what he has done by now. He has bent a false knee to Marduk, became a soldier or guard for him, and is trying to free his daughter."

Elisa shook her mane of hair. "How can you be so sure?"

"It's what any Kelt would do. I won't go into that mill of cursed Dis as it is certain doom. No Kelt would do that willingly and my father would think me a dumbass for jumping into the fire as well. No, I will head on that way and see what I can do with these ones behind me who follow on after."

Yana sighed loud again. "You will go unto your certain death, anyway. The twins and all the rest…"

"I'm smarter than they are." Rogan winked at them. "All

their guile and want hasn't been able to get me yet. I have a feeling they might not be as keen on killing me as trying to capture me and Aliene for further glory."

Looking over the great hairy elephant, Yana said, "I do truly hope you get what you are after, Kelt."

Rogan smiled at her. "You, too, Yana."

"I shall," Yana assured him.

For a long time he looked at her and didn't say anything.

Yana asked, "You wonder after my desires, and those of Elisa?"

"I do, but it's better if I don't know them, really."

"Yes?"

"In case I am tortured by these demon bastards, well, I'd hate to crap on your party."

Yana cackled loud and said, "And what a party it will be." Her thin fingers made a fist about her necklace of tiny bones and she kept laughing until the smile left Rogan's face.

"Mother," said Elisa with a halting tone, reining her horse back.

Bodyne stopped the wagon and the rest followed suit.

Rogan and Thyssen faced where Elisa stared, noting what she spoke of immediately. With a curse to himself for not seeing it earlier, Rogan studied the long form moving along a hill over a half-mile distant. For a brief moment, he thought it a giant, sluggish snake, but a moment's clarity showed this an illusion.

"Caravan," Thynnes mumbled. "Sneaky bastards."

"Just following a different path in the hills," Elisa theorized.

Yana took in a sharp breath. "On your guard, all of you." Her body trembled, her eyes closed, and her hand clutched her necklace.

The long organism stopped and a few men on horseback pointed their way. They swapped looks and spoke beyond their comprehending them. In a few moments, a rider on a shiny black horse flanked by two others clad in chainmail and helmets rode in their direction at a fast clip.

"Slavers," Yana groaned quiet.

Rogan grinned at her and said, "The feasting of swords isn't done for this day."

Elisa glared at him as the horses drew closer.

Winking, Rogan said, "Killer of giants, ya might have to kill a few runts."

Elisa replied quickly, "Those are no runts."

Indeed, the hulking man atop the black horse rivaled Rogan in girth and height, he guessed. Though his face covered by a wrap, Rogan guessed, by the sun-ravaged skin of his arms and legs, the man much older than he and probably harsher. The other two men on brown horses wore chain mail but different insignias. While the bigger man struck Rogan as a leader of some sort, the others wore similar uniforms, not that of military men, but more of standard issue guards.

"Travelers," the big man on the black horse stated, his face wrap falling, a grin emerging amongst the overgrown beard on his face. His eyes studied Elisa, then his grin faded as he noted Rogan, Thynnes, and the elephant. "What in hades is that thing?"

"Aliene," Rogan patted the top of the mammoth's head.

"What's an Aliene?" he asked, bemused.

Rogan frowned. "We are on our way to Irem."

"So are we," the man replied. "Want to come along with us?"

"I think are all right," Rogan told him.

His smile returning, his eyes looking over Elisa, he said, "Perhaps I should insist. It's safer in our caravan."

"She'll feed you your balls," Rogan warned him as the man's look fixed on Elisa.

"That might be worth the fight," the man replied, then looked back up at Rogan. "What's your business in Irem?"

"I don't recall saying," Rogan responded.

Yana muttered, "Just move on."

The big man leered at her.

"Just go away," Yana whispered.

The two guards with the man didn't speak or move until the big fellow gave them each a look.

"Let's get back," he grumbled. "These will be one of us soon enough."

The big man and the guards turned, but one of the guards didn't move as quick. This man paused, and stared up at Rogan. Their eyes locked for several moments before he went along with the others.

Thyssen exhaled and then sucked in air fast. "Gods, glad they moved on."

Rogan watched them go and then turned to face Yana. "Ma'am, I've changed my mind."

Releasing her necklaces and wringing her hands a little, Yana looked up at him. "Is that so?"

"Yeah. I'll go along with you."

Elisa raised an eyebrow. "No longer hungry for the Foundry?"

Rogan's look returned to the men riding away. None of them looked back. "No, I won't be going unto Dis."

CHAPTER THIRTEEN
Shaking Off the Chains

Lybeck praised whatever gods trod through the heavens for the sunlight still bathing the enormous facility far off to the left of Irem. Made of countless bricks, the walls of the place went on what seemed like a quarter mile and then curved. He supposed the edifice sported a huge oval shape or maybe an enormous rectangle. It didn't matter, as he had no intention of going inside nor circling about it.

The stone steps that ran up the side of the outer wall to a guard tower were tricky to navigate, and these allowed him to follow the twins up. When Urell stepped away from that upper wall's edge above him, turning to grip the guardrail of the steps and vomit out the day's meals, Lybeck near to came back down. The glares of the twins and the laughter of those unseen beyond seemed to push him up the steps.

When he reached the apex of the steps, the trembling face of Urell, such a strong man reduced to purging his guts, and the uncertain looks from the faces of the twins didn't give him happiness. From the stench escaping from behind the walls, his stomach turned. Lybeck looked down at the half-dozen men that stayed down by the horses and he envied them.

"Stop your laughing, donkeys," Batasta growled at the men beyond Lybeck's sight. "You can't be serious that you haven't seen him."

"Oh we are very serious," one of the voices replied. "No one could or would approach here and not be seen by us."

"Very much so," another man chuckled as Lybeck stood next to the twins. "Who but madmen or fools ride up to the Foundry of Dis?"

Lybeck saw the first man who spoke, a ruddy skinned bald man covered in boils, clad in light leathers. "Which one are you all then? Crazies or dolts?"

Binje stated, "We told you we are the Kaldwell twins, son of..."

The second guard, a shorter man with greasy black hair and a similar skin condition as his partner, laughed, and said, "Because you are twins doesn't make you special, big men. We get rid of twins every day." He grinned, and like his fellow guard, it was a yellowed, fractured smile well-suited for the horrors whispered of beyond.

Lybeck's hands gripped the thin stone curve at the top of the wall and looked over into the interior. The grand beauty of Irem just behind him in the distance paled to what spurted out of the earth. His guts churned and his mind wondered if the earth itself had pushed it further up, as if to reject it.

Though he'd seen the billowing smoke ejecta from afar off, he thought it the working of factories. Oh, part of his mind still wanted to assign these clouds to the smelting works in the left corner of the seemingly endless facility. From the carts and metal works going to and leaving this sector, he guessed at where the great foundry true to its name exited.

However, all of the many people working there, either by choice or under the lash of rough men like the guards, were scant in number to the others all about the facility. Buildings similar to the foundry extended far back, over a half-dozen in number, each holding smoking chimneys. Carts full of what looked like slop for swine went toward these facilities. Not far away, there were indeed swine farms, by their scent. Lybeck assumed this fed various people here. A guard down near the stacks directed a few carts to the pig farm and others to the chimneys…or what he guessed were incinerators.

"Gods," Lybeck gasped, trying not to wretch.

"Gods?" The taller of the guards giggled. "I've heard of them."

The shorter guard laughed but pulled a serious tone as he said, "Oh yes, very many indeed. I think they make up a few as they die."

"They wouldn't want to leave any out."

"Quite right," the second agreed.

Lybeck almost said the obvious, that the carts were full of people, but he stopped himself. He thought just saying it might make him puke, and certainly would elicit the teeterings of the guards. Still, he couldn't rip his eyes from the spectacle.

Lines of people, mostly older men and women, did a slow walk to a stone building to his left. A comparable line came out of the back of the same building and headed to a different smoking structure. Lybeck noted a few of the heavier people were being fractioned out to a different line. He also heard a call that the day's work would soon be over.

When he saw the one-wheeled carts exiting one of the buildings hauling women with huge bellies…pregnant…Lybeck turned away and held the rail alongside of Urell. Hands gripping the rail tight, fighting down the gorge in his throat.

Of course, the two guards cackled, but soon ceased. The first asked with a mock polite voice, "Soldier, you have kids?"

The other guard barely held his hilarity together as he wondered, "You want some?" Then they both burst out laughing. "Afternoon sacrifice is coming. I can maybe get you some leftovers if you want to get on your knees for me."

Hand to the hilt of his blade, Lybeck started to draw it out and turn, but Batasta stood very near him and shook his head.

Looming behind the guards now stood a figure much larger and devoid of boils. The immense figure could've passed for a larger version of the muscled Kaldwell twins, if they were totally hairless, and clad only in a loin cloth…and wearing metal gauntlets sporting blades on every finger.

The first guard cleared his throat and said, "Oh, you want to fight? Here is our guardian. Want to fight him?"

Binje said, "We came here to ask questions, not get into a pissing match."

The second guard popped up to say, "Pissing matches are after nine over by the altar for girl babies." He smiled again. "Goddesses love them I hear tell."

The first guard rebuked him, saying, "You're just making that up."

Batasta's rage flowed as he shouted, "I asked you all a damned question earlier. Do I have to call into existence my true enough grandfather? I shall use the guts of your guardian to divine his spirit."

"Yeah?" the second guard smirked.

A shriek from within pierced the air, enough to make all look back, save for the guardian. Lybeck watched as a young woman, naked, tan of skin, but dotted with bruises all about her body, ran into the open. He didn't know where she planned to run to, nor did she, but the urge to escape had seized her. Such it is with the young, Lybeck mused, they find hope even in the face of impossible horror.

From the rear of the building where she emerged rode a small figure…no two of them. Lybeck took them as children at first, but a blink of his eyes brought a grim realization. These two bearded dwarves rode tiny mounts, horses impossibly small.

The entire thing made him wear a grin of shock, until he saw they twirled ropes over their heads. These ropes weren't ended by loops like men trying to gather up a stray calf. These rope lines terminated in gleaming metal spades with extra points on the end, like miniature shovels. They rode at a rapid clip, their ropes looping, and the girl screaming and running…and it played out at first so comically silly all couldn't help but laugh…especially when one of the dwarves' horses stumbled, pitching the rider off, landing him face-first in the dirt.

With a dry voice, Batasta asked, "What is this lunacy?"

The other dwarf released his line and the rope flew, winding about her. The spade stabbed into her belly and the screams stopped…for a few moments. She, too, fell to the dirt, clutching at the metal in her abdomen. Her cries lowered and then ceased as the dwarf dismounted and strode up, hands to his hips, head shaking back and forth.

The other dwarf picked himself up, ran over, and shoved his mirror image at the chest. They started cussing each other.

One of the guards on the wall said, "You can't reclaim them all."

The guardian spoke up with a low voice, saying, "Tell them what they need and let them be gone."

The first guard let out a loud sigh and broke wind. "All right, all right. It's been a very boring day."

The second guard said to the twins, "No, we haven't seen nor captured any barbarians on mammoths, whatever the hell that is anyhow."

"A hairy white elephant," the first guard laughed. "Like there is such a thing."

Batasta frowned. "How in the hell did we miss him? There were many tracks leading this way, after all."

His brother shook his head. "He and others must've went on into the city. Rogan might have came this way and backtracked. The Kelts are a wily bunch."

Still angry, Batasta fumed, "All signs and feelings pointed this way, damn it all, that he'd come in here. I can practically smell his blood hereabouts." He glared at the guards. "If you deceive me…"

The guardian said, "They do not. There are worse duties here than to be on the watch towers."

Batasta turned to look at Irem. "They rode right up to the gates and went on through? Unlikely."

The guardian said, "They may have went to the other side of Irem, to the preparation baths. There is an entrance to the city that way as well."

Urell stood, wiped his mouth with the back of his hand, and mumbled, "Preparation baths?"

The first guard said, "If the girls are worth it, they clean them up over there and send them on to Marduk to get screwed to death. It's a long process, takes weeks I think, depending on his appetite or that of Zazaeil."

Binje said, "Well, we'll try and find that, then."

The guardian said, "We will send over a guard to escort you over so that you do not lose your way."

Batasta shot him a look. "I've had my fill of your guards."

"No, this is a new convert, a soldier. He will not give you trouble as these do. I will see that he is dispatched down and out through the walls."

The twins and Lybeck all looked to the guardian for a moment, but Urell headed down the steps.

Binje told him, "Kind of you."

The guardian replied, "You are not the only grandsons of God."

As the four rejoined the six soldiers, Urell spoke at last, saying, "What a godforsaken place."

Batasta nodded once. "Why do you think they built the wall?"

Lybeck coughed, still trying to hold onto his guts. "You would think the wind would carry that smell to Irem."

"Probably does," Binje said. "Probably serves as a good reminder to behave."

"Bastards," said Urell, going to his horse, head down and forehead flat to his saddle for a few moments before he climbed on again.

Stone ground on stone and a tall man appeared from the

walls. Lybeck couldn't even see how he slipped out and reckoned that was a good part of the defenses that way. As Lybeck climbed atop his mount, he took a breath. The big guard, clad in light leather breeks and a chainmail shirt, walked over to the twins.

Batasta said, "You will lead us to the baths?"

"Those are my orders," the guard said.

Lybeck rubbed his eyes and listened, trying to bury the sights of the Foundry, hoping his dreams would overlook them forever.

"Good," Binje told him as they all raised their eyes to see another guard ride up from around the bend in the wall, leading a rider-less horse. The big guard climbed aboard this mount once he stopped.

"We should arrive after dark," the guard said. "But this will be a safe place."

Batasta took a swig from his canteen and asked, "That is good. What do we call you, guard?"

"Ragnar," the voice came out flat.

Lybeck turned to face the guard and his mouth dropped. He gawked and then nodded at the guard. "Ragnar? Lead on."

The big man heeled his mount and they started away from the walls of the Foundry.

Lybeck still fought nausea and the temptation to tell the twins that the man leading them wasn't named Ragnar, but Jarek.

*****

From his position near the irrigation flow from the great bathhouse, Rogan cursed his cramped surroundings. Though he had a good view of the entrance to what the servants called the preparation sanctum, he could also see the city of Irem that loomed a stone's throw away. The setting sun did cast enough light to see the grand city, a sight his mind ached at taking in all the way. He recalled when they rode up to the locale.

As they rode up to the massive locale, they decided to take the path Yana suggested to a prep area for princesses.

"A cute name for a concubine perfume shop," Thyssen had quipped.

Seeing as the point of the place functioned to wash down and preen girls deemed good enough to serve sex to the aristocrats, kings, and wanton giants Rogan wouldn't argue with Thyssen.

Elisa, though, had snarled, "It takes them all weeks to get one proper enough for these people."

Thyssen shot back, "A week-long bath or clean up? I'd like to put some gold back for some prime trim like that."

She'd called him a pig and then ignored him when they approached the place.

His thoughts back to the present, Rogan's eyes traced the great city, the sun illuminating the area over Irem like a bubble even as it faded. He thought it mad to think of a city inside a covering or shell, but that almost is what his eyes testified to.

Irem needed no shell, for the walls and ramparts protected it well enough. These great bulwarks, though, didn't obscure the majestic pillars that stabbed toward heaven from its various quarters. All of varying heights, the stabbing columns thrust up with no real pattern, save for those that denoted avenues or areas about grand temples. Even in Shynar, Rogan had never beheld such complex masonry, round rooks of stone, triangular headbands about their entrances and more pillars shooting down in the earth like perfect teeth.

"What a waste," Rogan muttered. In his mind's eye, he thought of the sacred groves back home and places where they sacrificed to Wodan. Having been inside a few of the stone temples of other lands, he recalled feelings of coldness and suffocation. He looked up at the sky and searched for Wodan. "You who are so far away, Lord Wodan, have you ever been so distant from me at this time?"

Confidence ran through him that none of the altars or temples in Irem honored one-eyed Wodan or any of his sons.

Glad for just being alive, he hated having to wait. A man of action, Rogan loathed the games of these men and women. His burning mind turned back to their entrance into the bathing palace.

Elisa and Yana had went to the doors of the rather opulent building, made of polished bricks and sporting pillars decorated with the sketched faces of lovely women. Hulking male servants clad in white linen wraps were lighting outside censures when their group arrived. Thyssen had acted like they all belonged there and asked where to put their mounts.

What Rogan assumed were eunuchs directed them to go around back, once their brief frozen shock at the mammoth had subsided.

Thyssen said to Rogan, "You'd think they'd be a bit more horrified at such a thing as that hairy elephant."

Rogan looked over his shoulder as the three women went to the doors. "I reckon after you get yer balls cut off, only so much in the world can shock ya."

They quickly rejoined the three women, Bodyne taking a lesser role, waiting for them by the door as Elisa and Yana had stepped to the middle of the large room. Thyssen near to fell on his behind due to the polished floor. Rogan held him up by the arm as Thyssen's feet slid on the surface as he tried to steady himself.

"Why is it your father wants you in his army again?" Rogan questioned.

"One doesn't fight on a slick dancefloor, dickface," grumbled Thyssen and came near to spitting at the offending floor.

"Don't you!" a harsh voice near to screamed at Thyssen. The owner of the shrill shout moved across the slick floor like she skated on ice, stopping with impossible grace a few inches from Thyssen. Tall, thin, wrapped in a shimmering green robe, the white-haired lady poked both her index fingers at Thyssen's face as her eyes flared. "I don't care if you are from the Shynar Kings, I'll make you lick that spit up if you disgrace my floor."

Rogan himself thought of spitting but figured he'd let it roll.

"We are not…" Thyssen started to say, but Rogan gripped his arm tighter and cut him off fast.

"King Nungal sends his regards," Rogan said in a measured tone, mocking the polite talk of the region.

The ire of the tall woman dropped. "He better send more than that. You are a trifle early for the evening's princesses."

Thyssen pulled away from Rogan and stood up straight. "Well, sorry 'bout that but the weather favored us."

The tall woman grimaced at him, then looked to Elisa and her mother, who still bowed her head. "I assume you two are the brains of this party?"

Elisa let one gloved hand stay on the grip of her sword, but the other she made a gesture from her face and dropped the hand down, giving a slight curtsey.

The tall woman smiled and returned the gesture. "I'm Awan, controller of this house and liaison to Marduk. It's my eyes and orders that approve all worthy to be deflowered or married to the kings and gods, even if it be a brief time." She stepped closer to Elisa and looked at the tall girl's mother. "And you are?"

Turning toward her, head still down, Elisa said, "I'm Elisa. This is my mother, Yana."

The old woman then shrugged back her hood and looked up at Awan. "But you know me better by my birth name, Acilma."

Awan's head tilted and the refined lady let out a snort. "That's a name I haven't heard for…" Rogan walked up beside them to see the color drain from the Awan's face. "…for centuries…"

Yana smiled. "Hello, sister." Her hands let go of her canes, then shot up and criss-crossed in front of Awan's neck. An eruption of scarlet spewed out down the green gown of Awan as Yana drew her hands back, revealing tiny crimson blades, which she stabbed forward again, striking into Awan's kidneys on each side.

Awan fell back, blood spurting from her throat and sides as

she fell against Thyssen. The big man caught her and she looked back at him. He near to dropped her. Rogan couldn't help but wonder if the woman looked that shocked over her impended death or being in the gruff Thyssen's arms.

"Damn," Bodyne shouted. "What have you done?"

"Damn is right." Thyssen let the body go on down to the floor as a few more of the eunuchs appeared in the room, their faces stunned as Awan's life poured out onto the slick surface and staining Thyssen. "Yeah, what in hades was that for?"

Elisa drew her blade and glared at the eunuchs. "Just the start. You fuckers have anything to say?"

None of the eunuchs said a word.

The long blade tapped Yana's shoulder as the old woman knelt by Awan. Yana took her right hand in hers, tenderly, and then slit her wrist. Her eyes up at the servants, she slowly said, "Meet your new mistress."

The eunuchs took a knee as Yana stood up again, adjusted the boney necklace on her neck, and wiped her tiny blades clean on her own robe. Bodyne stepped forward and put the canes back into Yana's hands.

Rogan asked, "Sister huh?"

"What is it?" Yana peered up into his face and winked. "Surprised I'd really kill my sister?"

"Family hate is the worst. I reckon you have a good reason."

"I do," Yana replied but looked away from him, clearly done speaking to Rogan. She said to the nearest eunuch. "I'll need clean clothes. Speak of this to any and you will lose your tongues and an eye next."

The eunuch bowed and left, but the others stayed put.

Elisa said to the nearest eunuch. "You! They are coming in here from the city for princesses?"

"Yes," the eunuch answered. "Two will be for the visiting kings, one for Marduk, and one for Zazaeil."

"I see, I see." Yana then questioned them, "And you have four that are ready for this, I assume?"

The eunuch nodded fast.

Elisa grinned. "Good. Show us."

As this eunuch started across the room, Yana ordered the others, "Clean this up right and remove her. No word to anyone. All will carry as before. Hurry now. Are they due soon from the palace?"

The eunuchs all gave a nod.

"Then be quick." Yana then looked to Elisa. "Fortune smiles on us yet again. We must be hurried."

Rogan and Thyssen traded a look.

Elisa and Yana stared at them. "Thyssen, you can be on your way if you choose, as none of this concerns you now." She then looked over to Bodyne. "I'd run away along with Thyssen if I were you."

Yana faced Rogan. "You, though, come with us."

Rogan blinked, hands on his belt. "Ya think I wanna be a part of this play of whatever you have in mind?"

Elisa waved him to join them. "What you seek is here, Rogan the savage. Well, part of it, nevertheless."

Eyes narrowing at them, Rogan then shifted from boot to boot. "You say what? What lies are these?"

"She's here, your sister," Yana explained.

"Gale?" Rogan asked in a dubious tone. "How can you know?"

Elisa grinned wide. "My mother is a wizardess, you donkey."

But Thyssen didn't leave with Bodyne, they both followed Rogan and the women through the complex. They traveled down steps to a series of chambers lit by fireplaces and lanterns, and others open to the air. Once they reached the long bath house, dozens of girls lounged about, many in their mid-teens, a few much younger, but only a couple near to twenty years old.

The eunuch pointed to a hall beyond, where the scent of perfume proved so strong they noted it from yards away.

Rogan scanned the room, but heard a voice cry out, "You ugly bastard!" He turned to see a girl bounding toward him, her long auburn hair twisted in braids that hopped along. She leapt into his arms and Rogan caught her, embracing her tight.

"Gale, you little mongrel," he said and twisted about. "How did someone as rotten as you get in here?"

The girl drew back to go nose to nose with him. "Hah! Well, I remembered what papa told me."

"Be sweet as candy if you have to…"

Gale grinned. "…but rip their balls off, first chance."

Thyssen chuckled, "Damn, they have the same profile."

As Rogan dropped her to her feet, Gale asked, "Who's the fat horrible bitch with the toothpick spear?"

His big hand on her shoulder, Rogan explained to her, "That's Thyssen. He's a good fighter, but a bit of an ass."

Gale looked Elisa up and down. "Who is the mean cunt?"

Elisa sighed. "Savage girl, no doubt."

Taking a knee, Rogan embraced Gale again, then released her. "That's Elisa. Her mother Yana killed Awan a bit ago."

Gale looked at the old lady, her eyes flaring, and said, "I wanted to do that, though. Good. I hated her."

Yana winked at the child. "I hated her more."

"I believe you," Gale's admitted. Her blue eyes traced the face of the old woman and then a wry grin crept onto her face.

Rogan asked, "Where's father?"

Her hands curling into fists and bouncing off her waist, Gale replied, "He's a guard at that shithole Foundry of Dis."

"Wodan's ass," Rogan grinned. "Yeah, I wondered if he fell in on a patrol for them. First things first, I have you now."

Her right cane waved away from Rogan and Yana said, "Thyssen and Bodyne, just go. This isn't going to be pretty."

Rogan asked, "You have some kind of plan that doesn't involve me? I dunno about all of this now."

"Oh, it might. You see, I could use you all."

"What do I get if I help you? I just want my sister and father, to get out of here and escape alive."

Smiling, Yana blinked. "Life is overrated, savage, especially after several hundreds of years." She turned to the servant women, who bore a fresh gown to her. "Clean me up and my daughter." She then looked to Rogan. "Turn the little barbarian girl into a princess too. We are going to a party."

Thyssen regarded Yana and said, "That's some hate for a sister."

She returned his look, but no malice swam in her eyes. With a very placid look, she said, "You surely have siblings."

"Surely," he replied and pointed at Rogan. "Prolly not as many as that ol' stud man over there."

Ignoring his jest at the Kelt, Yana asked, "Do you adore them all?"

"Not really, no."

"Twin sister hatred, sibling animosity, really something, aye?" Yana sighed, limping over to look up at the two big men. "I've heard tales of twins born, one gripping the other's ankle as they come out. Such stories…"

Thyssen asked, "Is that what happened with you two?"

While Rogan rolled his eyes, Yana's mouth curled into an arid expression as she answered, "How would I know? I was an infant."

"Asshead," Rogan had taunted him.

Yana went on to say, "Such tales are carried by parents and thus, rivalry or animosity is sown between twins, one better than the other, one more evil than their twin. That is terrible parenting there. It sets a cast out and can ruin lives."

Thyssen said, "Twins? You two…" He stopped talking as Rogan groaned louder.

Yana stared up at Rogan. "Bright one you brought along."

"We are lucky he isn't a twin," Rogan agreed.

"Piss in your scabbard," Thyssen snapped at him, then said to her. "All right, I understand not all twins are the same, just born the same time."

She threw both her thin hands up. "The world is a tainted place, so poisoned beyond repair. It should grieve God above that he ever made it. Some people the world is better without."

One of the eunuchs walked in front the front door carrying the box where the black stone rested. Yana hobbled over to him, opened the box, and withdrew the stone. She then made it over to where her sister's body lay. She half knelt, half fell to the floor and raised the rock up. The men both stepped forward, hands out, but Elisa only laughed as her mother dropped the stone onto the mistress of the house's head. Yana did this three times, caving in the skull of her sister at different angles. The men dropped their arms and stepped back.

"Why?" Thyssen gasped. "You fear she will rise again?"

Breathing hard from her act, Yana replied, "No."

"Symbolic?" Thyssen searched for an answer.

Yana turned and looked up at him again. Her look made Rogan grin. "No, I just wanted to do it."

Rogan sniggered and turned about in a circle, giving her a short bow.

"Damn," Thyssen said. "And you are the savage."

Elisa took the stone, cradling it under her left arm, and helped her mother up with her other gloved hand. "The stone is a gift of the gods, fallen from heaven and those fools will want it. If they don't want what we can offer in the flesh to get in, we shall deal this. That was the plan to start with."

After she walked on back over with Gale, Thyssen looked down at the remains of the pulped woman.

Yana groaned. "She had such dreams. She deserved to as she was the pretty one, the chosen one, the one to bear the true son of god from God himself, not one of these evil little demon shits. But, she didn't get to bear the savior of the human race, but a line of fools with no vision."

Rogan said with a soft tone, "You didn't bear the savior of humanity?"

Looking at Elisa, Yana smiled. "No, my child will not save all of humanity." Her grin faded as she touched her stomach. "Only one."

Back in the present, Rogan opened his eyes, looking out from his hiding place, knowing that the cleaning process went on even as he hid outside. He couldn't breathe or move as he watched the litter coaches stop and the kings get out.

Kamala-ur and Nungal exited, stretched, and were greeted by Yana outside. Thyssen, clad in a white wrap, freshly shaved and clean, stood with her.

"Those bastards."

He breathed deep and looked back to Irem and wished Wodan would let the ground swallow it all up.

CHAPTER FOURTEEN

Angry Heart

As the sunlight waned, the hooded guard led the party back to the well-travelled road. Though he secured the hood and kept his face drape tight, the guard turned to see those coming up behind him.

Lybeck kept a close eye on the big guard, he felt confident the man was Jarek, the Kelt tribesman, the father of Rogan. His glowing blue eyes, so alien to this place on the earth, pierced him icy. Lybeck speculated how the other men didn't pick up on such a thing, or his size. Many said that regular folk don't look a slave in the eye or note them well, but he didn't know. A few times, Lybeck looked over at Urell, who still held his gut, half ill by the sight and, now, the strong memory of the Foundry. Urell would distinguish Jarek as well, Lybeck pondered, but his mood and ill state kept his eyes from such a revelation.

Jarek eyed Lybeck but once, not keen on making it obvious they knew each other. His piercing look told Lybeck volumes. He suspected Jarek might kill him and Urell first if he made such a move. Surely he wouldn't, knowing the twins would slay him. *The savages were crazy*, Lybeck thought and that wildness inside might be enough to make him happy to die in battle just to take him out.

Lybeck made no move. Part of him wondered why he didn't disclose this to the twins at first, but the other part of him, down in his soul, he let it roll off into nothing. Some part of Lybeck wanted to head down the open road off to their right at full speed, consequences be damned.

Jarek, though, stopped them as the road forked.

Binje ceased riding, moved his horse about, and grimaced at Jarek. "What goes on now? What is it, Ragnar?"

Ragnar/Jarek replied, "There is a travelling party set to stop at the prep baths. Can you see their standard from here?"

Batasta joined them and the twins squinted together. "You've got brilliant eyes to see that far as a regular mortal man."

His voice cutting, Jarek stated, "My eyes have not dimmed just yet."

Binje looked at his brother. "Damn my eyes! The kings Nungal and Kamala-ur. See that, brother?"

"The opulent wheeled coaches denote royalty, along with their host of guards and by their standards," Batasta answered, thumb tapped his bottom lip. "Wonder why they have come to Irem now? Why didn't they tell of such a venture before?"

Binje speculated, "Didn't they say all the sons of god were due to come near here for some kind of meeting?" He then looked at the guard and demanded, "Isn't that so? We have heard such things."

"You are mistaken," the deep voice of Jarek replied. "That is but a story, at least at this time. Nonetheless, the sons of god are a skittish bunch."

"Skittish?" Batasta eyed him close.

"Paranoid, then," Jarek said with no quarter given. "They are careful not to all be in the same place at the same time. Such things of a grand meeting are stories set to attract a certain element, perhaps that of the heavenly host. Who can say?"

His gut settling a bit better, Lybeck summoned up a cluster of nerve and asked, "Why is that, guard?"

Jarek didn't look at Lybeck as he answered, "Many fear an ingathering in one place or such wanted men, or god-men, as they fashion themselves."

Binje raised an eyebrow at him. "Wanted by whom? The heavenly host?"

Jarek replied, "You know the sagas. There are always tales of headhunters for them, and by those far worse than men with big balls."

"Fools," Binje stated with a nod.

Jarek gave no opinion on that, but said, "Some say their guilt-ridden demon fathers would like them scrubbed off the earth for their sins on the ground or far worse foes seek them out for a prodigious ending."

"Worse?" Batasta asked.

Jarek pointed to the sky with his right index finger and the twins laughed.

"The heavenly host?" Binje chuckled. "Do you believe that?"

"It doesn't matter what I believe."

"Why?" Batasta questioned further. "Because you are a slave?"

Jarek gave him a forbidding look. "Because I don't believe in their gods. Besides," Jarek snorted and lowered his hand to his lap, "you couldn't accept a thing these god-men say from their fathers at all."

"And why is that?" Binje asked, his humor turning to indignation.

"Because all demons are lying bastards," said Jarek and locked eyes with Lybeck, who looked away from him.

Urell awoke from his haze to join in talking with them. "Well, shit damn." He didn't look at Jarek directly, but with his face covered, Lybeck doubted he would recognize him. "Now what the hell are we gonna do? They, those damn kings, will be pissed if we show up without Rogan in chains, or his balls on a stick."

Shaking his head, Batasta answered, "You live in such fear of these kings, man. No wonder your guts betray you when challenged by the appalling horrors of life." He pointed at the other side of the preparation bathhouse. "Look, there, all of you! That's no common horse being led out to join them."

Almost standing in his saddle, Lybeck gasped and said, "The mammoth."

The twins asked as one voice, "Where's Rogan?"

"Is it a white one?" Urell drew out his scope and scanned the area with it. "Yeah, it is ivory in color. Same one that killed our men."

"Damn," was the only word to escape Lybeck's mouth.

Urell added, "The guy leading the elephant isn't Rogan, even though dressed in fancy linens and acting a fool."

Binje said, "He would look out of place, that Rogan."

Urell said, "But that man who is leading the mammoth is no eunuch. He is some sort of fighter, a tough guy, but acting the part. I can tell, sirs, look at the way he walks, like a soldier, not some cunt slave with his balls cut off."

The twins peered close again as the light of day seemed to wane more.

With no warning, Urell threw his scope at Lybeck.

Pinning the object to his chest, Lybeck frowned at him and then raised the scope to see for himself. "That man…"

Batasta glared at Lybeck. "Yes?"

"He's out of place indeed. I don't know him by any name, but Urell is right. He's no eunuch at all. I've seen him before, but cannot place it just now. He doesn't belong here at such a place where women are scrubbed in their nakedness."

Urell stared at Jarek, and jeered him, "Who does, huh, Ragnar?"

The guard said nothing, as Urell just acted the part of an ass, still oblivious to who the slave might be. He earnestly didn't care who he might be really, which proved a perfect cover for Jarek.

Batasta said, "Whoever the leader of the mammoth is, he talks to the kings or whoever lies within the carts."

Binje rejoined his brother, saying, "Who else would ride in such opulent things and carry a small army of guards? It has to be them, the kings."

"Which is why I stopped," Jarek said.

They all gaped at the guard.

Jarek said, "I'm here to lead you to the baths, not into an uncertain doom. I don't know the nature of your business at such a place, nor do I care."

Batasta smiled. "It was prudent to stop."

Urell spoke up to say, "Those rich fuckers, they might well be pissed we are empty handed now."

After a mocking belly laugh, Binje said to him, "You're fears are droll. It's not a wonder you don't gag at the scent of your own piss."

Teeth clenched, Urell's hand gripped his pommel, but he dared not draw on either Kaldwell.

Lybeck threw his scope back to him and broke his ire. "Damn it all. Well, they won't be delighted, for sure."

Rubbing his chin, Batasta said, "But it appears they are being given the mammoth. That's what Marduk and the rest wanted, right?"

Binje said, "The kings will take the beast to Marduk."

After a sigh, Batasta said, "And we don't have the Kelt's head or balls to show for it. There they will ride in for a great pat on the back."

"But if the mammoth is there," Binje reasoned. "Where is that Rogan?"

A smile on his face, Batasta said, "This is very true that he must be nearby, here or in the baths, right?"

Binje said, "Good diversionary tactic, that man and now a short woman there going with the mammoth and the kings. I think he is here or within, and the gift of the mammoth will divert them away from him."

Batasta said, "If Rogan is here, they just moved the kings and their small force away from him. What does he want here?"

"I wonder," Lybeck brooded. "Why is he there, in the baths?"

"Fuck," Urell swore. "Why anything at all? I'm tired of this damned game. I want to see Rogan dead, this very night."

Batasta cleared his throat and said, "Let that force from the kings move on and we shall ride down to see this prep place and what it holds." He hard leered at Urell. "If Rogan is there, you can kill him if you wish."

Binje chuckled, "If you can."

"I fear no man, and not some ruffian bastard."

Watching Jarek, Lybeck didn't see him flinch or react to Urell's boasts. Though older than himself, Lybeck understood Jarek a dangerous man, plus he sat atop that horse, armed with a short sword and flail. Lybeck kept looking at the flail that hung off the horse's saddle as a side weapon. Jarek's gaze scanned in the distance, but every so often returned to Lybeck. Hand resting on a long knife at his left hip, Jarek's hand flexed on the handle.

Batasta waved his left hand, saying, "They are moving along now. Let us ride down slow and see what there is to see at the prep house."

As they began to ride, Binje looked to Jarek. "This is a place where women are prepared for the kings or giants?"

Jarek's reply fell out slowly, saying, "That is so."

His grin wide, Binje turned to his brother. "Perhaps they can spare us a few girls as children of the giants?"

His mouth twisted a little, Batasta reminded him, "Mind on task, brother. We are not sure what lies in wait for us there."

"But if it's a bunch of pristine maidens…"

Batasta sighed loud. "We shall see. Careful or that wandering cock of yours will be the death of you."

Binje wiped his mouth with the back of his hand. "No rotten whores in there, just think of it! All bathed up and trimmed nice? God of goddesses!"

Again, Lybeck eyed Jarek. The big Kelt gave no reaction.

No more words passed between any of them as they gradually rode to the preparation house. Lybeck kept his eyes forward, trying not to look over at Jarek. The big Kelt didn't regard him again on the short journey.

They arrived at the perp house and no one dismounted. Batasta turned to the six soldiers behind them and said, "Check out the area, investigate the stables where that big thing was quartered. Search the place and hold a perimeter."

As the six trotted away, the twins dismounted.

Lybeck and Urell stayed on horseback as the doors opened before the twins. An icy sensation crawled up Lybeck's chest as the light poured out of the long building. He cursed himself for being foolish at the terror feeling, as what stood in the doors looked like nothing to fear at all.

An elderly lady clad in a shimmering gown filled the doorway. Behind her stood a remarkably tall woman, her nakedness hardly covered by a light white wrap. Lybeck thought her an enchanting beauty, heavy makeup, wearing lacy leggings and gloves. A small girl, maybe over ten years of age, held the gloved hand of the tall woman. Her auburn hair, pulled back into braids, almost glistened in the light of the censures.

Almost drooling, Binje looked back at them and winked.

Lybeck and Urell exchanged a look.

Urell said, "I'll go help the scouts secure the perimeter."

Clearly not wanting to watch any debauchery in the offing, the red-haired man trotted away fast.

His stomach turning, Lybeck hoped Batasta could control his brother. When he looked at the three females, a strange feeling washed over him. His eyes rested on the young girl. She had eyes of glacial ice and couldn't hide a bloodthirsty look. Lybeck shook his head, dismissing his fears, thinking he had imagined it. But that smile of the tall woman, so kind, so seductive, made his skin want to crawl away.

*****

Rogan suppressed his laughter at how easily the two soldiers died. The two men, part of King Nungal's detail assigned to his pursuers by their insignia, had rode around the stables in the rear of the prep house very slow. Both men, not really looking around, but talking to each other, didn't see any of Rogan's actions coming.

He jogged up between them and jabbed his sword through the soldier on his right's back. The insertion, like his father taught him, went up under the short ribs and surely struck the heart. The blow went quick and out like lightning. Rogan wondered if the man even knew he had been killed before he opened his eyes in the afterworld.

The other man turned as the blade came out. Rogan gripped the sleeve of this soldier, pulled him from the saddle, and drove his blade into him as he fell. The soldier on his left hit the ground hard with his head, but didn't fall free of the horse.

Upside down, sword through his belly, Rogan kicked him in the head. The sword slid out of the soldier, who gave out a gagging sound, falling a bit more from his horse awkward, foot still in the stirrups.

Rogan's blade thrust fast again, jabbing into the other soldier's chest. The blade went through and smashed into the ground, and the man didn't die. His eyes flared, mouth open, his cry began to rise until Rogan stepped up, boot on his face, withdrawing the sword and stabbing down like a spear.

He struck the heart direct this time and twisted the blade fast. Blood spurted active as his foot fell free of the stirrup and Rogan strode off him. The fight departed the soldier and Rogan started to move out of the open, to where the mounts were tethered in the back.

Going low, he tried to stay hidden, seeing the king's party off in the distance. He'd heard another group come up to the door of the prep house and he planned to return to see who had approached. By these two guards, he assumed more of that small army lingered to look around the place. Hoping he didn't give them away, Rogan started to turn to the other section of the long prep house.

"You are him!" a voice shouted out.

Rogan turned and set his boots. Sword out, he stood face to face with the ginger-haired soldier he'd served under in the merc army.

"Urell," said Rogan, not hiding his earnest surprise at seeing him, but not letting his shock take ahold. "Well, hello there, you backstabbing sonofabitch." His humor gone, Rogan snarled, "You betrayed us all."

Sword out as well, Urell armed up a small, triangular-shaped shield with his left hand and said, "Cuss me? That's so rich. C'mere here. I'll teach you to mind you betters, you Keltic punk piece of shit."

"I'm a fast learner," Rogan promised. "Fooling me twice is tough."

Urell stepped closer, sizing up the huge youth. "Damn you to hell, you and all of your blood kin."

Rogan didn't answer him, but mirrored his moves.

"I've came a long way to kill you."

"Kill me then, you coward," Rogan ordered, suddenly not moving. "I've got nothing better to do."

"The nonsense I've seen," Urell spat and moved forward. "The fine woman I've seen die because of this trip after you."

Rogan probed out with his blade and Urell brushed it aside. "I don't care."

Urell said, "The people who have died all because of you." He swiped his weapon at Rogan's left arm, but the Kelt slapped the shot back with his blade.

"What about those that died because of your treachery," Rogan retorted and stepped forward, striking at the shield, jabbing it and getting Urell to stab forward, to which Rogan blocked with a great dig. He followed that move back, rushing forward, fist tight on the handle, swinging his arm out to strike Urell's face.

No amateur, Urell motioned back, and the blow from Rogan missed. His counter strike with his blade went fast, trying to chop Rogan's left shoulder. The big youth twisted, avoiding the sword dropping, and kicked for Urell's groin. The move didn't hit any balls, but landed on Urell's upper thigh. Urell staggered a step, brought his blade up, and clashed in tight with Rogan's weighty sword.

They struggled for a few moments until Urell relented and fell back, rolling and getting up quick.

Rogan cursed him, as he had planned to overpower him and bash his head through that pale skull. He cussed Urell to himself as he understood the soldier, while reckless and an ass, figured Rogan ran more powerful than he.

"Stupid Kelt," Urell spat. "Attack and defend, you have no style."

Rogan grinned. "You dance like a silly bitch. I don't know to kill you or throw coins in a cup for you."

"Come on, you damned kid," Urell raged, a wicked grin appearing in the middle of his red beard. "Show me how strong you are."

Rogan didn't bite on his challenge, but circled around him.

Urell set himself again, and probed out a few times. His shots didn't strike home anywhere, but he just threw a few jabs. Suddenly, Urell made a bold move, a great overhand arc to which Rogan had no choice but to block it with his sword.

Urell's blade broke in half. Both men stood stunned for a moment, but as Rogan tried to slash and kick him, Urell leapt backwards, pulling another blade from his back. This sword, a shorter model, looked better suited for up close fighting.

"My father makes better swords than your mother," Rogan taunted him, brandishing his blade back and forth. He then took the initiative and powered forward, meaning to run Urell through with his heavy blade. However, Urell twirled, side-stepped him, and spanked Rogan's ass with his fresh blade as he passed.

"Your father should teach you the art of fighting," Urell admonished him as Rogan lurched, left hand to the ground to steady himself.

"He did," Rogan assured him, and came up with a handful of dirt, flinging it up into Urell's face.

Blinded a moment, Urell defended the sword shot Rogan came at him with, but couldn't stop the left-handed fist of the Kelt as he struck him across the face. Urell wobbled, but soon put his boots flat, his sword blocking the big blade again and again.

When Rogan stepped back a yard, he saw blood leaking from Urell's nose. Again, they clashed and Urell cursed him, saying low, "Say her name." He said that many times. Rogan didn't ask any questions, but soon in the fray of clashes, Urell hollered out, "*Kylene*, say her name."

Moving back to gather himself again, Rogan muttered, "You're batshit crazy."

"Say it," Urell barked, sucking in air. "Kylene!"

"That your mom, lover, or sister, or all three?"

"Shut up!" Urell raged, spit flying from his mouth.

"Did I screw or kill them all? If not, I can do that once this is done."

Maneuvering in a little, Rogan slashed out and Urell parried the shot down, then swiped across his body with the shield. The shot to Rogan's head didn't land, but when Rogan rushed him, Urell shouted and fell back, pushing him with his sword and shield.

Rogan's superior weight hard-pressed Urell back on his shuffling feet, and they both went down. Swords crossed, pinned between them, Rogan's left hand gripped over Urell's fist that held his sword handle. He then tried to ram his head into Urell's face. However, this time, the small shield did find its mark, braining Rogan across his oncoming forehead.

Groaning, Rogan progressed back off him, but didn't release either sword. His great strength pulled Urell with him. This move did shock Urell as he flailed, trying to strike him with the shield and free the sword from his grasp.

His head swimming with stars, Rogan still held on, and tried to wedge his blade further on Urell's. He could feel both blades pinned against their bodies constrict. The small shield came down again, this time the bottom point stabbing into Rogan's right shoulder.

The blow fell awkward or Urell would've broken his skin. Rogan released his hold on Urell's wrist and slipped his left arm under Urell's armpit, gripping him tight like one would hold a woman snug in an embrace.

Urell cursed and prepared to strike him again with the shield. He froze when Rogan's right hand blocked the shield. The shock came in revelation that Rogan had released his own sword. Blow blocked, Rogan's hand dropped, but not to his sword pommel. Terror gripped Urell and he struggled to get free.

Rogan grabbed the handle of the dagger on his right hip and yanked it out free of the holster.

Fully aware of what came next, Urell pushed back with all his might and separated from Rogan a few feet.

Rogan's left arm slid out a bit, but his fist then released the hilt and gripped a handful of Urell's tunic, holding tight. The moment was all he needed to drive the dagger down into Urell's thigh. Rogan drove the small blade in deep to the top of his knee, letting go of the dagger once it set far in the meat of Urell's thigh and struck bone.

Too close together, Urell couldn't do more than push at Rogan with his blade. Rogan balled up his fist and brought it up, striking the red beard with all of his strength. Though he could've swore he felt the jaw break, he didn't wait to look close at the result.

He saw his sword fall to the ground, but reached across his body and pulled out his other dagger. With a backhand swipe, he buried this dagger in Urell's chest just below his sternum.

Again, Rogan put his arms about Urell, but picked him up off the ground, turned, and slammed him to the ground.

Urell flailed all his limbs, still trying to raise his sword as Rogan's boot stomped on the dagger, sending it further through Urell's midsection.

Rogan scooped up his sword and turned to face his adversary.

Urell's eyes and mouth were wide, but blood bubbled from his lips. His right hand darted up, holding his sword aloft.

Rogan cut Urell's arm off at the elbow and the blade fell. He put his boot on Urell's gagging throat and retrieved the dagger from the man's thigh. It took some digging with his sword to get his other dagger back, but in time he accomplished this.

Floundering, blood gouting from his belly, thigh, and ruined arm, Urell tried to speak, but too much blood throttled him. He coughed up more blood many times and snorted wet through his nose.

"Lay there and bleed to death," Rogan told him as he turned away. "Like all traitors should."

"Why wouldn't you die?" Urell choked out, his words drizzly and in spurts. "You were supposed to die."

Stopping, Rogan twisted his head to look on him. In his gut, he felt a memory suppressed, one of his father's huge hand striking his backside after he'd took a handful of his hair. Jarek had shouted into Rogan at an early age to command, *never look back!* Yet, here he stood, defying his father's rules, one he slapped into him at age five and then again, when he was but a teen. He could still feel those strong hands in his hair and on his buttocks.

Urell sputtered out, "You and all of your inbred kindred. Trash of the mountains, you were supposed to die." He gagged again and then drew in an arduous breath. "Just line up and die for the kings."

"Sorry I disappointed you."

"But you made it, damn you to hades." Urell choked again, sucked in wind, and spat out bloody words, "Coming all that way for gold, adventure in war against a weak foe, you thought, and all the women you could chew on."

"Shut up and die already."

His body shaking like he froze to death, Urell vomited again and then started to laugh. "How's that pussy now, boy?"

Words, Rogan told himself, *the fool uses his dying breaths to taunt him.* "You ought to pray now rather than curse me, dead man."

"Fuck you and all of your kin."

Rogan said, "Wodan leads us where he must."

"Wodan?" Urell cackled, trying to breathe. "Piss on him. He sucks cocks just to get into hades!"

"You shut your ass."

"Hah. You trash, you white skinned shits…so big, strong and stupid…"

Trash. Rogan didn't like the term used for his folk, not one bit. He also didn't care for the mental image of what his one-eyed god did to gain access to an unpleasant eternity, but he shrugged that off.

"Trash?" Rogan snarled. "How does it feel to be beaten down and killed by a son of Wodan?"

"Kylene…"

"By a Kelt piece of trash?"

"Kylene…" Urell whispered again, weak.

"I did out-fight you and I did out-think you. Stupid white trash piece of shit, huh? Good luck sucking cocks in hell your own damn self."

Urell mouthed the name again, eyes wide.

Rogan turned his back and heading back to the prep house. This time he didn't look back.

CHAPTER FIFTEEN
When Death Calls

Blood ran through Lybeck's right eye and his hand flopped on his lap when he tried to wipe it clean. His mind registered reality as he blinked, the sting of the blood sharpening his focus. He tried to look down at himself, unsure how his hand dropped to his lap…why he had a lap…as he stood only a few moments before. His mind didn't add up why his ass sat flat on the polished floor, nor why his back reclined on a stone pillar.

The joints in his body felt numb, and again, he failed to raise his hands. His sword remained in the scabbard as blood leaked from his head to his face. He felt certain it was his blood, as a dull throb pulsed atop his hairline. Unsure if he'd struck it on the column before falling to this prone positon, Lybeck took deep breaths, working even at that, for his body still felt strange all over.

His mind freer than his form, Lybeck started to recall how he got there, mainly, as events before his bloody vision reminded him of it. He saw that older woman in the shiny robe that let them into the place cross his vision, and he remembered the light from her hands causing him to go to this reclining place. Oh, the woman didn't just aim at him with what looked like a pan full of wasps belching out of a censure, quickly turning to light and exploding into a countless hail of dust motes…all striking the Kaldwell twins and himself.

He remembered Batasta behind him was struck and stumbled back to the doors. Binje had fallen to his left and rolled over many times, but he took the brunt of it, flying back to his right and striking the pillar.

Whatever else happened before him, the tall woman and older lady seemed to have no interest in him, well, that small girl didn't either as she knelt, looked him in the face, and spit on his forehead. He felt that spittle fall, a tiny pinprick of wetness near the warmth of his own blood. That young girl dismissed him, not worthy to deal with. He felt a weird sense of joy in that, for she had him dead to rights if she wanted to cut his throat. A little girl to cut his throat? Yes, his mind felt positive that little girl could and would do it. Besides, he thought he saw a blade in the folds of her gown.

Off to the edges of his vision, he saw the eunuchs standing, but they just did that, stood. They made no movements on what transpired before him.

Binje lay flat on his back, but for a few moments, as he bowled over to his hands and knees. As he shook his head to free it of whatever spell still plagued Lybeck, the tall woman kicked him in the side of the head.

Lybeck thought it an odd blow, as she looked to wear odd slippers with heels on them. Binje's head moved from the shot, as she did have large feet for a woman, Lybeck surmised, but the balled up fist that fell on the top of Binje's head caused him to sink lower on his all fours.

"Gale?" the tall woman called out and the little girl with the hungry eyes appeared to his right. "Bring me my sword."

"Yes, Elisa," Gale replied and turned away.

With a guttural roar, Binje sprang from his position on the floor and tackled the tall woman, Elisa. The move didn't go as Binje wanted, Lybeck guessed, as his arms missed her midsection and flailed about her hips. Lybeck figured the effects of the lurid spell or the head shot lessened his move, but not Binje's resolve, as he tried to bite her hip as his boots skated on the floor.

Elisa wore no look of pain or shock at the sudden move, but reached down with her gloved right hand and raked at Binje's eyes with her fingernails. Lybeck hadn't noted the gloves let her fingertips out of their housings until that moment.

As tough as Binje lived, he screamed at his eyes being touched and let her go. He didn't back off, though, nor did Elisa fight to get away. She simply turned about and kneed him in the jaw. Lybeck admired her lack of fear. Again, Binje's head snapped back. He had little time to recover from that shot before Elisa kicked him low in the groin, causing him to move his hands from his eyes to his crotch. This time, Elisa stepped away from him and walked back some.

"Thanks," Elisa said to Gale with a steady voice. The girl held out a long sword in a leather-bound scabbard to Elisa, who drew it free like she'd done it countless times.

Lybeck's mind still reeled and his body still didn't respond as he pondered the tall girl, all dressed like a bride or sexual toy for the kings, yet fought and held a sword like a warrior. He felt silly in his head, for she obviously *was* a warrior. Elisa turned to Binje and gripped the hilt with both hands.

Elisa swung the blade in a swipe intended to remove Binje's head, but he twisted his body, slamming himself to the floor and progressing over twice. When he came up to his knees, his hand rested on the handle of his sheathed sword.

Binje grinned at her.

Lybeck heard Elisa chuckle and then say, "Draw it, Kaldwell."

A twinge of inquisitiveness birthed in Binje's eyes. Lybeck wouldn't name that look as fear, but cupped with a tinge of uncertainty.

Binje drew out the sword and stood up, shaking his legs a bit to free that groin shot more. "You know who I am?"

"Batasta Kaldwell's horny, ignorant brother," Elisa said, stalking him some, but they mirrored the moves of the other, circling before Lybeck's eyes.

"I won't kill you," Binje promised. "I'll maim your big ass then screw you to death, honeysuckle, very hard."

"Big words," Elisa noted, eyes unblinking. "Going to talk me to death?"

"C'mere," Binje's smile widened. "I've got something for you."

Lybeck's mind burned as Elisa charged forward, thrusting her sword, to which Binje blocked, and she swung her left fist, which he also pushed off with his forearm…and the backstroke of the sword with his blade and dodged the second shot to his balls.

Again, they squared up and encircled each other. Binje stepped nearer to Gale, who proved wise in that she fled out of the room so he couldn't grab her for a hostage.

This time Binje struck forward, stabbing out and then swinging, slashing fast in three moves that blinded Lybeck with their speed. Each shot or move was met and parried away by Elisa, who looked to be smiling back at Binje.

"You set a trap for us twins?" Binje asked.

"Ignorant to the last." Elisa speared out again, only to be rebuffed. "You overestimate your importance."

"I doubt that," Binje said, his smirk intensifying. He once again hacked and stabbed, only to be met and pressed back.

"You are just unlucky," Elisa assured as she lunged out again, to feel Binje repel her yet again.

"I don't feel unlucky, like your mama," Binje chuckled, not changing his stance toward her, but withdrawing a knife from his belt and then turning to throw it, end over end out of Lybeck's sight. Binje turned in a circle and returned to fencing with Elisa.

"Dumbass," said Elisa, her smile transforming to a scowl. "Can't kill an old woman, never gonna kill me."

Binje moved forward and again slashed twice, but didn't

relent this time. He kept chopping back and forth.

Elisa continued hindering his shots, but couldn't keep backing up much further. Wise enough to see, Binje tried to pin her to a corner, Elisa turned a semi-circle, still trading shots, moving out of the path of the trap.

Laughing at her moves, Binje kept going, each both strong and hard, each one being pressed back. In the midst of the attack, Elisa pushed back tougher than Binje struck and the assault changed. Lybeck couldn't believe such a thing happened, but she reversed the moves, striking after Binje, causing him to move backwards.

"Hey, big bitch," Binje shouted amidst the blows, but Elisa didn't answer. "Hey, I think I love you."

Elisa never spoke but kept her exchanges up, pushing him back to one of the columns across from Lybeck. They swapped shots twice and then the clash ceased as Binje and Elisa's blades locked near the guards.

Both were holding their blades by the hilts and they stood, face to face, for a few moments. Lybeck thought Binje would kiss her. He didn't, but put his thighs together, tighter to avoid a low blow he probably figured to arrive soon. Elisa, though, drew back a little when she kicked her left foot out, locked in with Binje's ankle, and then fell backwards. The move would've yanked a normal man back, and probably flipped him over her head. However, Binje, who fancied himself a quarter god, only staggered a few steps.

Binje did look at Lybeck about then, perhaps for an assist, but his expression showed how quickly he dismissed such an idea. In a way, Lybeck thanked what gods there might be as they thought him done for and avoided him.

His steps stomping like he stalked something defenseless, Binje trod over to Elisa as she swung a leg whip at him. He jumped in the air, avoided the swipe, moving his sword to his left hand, but anticipated her coming sword jab. It amazed Lybeck the swiftness at which that Kaldwell moved, so perhaps there was salt to his semi-godhood claim.

He dived on Elisa, and looked to impale himself on her willing sword. Nonetheless, he seized her by the throat and pinned her down with his right hand. Elisa's blade, slid under his left armpit, was pinned there by his meaty arm.

"Got you," Binje grunted, his grin of victory impossible to suppress.

Elisa struggled under him, but couldn't budge that blade, nor dislodge her heavier opponent.

The veins in Binje's right arm protruded heavy as he bore down.

"Keep fighting me," Binje told her as her legs kicked and her left hand tried to gouge at his eyes. "It's making me hard."

He then looked up and wore a face of panic.

Lybeck saw an emerald glow over to his right, just out of his range of vision.

Binje's look of alarm lasted but a moment, and he moved back, pulling Elisa off the floor. Lybeck didn't guess the move a blocking mechanism until he heard Yana curse and throw her glob of green light away from impacting on her daughter...but in his direction.

The oblong greenish glow flew out, splattered on the column on which Lybeck reclined, filling him with paralysis anew. Some of the liquid cloud popped off and did go near to Binje, who flipped Elisa about to avoid the substance, but not letting go. The move allowed her to use her long legs and she overturned atop him. Both dropped their swords in the scuffle, but his hand remained on her throat. Now, his other hand joined the hold.

"Damn you," Binje cussed her. "My grandfather is a demon. Who are you, girl, to be the death of me?"

Elisa's hands rapt the wrists on his long arms, but her knees moved up fast under his armpits.

Lybeck tried to cry out loud and warn him, but his mouth only hung open, dry and wordless.

A small shape jumped onto Binje's head, causing him to cry

out and release Elisa. His hands went about the body of young Gale as she looked to have tackled his skull. At first, Lybeck thought the child had cried out in pain when Binje's hands went to grab her, but he soon learned the Keltic girl shouted in some primal victory shout the barbarians used. The little girl howled for *Wodan* as she twisted her shoulders. Binje's threw her off and Elisa trundled off him and struggled to breathe.

Lybeck's bloody vision clearly saw Binje's body shake and try to rise, but then to reel on its side. He looked Lybeck's way, but didn't move nor say a word. Lybeck saw the hilt of Binje's own knife protruding from the right side of his head…no, his ear. Just guessing the blade six inches long, an inch hung out Binje's ear by the handle. It didn't much matter how much hung out, the five inches inserted into Binje's brain is what counted.

Gale stood over Binje and spat on him.

Her hands rubbing her neck, Elisa slowly climbed back up to stand. Yana joined the girls and Lybeck closed his eyes. He held his breathe and hoped they thought him dead.

Yana said, "What happened to his brother? He flew out the door and they closed up, but he didn't come back inside."

"Damn," he heard Elisa say as darkness swallowed him up.

*****

Rogan moved down the side of the prep house away from where the parties had departed. His ears easily directed him to where he needed to go, and the grasping howls of pain were better than a blazing beacon in the night. Sword at the ready, and carrying the triangular shield of Urell, Rogan slowed his pace to peer about the edge of the last wall toward the entrance of the prep house.

The howling man proved to be one of the Kaldwell twins. He didn't know which one, nor did it matter. The big man seethed in anguish, pulling himself to his feet, trying to paw at himself.

By the light of the censures and the waning light of day,

Rogan could see the long threads of a flail had wrapped about the Kaldwell, one of the spiked balls of the weapon had pierced into his left eye and cheek. Another of the flail's tails had stuck in Kaldwell's right shoulder blade, another into his sternum, and the last of the four hung away from his thigh, where blood oozed from a glancing wound. The Kaldwell brother ripped the spike from his chest and shook his shoulder like a man fighting a pesky itch. Rogan smiled when he beheld Kaldwell's assailant.

His father held the flail handle in his left hand and herded the big man like one would a wild horse. Jarek, no small man himself, stayed away from the Kaldwell's swinging arms like a dancer. The old warrior brandished a short blade in his right hand and jabbed it into the Kaldwell's kidneys on the left side. The sword tip went in but a few inches, but Jarek tore the kidney out with precision. Blood and piss spurted out.

The man stormed further, gripping the tails of the flail and trying to pull Jarek to him. A wise man in battle, Jarek knew when to release the flail handle. The Kaldwell twin's face appeared wide open, flabbergasted, not expecting the loss of the man holding the weapon.

Jarek took a knee as the big man spun, and then inserted the nose of the sword in the back of the man's thigh.

Rogan near to laughed out loud as his father hamstrung the Kaldwell. He kept his humor tight in his head as the big man took a knee and yanked the flail spike from his eye, ripping loose his eye and half his left cheek. As blood and a gray gruel ran into his open mouth, Kaldwell reached for his sword.

Jarek hopped about him, gripping his own blade's handle with both hands, and hewed at the scabbard on Kaldwell's thigh. The shot fell awkward, but took off three of the man's fingers at the second joint. More blood shot out, as did more curses, but Jarek didn't stop there. He chopped at the side of the man's head.

While Rogan wasn't certain if Jarek tried to behead the Kaldwell twin, a truly big task as thick as that neck went, but whatever his mission, Jarek went on after him like an instructor.

He didn't relent, but kept chopping with the small blade, ruining the Kaldwell's ear, creasing his skull, slicing open his copious neck, and then swiping off his nose as he turned his head to face his attacker.

The Kaldwell then roared and jumped at Jarek.

Rogan came out of hiding, ready to run in to aide his sire.

Jarek, though, didn't retreat at all but charged the bleeding man. He rammed the small blade into Kaldwell's abdomen and then curled his left arm about his neck. Jarek gripped him about the head, holding what was left of the ruined ear, then pulling the head to one side.

Jarek bellowed and buried his teeth in the Kaldwell's throat, biting in like a mad dog. He worked the sword into the Kaldwell's guts and still held him as he heaved his head back, ripping a vein loose from the man's neck.

"You…" the Kaldwell croaked, hand to his neck, blood spewing between his ruined fingers. The man looked down at his gut at the sword Jarek had left there. Before he could raise his eyes to face Jarek to grab at the sword himself, Jarek tackled him again, shoving the blade on through until it burst through the short ribs of his back.

His face a veneer of hurt, Batasta's eyes locked to those of Jarek. His right hand curling into a fist, Jarek struck Batasta cross the face, landing a rigid blow to his mouth. Batasta's face moved, but popped right back to face him again.

Once more, Jarek smashed his fist into him, hard on the chin, then followed the shot up with an awkward blow to the forehead, then another to the mouth. Yet again, Batasta looked up at him, the misery obvious, but giving no quarter to the elder man.

Batasta smiled.

Jarek drew back and put his boot on the handle of the blade and shoved it down at a cruel angle, delving more on through Batasta. He then stepped back from the Kaldwell twin, his back bent over, hands on his knees for a moment while he took in deep breaths, but quickly stood up again.

Unable to rise due to the wounds to his thigh, Kaldwell again reached for his sword, but fell over, coughed and choking, blood pouring out of his wounds.

Jarek wiped some blood from his beard, took a few more breaths, looked up, and spied Rogan. "Thank you for your help."

Rogan answered, "You didn't seem to need it."

Kaldwell contorted on the ground, dying, but not going at it easily. His unfocused eyes scowled down at the weapon sticking out of himself and a look of misunderstanding set across his face. In another moment, a guise of ominous fatalism locked in and his eyes seemed to sink back in his skull more.

Jarek admitted, "He flew out the doors in a magical haze of some kind. I picked my spot with the flail and got the best of him fast."

"Well done."

"He'd have outlasted me in a straight fight," Jarek confessed, taking another breath. "But he had to die."

Kaldwell gasped, "The gods will...avenge me...my brother..."

The doors to the prep house opened and Elisa filled the space. "Your brother is dead, Batasta."

After a few wet breaths, Batasta smiled at her. "Our grandfather was a devil. He will avenge his fallen grandsires."

Yana moved to the steps and said, "That is a lie."

Batasta gazed up at her, his face in misery but also confused.

Yana said, "That demon may have fathered a few Nephilims, but those that claimed to be your mother or father? They are liars."

Batasta spat more blood out. "Curse you, be gone and let me die." Eyes shut tight, tears rolling out the sides, he groaned, "Just let me die."

Yana insisted, "A demon breeds a giant, or a girl to be cast away to the desert, but if those children try to father another bunch, they are tiny freaks. You cannot be real grandsons of demons."

Eyes open again, Batasta laughed and gurgled. "So you say to me at such a time, you filthy old bat." His laughter made Gale back up a little and hide behind her father. "I speak to my grandfather every day and he says…"

Yana walked over near him and said, "Demons lie."

His eyes flared at her and Batasta choked out a last breath. He moved no more, save to break wind loud as his sphincter released.

"Well then now," Elisa said, cracking her knuckles. "Those are two less for us to worry about."

Gale stood by the door and said, "There were others with them. They went around the place here."

Rogan spoke up to say, "Yeah, I got two of the soldiers and that red-bearded fuck Urell."

While Jarek nodded, Gale said, "Binje Kaldwell lays dead inside, but there is another with them still…" She turned and then looked back at them fast. "He's gone."

Yana turned to face the girl. "The bloody man on the pillar? The older man?"

Gale nodded fast and pointed into the house. "He's gone."

Rogan joined them at the door. "Wonder who he was."

Gale said, "He can't get far. Yana stunned him with her powers and his head had been bloodied."

Jarek picked up the flail and gave it a smile.

Rogan said, "I don't recall you using one of those."

Shrugging a little, Jarek replied, "One makes the best of a situation." He then pulled out the short sword from Batasta. "Like this damn runt's blade. It worked, though."

Gale stood between them and said, "We need to get out of here."

Nodding, Rogan agreed. "She's right."

Jarek grunted his agreement, too.

As he looked toward Irem, Rogan noted the two women trading a glance. He then said softly, "Damn, they took Aliene."

Yana stepped up and said, "Your friends Thyssen and Bodyne went along to give the story better credence."

Grimacing, Rogan cursed under his breath, then louder. "Shit."

Elisa asked, "Who are you missing more? Your so-called friends or your ugly assed white elephant?"

"I can find so-called friends any damned where," Rogan replied. "Aliene is the hard one to replace."

Gale asked, "I wonder what they will do with her."

"What?" Rogan gave her a confused look.

"Yeah, like, they want to collect odd things or brag to their demi-god brothers over their possessions, but what will become of the mammoth?"

Jarek offered the girl, "Like any possession of these fake gods, like a child, woman, or a horse with two heads, Aliene will be amusing for a while and then probably set out to pasture or to be eaten, if she is lucky."

Rogan faced his father. "Lucky?"

"Yes," Jarek cleared his throat. "Those bastards will try to screw anything."

"Wodan wept," Rogan muttered while Gale grimaced.

Jarek sighed and said, "Are you that devoted to your pet elephant or these friends that are not Kelts?"

Yana rolled her eyes and Elisa said, "Savages, indeed."

Eyes wide, Rogan raged, "Ya'alls should talk. You keeping little secrets bout whatever the fuck it is ya got in mind to get here. Thyssen and I were gonna part ways anyhow, once I found my dad and sister. Well, I found them."

Lips peeled back in a snarl, Elisa snapped, "You will leave your friend to the mercy of those in the palace?"

"Thyssen is a good bullshitter. He'll be all right."

Yana questioned, "What of Bodyne?"

Quietly, Rogan said, "She'll be fine."

Jarek's ire raised and he asked Yana, "Who the hell are you, anyway? Why should I care about your lives?"

After she looked Jarek up and down, Elisa faced her mother and quipped, "Hard to believe that's Rogan's father, aye?"

With a boney hand, Yana waved her off and approached Jarek. "We could use you all in our endeavor."

His blue eyes gazing down at her turned colder. "I bet you could."

"It's true," Yana said, eyes sparkling in the night.

Jarek's jaw ground and he said, "That's what all in these southern lands do to our folk, use us." He then looked at Gale closer. "Why are you dressed up like that?"

Gale shrugged and looked at Yana.

Her withering face creased more as she stepped closer to Jarek. "You, your son, and daughter would be a great help in what we have planned."

Rogan's laughter didn't deter the serious tone Jarek kept. "And what is that, fair damsel? What is it you and your daughter are out to do here? You must be out to kill someone, for why go through this much to get here. You aren't here to kiss someone."

Yana smirked. "You are wise. I see why you are the chief."

"We have many chiefs, I am no king," Jarek replied with a sardonic voice. "Irem is ruled by that demon in flesh Zazaeil and the Nephilim Marduk."

Elisa's eyes looked Jarek up and down. "You know much of this place, for one who has not been here very long."

"You think us savages or fools," Jarek said with bile in his tone. "But even an animal learns from his new place of living, be it a yard, or a cage."

Yana nodded. "Indeed."

"The tales of the swine in Irem are rife in the Foundry, their love of women and hunger for the flesh of infants." Strong humor then spread on Jarek's face. "What do you two women have in mind? Don't cloak your words in pretty tights for me. To challenge the gods that walk the earth?"

"Oh no, not a challenge," Elisa said, her tongue ran over her lips.

Rogan asked, "Then what the hell are you about?"

Yana's tone went very serious as she said, "Deicide."

CHAPTER SIXTEEN
Lord of This World

Lybeck woke up in the saddle. He'd slept when riding a horse in the night before, so this act didn't strike him as completely alien. Nevertheless, his aching head tried to recount how in the hell he came to be on horseback and in the company of the king's troops.

His mind reeled a few times and his thighs squeezed in to keep him from falling out of the saddle. Night near to have fallen as they rode on slow through the walls of Irem.

"Are you all right?" a voice called out to him from his left.

He looked sideways at the older fellow in military garb of the house of Kamala-ur. "Yeah, I'm fine."

"You look a fright, still," the older fellow said. "I can reapply that head dressing if the blood starts up again."

"I'm good," Lybeck insisted. "Just a few buzzards in my head."

"Hope so. They will feed us like the kings once we get up there in the lair of the gods," the older soldier related.

"Lair of the gods," Lybeck mumbled, eyes ahead, impressed by the series of curtain walls they passed through to enter the city of Irem. "Damn it all, that sounds like a hell of a place to visit, much less get a seat at."

"They don't call it that," the older man said, his eyes gazing down the streets as if he could see where they were bound.

Lybeck figured that, but his head still ached and swam.

"We just came along with Nungal and Kalama-ur from way back home," the soldier went on to say. "Try and keep up, sir. You were assigned with those to bring in that accused rogue mercenary, huh? Like the others we picked up outside the prep house?"

Lybeck said nothing, but just backstroked in his own mind.

"I bet you are really hungry for a good supper, then."

"I suppose so, yes."

"Life on the open road is much harder than travelling with the entourage."

"Yes."

"All that hard-tack and jerky. It's all right travel food, but you are truly in for a good treat with the birds and butter they will make for us."

His gut churning, Lybeck wished he'd quit talking about eating. He did admire the masonry of the access towers, and then the simple places along the main avenue that ran into Irem. He lost count of how many inscribed pillars lined the open streets before great brick buildings took over the avenues.

After a few additional breaths, his head shuddered, trying to make sense of how he came to be in the column. His mind whirled back to the scene in the prep house, of that tall woman and the little girl slaying Binje Kaldwell.

A deeper part of his mind couldn't quite grasp that the mouthy, but tough, fighter lay dead in that prep house. He wondered if Batasta also had been killed, as they rushed outside to see his fate. When they did, he took his chance, or must have. Lybeck tried to remember faking unconsciousness, and then running out through the baths, but the exact images eluded his aching mind.

The old soldier with him commented, "Your horse even

looks tired."

Lybeck almost admitted the mount wasn't his, that his horse still stood tethered outside the prep house…that this animal wandered by the stables out the rear of the bathhouse. He recalled seeing it, didn't recollect getting on it, but did remember seeing two dead soldiers on the ground nearby. An image of Urell, dead and cut up bad, also haunted his mind, He didn't know if that image rang true or if his brain threw it in to ponder.

"Been through a long trip, huh?"

"Yes," Lybeck said, his mouth so dry. He searched about his belt and self for his flask, or for a canteen on the horse, but came up empty.

"The animals will be cared for as well. They run a real high end joint up here, don't ya know?"

"Good."

"Better just stay with us and forget all the rest of those fools you traveled with. The others that came along with you are glad to be here."

Lybeck eyed him, and then tried to see the other soldiers from his group that had went around the perimeter of the prep house. He didn't see them, so he relaxed back to the saddle of the alien horse. He reckoned the other Kaldwell twin met his fate or these men wouldn't have deserted so easily.

The old soldier said, "That man with the spear brought the hairy elephant out to us. His story was that that rogue Rogan died at the Foundry of Dis, that the guardian slew him when he searched for his father."

"Yes?" Lybeck replied. "Unlikely."

The soldier nodded. "That guy has his elephant, though. Must be dead, for real. How else did he give it up?"

"I don't know."

He snorted. "I say he is dead."

"I can't say, but we never went to the Foundry for long."

"Good idea." The soldier's eyes rolled towards the heavens. "Anyhow, here we go to be fed like aristocrats, or at least half-assed like them."

Lybeck managed a weary smile, glad that he wore the right colors, and glad to be taken in so easily by the soldiers.

"What did you say was happening at this Lair of the Gods?"

The soldier fished in his belt and pulled out a small flask. He took a hit off it and then offered to throw it to Lybeck.

Lybeck shook his head, unsure if he had coordination enough to catch it.

"I hear tell it's a big banquet. The kings were on their way there even before they had the elephant to give to Marduk."

"They have these banquets often?"

"Once a week," the soldier confirmed. "They eat and that demon thing Zazaeil and Marduk cover a bride before anyone who wants to watch."

"Damn."

"Yeah. I hear tell an orgy breaks out sometimes after the sight. That's among the fancy folks, not us soldiers. "

"You'd think as they are giants, they would slay a woman with their manhood."

The soldier drank deeper this time and said, "That's what usually happens."

"Crap. And the aristocrats think about fucking after seeing that?"

"Rumor is."

His mind clearing a little, Lybeck said, "Bastards."

"Yeah, we're just there for the food and drink."

"Sounds good."

"Where is the rest of your big party?"

Lybeck asked himself that a few times. "Quite a few died on the way. I'm not sure if the rest went into Irem by another means."

"Ah well, it'll all come out in the wash, yes?"

"Yes."

"Ah, heaven," the soldier said, taking a swig of his traveling wine in the designated ration for the soldiers. As he said this, the other soldiers near him took out their flasks and joined him in the toast.

"Impressive, place," Lybeck agreed with their sentiment, looking at the pillared architecture and many grand buildings that led down the main thoroughfare of interlocking stones.

"You misunderstand," the soldier laughed. "Irem, the city itself, is a twisted meaning for Heaven."

"Someone tried to make heaven on earth?"

"Yarns say."

Patting at his tunic again for his own flask, Lybeck answered, "Never a good idea, I'd have to say."

"Screwing with the gods never is. I hate to even have wine with their bastard children," he said, winking at Lybeck. "But my belly is empty and my mouth will be plenty dry by the time we sup with those fuckers."

As they traveled through the city of Irem, the censures at the bases of the pillars added light to the city with similar light sources at each street corner. Lybeck saw several guards and slaves adding to certain censures, probably bidden to keep them going every so often with some additive. He didn't understand what they supplemented to the long-burning bowls on extended platforms.

Looking up at the pillars, temples, and street corners the greenish light illuminated, Lybeck's eyes grew weak trying to understand what substance they used to accomplish such a feat. Still, onward he went with the rest into the great city, lit up in the fallen night by such perceived magical means.

Lybeck found it curious that the city, while inhabited by people like himself, the alleys, domiciles, and buildings all bore huge doorways. He thought this so superfluous until it dawned on him it came that way to allow for the giants who lived there.

"How many are there here, those like Marduk?" Lybeck asked him.

"Oh, not sure. I know Marduk and that Zazaeil are here most times. At certain times a few more gather and meet here, but this really seems out of season for that."

"Yeah?"

"Usually at the change of seasons, or top or bottom of the year, that is more likely. This is just a usual night for them to drink a lot, screw a few powdered princesses and brag about those they know from beyond the stars." The men all gave a vain cheer and toast to the sky and stowed their flasks.

"I see."

"These are all regular places, along this avenue now, but they lead up to that big-assed octagon-shaped palace?"

"Yes?"

"That there is the Lair of the Gods."

Lybeck took in the place he had to guess had eight sides from the soldier's words. The stone structure, so immense, couldn't be taken in from their angle or any place, save for if one had wings. His mind spun at the size of the enormous building, made of blocks, but in some places sheeted over with a thin layer of some form of rock in other places, the bricks glistened like they were painted with a glaze put on food. The huge dome that stretched over the top, that baffled him as such accomplishments in engineering went beyond his imagination.

The avenue leading up to it held common shops and even what looked like a tavern, but all well-maintained. He saw not a bit of animal feces in the street, and supposed the area quite high upkeep. Noting the treading of the mammoth ahead of them, going for those huge doors, Lybeck wondered how that would sit with the maintenance folks of the street.

A great creaking echoed and the massive double doors parted. His heart flittered as countless lights from lanterns and censures lit the inner spaces brilliantly. The mammoth and the rest gradually headed inside the inordinate hall and Lybeck's mind concentrated better than it had.

Just inside the doors stretched tables for dining, aloft from the rest on a dais, where the eaters would have their backs at the wall and no one facing them. He saw other banqueting tables across the way, all well set up, but these also were set up in waves, facing the hall, thus nothing obscured their view as each table line sat on a riser. Far toward the end of the hall sat longer tables, setting facing each other, all on a regular level. He assumed those spots good enough for common soldiers like himself.

In the left side of the hall another raised platform held a tall rectangular pedestal, several yards long. Trying to fathom what it was for, Lybeck noted the cushioned surface and figured it a lounging place for one of the giants.

As the long doors behind them ground closed, another set of tall doors opened off to their right. Through the huge opening strolled Zazaeil and who Lybeck assumed as Marduk. Zazaeil stood a bit taller than Marduk, but the demon's gait couldn't be much more arrogant. His bare feet slapped down and his hips rolled like a gyrating whore. He seemed even more imperious than when he saw him at the sea port, the way he shifted his shoulders, and kept slinging his long hair back over his shoulder.

Demon in human flesh, his mind reeled. *Gods let me escape this place.*

Marduk, though, looked like he did on all the reliefs carved of him across Shynar. The Nephilim indeed stood tall, well-proportioned, muscled and perfect like every other giant Lybeck had ever seen. His hair, black and curly, sat above his shoulders, a little tighter than most reliefs of him, but this squared beard looked almost comical to Lybeck. He thought the squared thing an artist rendering, like that on Zazaeil.

"No wings," Lybeck muttered.

"What?" the soldier hissed, somewhat panicked.

"Marduk has no wings."

"Shut your ass!"

Marduk's head tilted and turned their way. He then looked back to where he and Zazaeil walked.

Lybeck gave the soldier a caustic look. "He's across the room."

"He might've heard you."

"So what? I'm amazed he's got no wings like the portraits and statues."

Still walking beside the demon, Marduk smiled.

*****

Rogan held onto his handgrip and tried not to stare too much at the passing walls of Irem. He looked to his left, where his father also held a handgrip on the grand litter that carried Elisa through the security walls of the city. He thought his father looked damn silly dressed in the robes of a eunuch, but then again, he wore the same togs, so he probably appeared just as inane. The hoods obscured their faces, so that might help, he figured.

"This will never work," Rogan told Yana when they were at the prep center. "It is what they call utter madness. We will be caught in short order."

Yana assured him, "They don't look into the faces of servants, especially eunuchs. It's sort of a pity thing."

"Yeah, I guess." Rogan looked at the two eunuchs that carried the front of the litter and couldn't argue with her idea of those aristocrats and their pity.

He again clutched his hand-hold, feeling somewhat reassured as it was the hilt of his sword. His father also held his own weapon, but looked over his shoulder a few times at the other litter, that carried his daughter.

Rogan figured they would indeed get inside easily enough, but their assurances that they would take out the gods, he thought mad indeed. The idea that they walked into certain doom just on the slight possibility that these woman could slay the demon and its offspring, all of it made him near to nauseated.

"We need to get away from these terrible people," Rogan had told his father when he pulled him away from the women at the prep center. "We need to leave them to their crazy ideas and run away."

"Where shall we go?"

"Go?" Rogan fumed, not caring who heard him. "We shall go home. Fuck those women, fuck this world, and fuck them all. We need to get out of this foolish place and head back to the land of ice and snow."

Yana had interrupted to say, "Paradise, to you, yes?"

Rogan leered down at her. "Paradise enough."

"Runaway and be cowards," Elisa shouted, her ire riding as high as she sat in the litter as a perfumed noblewoman. "Who needs you all?"

Yana spoke softer, saying, "Jarek, you saw the abomination that is the awful Foundry of Dis?"

"Well, yes."

"You saw it on the inside?"

Jarek nodded. "So what? These people are pigs to let all that go on with no real fight. They don't gang up and attack those rotten bastards. If I had stayed their longer, I'd have cut all their throats."

Yana said, "Overpowering Marduk is one thing, but his kindred would soon come and destroy all them. Getting past Zazaeil, that is the problem."

Rogan retorted, "And you two can kill a demon?"

Elisa said, "He wears human flesh."

Jarek pointed out, "But he can jump into another body, another form."

Gale blinked. "Imagine him jumping into Aliene."

"Great," Rogan mumbled. "A possessed mammoth?"

Elisa and her mother smiled. "We will make sure he doesn't escape."

Rogan shook his head. "How?"

His eyes closed a minute as they marched, he shuddered again at the revelation they gave him. He still didn't care for a chance they took, nor his father's words that the devils needed to die up in the great octagon palace. However, his father still was his father. He couldn't just leave Gale and him to this irrational venture and run away. Bull-headedness ran in his family, he ruminated, so he relented.

Through the pillars and down the great avenue they marched. They picked up more security from the palace as they went, as the gods wanted what they were promised. His eyes grew wide as he marveled at what the glow from the censures testified to. They glowed bright and showed many things that amazed him, the temples, and just the reality of the unnatural glow they gave off.

Rogan had to hand it to Gale, she showed little anxiety in the face of what awaited for her and the possibility of it all going tits up.

Yana rode side saddle on a small colt, leading them all to the palace in the robes of her dead sister. No one seemed to question if Yana was her sister, but perhaps none here knew the difference.

His mind afire with the stone work and amazing avenue they went down, Rogan came close to being struck dumb at the sight of the octagon palace.

"Lair of the Gods," Jarek said to him.

"I don't care if it's their pisspot," Rogan replied. "I don't want to be here nor do I think any god should be inside."

Elisa spoke up from her position on the litter to say, "Steady on, you puerile pricks. Just lead on and be good servants."

Jarek sighed. "Listen to the princess."

Rogan said, "If she's full of crap…"

"It's not her crap that I really worry about," said Jarek and shook his head a little to shut him up. "We shall see if she has the guts to carry it all out and if it does happen to be true, her words, well, that will be an interesting happening."

They moved on down the avenue and Rogan spotted a group of men by a hitching post, all holding tankards in their hands.

"Fancy a drink?" Jarek asked softly.

Eyes forward again, Rogan said, "An ocean of it."

"After this is over, we shall drink to their health a very large lot."

Eyes closed again, Rogan hoped that wasn't in Valhalla.

They saw the great doors open, and the even greater light spilling on out. Their small party entered in the abundant hall and they saw all of the people, filling the tables and having a drink. No one ate just yet, but the mutterings and talking had begun in earnest. Far down the way of drinkers, Rogan saw a prodigious number of soldiers, all imbibing as well and none ready to go to war. Each man, to his eyes, looked to be relaxed and at ease.

"We are fucked," Rogan said to his father as they headed over to their left, toward the raised dais of the giants. "Look at all these people. I thought in a pinch we could fight our way out of this ass-bandit meeting. But look at them all. We are fucked if they all draw steel at once for real."

Yana slid off her pony, rubbed her behind, and admitted, "I hadn't foresaw that, damn soldiers and others."

Rogan shook his head. "If they but had one throat I could just slit it and get 'em all dead fast like."

Yana looked up at him and then at the crowd. "Good idea. They are gotten rid of easily enough." She reached back onto the pony and grabbed her satchel and slung it over her arm. Once they set down the litter on a smaller cushioned platform, Yana walked to Rogan. Her hand on her small necklace, she said, "You, killer, come with me."

Rogan looked over and saw who must be Marduk and Zazaeil reclining, drinking from oversized goblets. Both yawned, as if too bored to get up and look at the prizes that had arrived for them.

"Kelt killer," Yana hissed at him. "Snap out of it and come with me."

Rogan gave her a mock bow and followed along. Out of the corner of his eye, he spied Jarek shadowing Gale, who sat on her own litter, adored and perfumed like a princess.

"Come along," Yana led him past the reclining giants like

they were nothing to fret over and into a wide hallway the gods would've had to crawl to pass through. From the strong scents, Rogan could tell they headed into a kitchen area.

His eyes closed for a moment, thinking about those two giants, and the arrogance that sweated from each pore of their selves. That devil, Zazaeil, Rogan's hard heart near to shuddered at his look. He thought himself lord of this realm, if not the world. Rogan feared for his life more than any time he drew breath. His guts churned, but he willed himself on, pushing his distress down deep.

The hall opened into a vast area vented to the outside where numerous grills turned countless fowl on metallic rods. Dozens of servants clad in aprons scurried about, making sure all of the food stayed properly prepared.

"Enough to feed an army and more," Rogan quipped, thirsty for wine but not wanting to risk stealing any.

Yana went to a long cutting block and slammed her satchel down. Many of those who prepared the meals for those outside gave her a wide berth.

Rogan wondered what fear they had for her sister that they gave her such a good clearance.

She rooted in her satchel, drawing out a large mortar and pestle. Her dark eyes looked up into his.

"What are you about?"

"Going to make some magick," Yana explained, reaching for her necklace, but this time ripping it free of her withered neck.

Eyes narrowing at what she did, Rogan watched as she took the tiny bones off the string and pushed the jewels at him. Yana placed each bone within the bowl of the mortar. After a short breath, she went to work.

"Grinding up bones?"

Yana smirked and put the pestle in the mortar. "Bright boy, you are, too. I see why women might like you more than for your body."

He laughed a little, watching all the preparations that went on around them in a near frenzy. "Too bad you didn't have some of those bones I gave to…" his voice stopped and his eyes widened at her.

Yana peered up at him again and winked. "Now you catch on, Keltos killer." She ground the bones around swiftly, then reached her right hand down into her robes. "Curse the luck, damn it all to hades."

"What? You drop something?"

"No, damn the gods." Again, her hand moved around in her gown down low. She glared up at him once more. "Give me a hand, big fellow."

"With what?"

"Get around behind me. Do it now."

Rogan stepped behind her and looked over the tiny woman. Confused, he asked her, "Yeah?"

"Rub my shoulders."

"What?"

"I said rub my shoulders, massage them and my back, gentle like. I'm brittle so don't break me."

Hands out, Rogan hesitated.

Yana sighed. "I'm not asking you to mount me up here right well, you savage, just rub my damn shoulders."

"All right," Rogan responded and applied his hands to her. Her skinny shoulders were threadbare, and his thumbs easily slid over to her neck bones. He didn't apply much pressure, but gently massaged her shoulders and then ran his thumbs down her spine. It wouldn't take much for him to crush her neck and feeble self unto a certain death or paralysis. He felt her body tremble.

"That's a good ruffian," Yana near to groaned, shaking. "You are full of talents, savage. That always did it for me in ages past."

He peered down at her and saw her hands not mixing in her bowl, but still with a right hand delved deep in her gown. In a few seconds, her hand emerged and she wiped her fingers into the side of the bowl.

"What the?"

Yana said, "You can stop now." She started to grind up the tiny bones to fine powder and said, "That always got me going as a youth."

Hands away from her, Rogan didn't know what to say.

Yana ground away in the mortar and then said, "See? Magick."

From the small bowl he saw a full measure of fine powder, one that glowed bright yellow like fire.

"How…never mind," Rogan said, his words lost.

"Fetch me a seasoner," she ordered him and pointed. "One of those shaker bottles full of herbs will do."

Rogan turned and the servant boys stood back from him as he snatched the shaker off the table. He gave it to her, eyes not leaving what she did.

Yana unscrewed the top of the bottle and dumped out whatever lay within. She then put all from her mortar inside the shaker.

"What now?" Rogan asked as she screwed the top back on. "I'm waiting to see such amazing things by such a wizards as you."

"Now?" Yana grinned wide. "We spice up the many meals for those pretty bastards out there."

"Remind me not to eat a suppertime made by you," Rogan told her. Still, his stomach growled but his desire to feast on what she made ran at nothing.

Yana worked the shaker with the coyness of a masturbating whore. "No worries on that, killer."

CHAPTER SEVENTEEN

Sins of the Father

Lybeck drank deep from the tankard of ale they furnished him, along with the other soldiers at the tables in the back. The craftsmanship of the tankard earned his admiration, and he set the stein down with meticulous care out of respect. He squinted his eyes as the old soldier chortled.

"Still feeling it, huh?"

"Yeah."

The soldier paused as dozens of servants arrived carrying platters of food. "You look a fright, all of a sudden, even worse off than when we patched you up and set you right on the horse again."

"Ale in my belly has woken me up again, I guess," Lybeck tilted his head as he looked down at the plates. "What is that exactly?"

"Quail, filled with butter, wrapped up right with a pork strip of bacon, fried on done right." The soldier winked and could hardly stop his mouth from drooling. "Make a puppy pull a wagon, praise the gods above and below."

Pushing his chair back, Lybeck grabbed his belly with his right hand and grimaced. He then said, "I have to find a privy."

The soldier shrugged. "Suit yourself. Out through there into the kitchen. I'll save you yours, sir, but hurry. It's really good." He bit into the breast of the small bird wrapped in bacon. "The rest will eat up the scraps."

His stomach heaving as the scent of the cooked meat filled his senses, Lybeck arose and tried not to run for the kitchen door. If anything, taking a few steps cleared his head, but it also showed him a few things he'd been missing.

The husky spearman and the short blonde woman who'd delivered the mammoth to Marduk headed out the kitchen door, way in front of him. He watched them walking casually and then start to flee down the hall. Their running gait made some fear rise in his gut and unsettle whatever churned in there.

He sensed no terror in the big room, though, only revelries as the eating commenced and the lute music began. For a moment, he thought himself a dupe for such thoughts and that his senses made him afraid.

Lybeck stopped and took a breath, then locked eyes on one of the eunuchs walking with Yana. The tough Kelt Rogan didn't play the part of the serving eunuch well, he even wore his boots fashioned in a realm far away from here as well, but no one called him on it, as who looked at a man close with no balls? Lybeck shivered, thinking of the young Kelt warrior before his eyes. Rogan had balls, balls to spare, and the idea of fighting him made Lybeck want to be sick even more.

At the entrance to the kitchen hall, Lybeck stopped and looked at the inordinate hall. The tables of aristocrats along the walls dug into the quails much like the soldiery did. He bet they had respectable wine and not pissy ale like the regular men had to sip on.

He looked over at Nungal and Kalama-ur, sitting with their heads back in their chairs, not eating. It took him but a few moments to see that serving girls had knelt before the kings to provide a sufficient bit of pleasure. Both old men beamed and grabbed their wine goblets, sucking down the wine as willing as the serving girls had sucked down their warm seed. Their mouths red with wine, the goblets slammed down and echoed in the hall, giving rise to mocking applause from Marduk as the giant walked around his dais. The dark-haired serving girls arose, refilled the goblets from their decanters, curtseyed, and skipped away.

Marduk found this very funny but Zazaeil didn't smile at the display. The demon in flesh appeared to have his interest elsewhere, as the tall girl that came out of the prep house walked about the demon's dais, hips shifting. She walked with her hands on her bounteous hips, shaking her ass as she stepped forward. Lybeck thought Zazaeil's head would turn a complete circle to follow her in a moment.

A laugh from the Nephilim, Marduk's deep voice echoed out "She has goodly hips, Zazaeil."

"Yes, indeed."

Marduk reached out to the small girl offered to him, his index finger tweaking the dangling metal stars in her earlobes. "Perhaps she'll live through it."

"Perhaps," Zazaeil sighed, trying to feign disinterest, but his eyes told Lybeck another story. Not everyone just wanted a woman to destroy like the other giants. This devil saw a challenge in Elisa's smile and her winks taunts toward him.

The servants who brought the food started to shoo the eunuchs away, arms waving, saying, "Go on along now. Don't torment yourselves for what is to come now. Go on, now, you half-men."

The real eunuchs did start to shuffle away, but Jarek and Rogan lingered, of course, not departing the area.

One of the servants, a short man with slicked-back black hair, pointed into their faces, saying, "There is no more reason for you to be here, either, skinner men. Go on. Unless you want to stay and carry out the bodies later?"

Rogan and his father said nothing.

"Is that the prodigious prize you look to be here for? Such a fun thing, will you get more food for that or a pervert pleasure in carrying out the ruined women?"

Rogan looked at the little man for a long time and Lybeck thought the two Kelts pondered crushing him between them. They did no such thing, for in a moment, the first cries in the room began.

At first, Lybeck thought someone drank too fast and coughed on out in pain to clear his throat out. Then, more of the rich of Irem made a similar cry, and soon, far worse rang out amongst the soldiers. The cries rang out and echoed all over. Then, as if one unlimited voice existed, they hollered together. He wanted to run and not look back, but Lybeck took a few steps back, trying to understand what happened.

All through the hall, the men and women of the upper class bolted up from their seats, clutching their bellies, trying to vomit. The soldiers he'd just sat alongside, including the older man who befriended him, did likewise. While the servants ran about in a panic, Lybeck noted that Marduk simply sat on the dais nearest him, looking at the young girl brought over to him by the aging eunuch. Zazaeil seemed only mildly perturbed, as his focus grew stronger on the tall woman given to him.

A few of the dining class fell over tables near to him and Lybeck saw a calamitous reality. From out of the silken clothes of those who ate, climbed out a mutilated fowl. His heart pumped fast as the somewhat regenerated cooked bird took on a more ghastly appearance, not that of a benign quail, but something more like a bat crossed with a lizard.

As these creatures clawed and chewed free of the stomachs and guts of the people in the hall, Lybeck stared at Rogan. The big Kelt paid him no mind at all, but seemed fixated on staying near the litter he'd just carried in the room. If anything, Rogan wore a look of shock, as if this happening came as a new revelation to him as well.

The crippled old woman in the green robe wore a grin, and rubbed her small hands together. Her face, a look of triumph if Lybeck ever saw one, near to beamed across the room. The look soon faded as she walked near to where Zazaeil's dais lay.

Lybeck then looked over to see that Nungal and Kalama-ur weren't getting their guts ripped out. They both peered into their goblets and then at the dinner trays with caution, then at each other in earnest terror. Their quail lay on the platters, not a bite being taken out of them by their intended.

Some of the servants fell at the feet of Marduk and Lybeck heard one exclaim, "My lord, we are undone! Someone has worked bad magicks on us!"

His grim eyes of the demi-god left the little girl before him and took in the sight about him. "I can smell it, yes, and not just bad food for true." He then looked over at Zazaeil. "I think the party is over for all of them."

Zazaeil didn't take his gaze off Elisa. "I disagree. The celebration and consummation are just getting going." The demon then glanced at the room and the edges of his mouth drew down a little. "Damn fools. What are a few dozen more humans for Hell?" His focus returned to Elisa. "You don't seem put off, little one?"

Elisa's sly smile widened. "I'm not so little, great god of Hell, lord of this world, and I didn't have the dinner." Her painted nails tapped her stomach once and then fell away. "I wanted an empty belly for you, dear."

"Did you now?" Zazaeil smirked, eyes on her, not caring about whatever happened in the long hall.

Her voice soft and child-like, Elisa asked, "Really now? Are you gonna put a baby in my belly?"

Lybeck thought the demon's body seethed like a stoked furnace in a smithy, as a red glow frothed off his flesh.

Marduk, though, seemed a bit more concerned until Gale reached out and touched his kneecap. Her tiny hand then ran down his calf and she knelt at his feet. The girl smiled sweeter than Lybeck thought possible, as he knew the girl a true viper. She took her right index finger and playfully counted his toes, singing as she did so.

"Ten, eleven, twelve. My, my, you are a son of a god, no?"

His focus away from the deaths all around and back on her, Marduk stated, "It'll be a shame to slay you with myself."

"Really, honey?" Gale cooed.

"You look delicious," Marduk told her.

Gale winked at him and Lybeck's blood froze. Can't they see this is a deception of some kind? Are they so arrogant they don't think a couple girls can't harm them for real? Lybeck saw the wizardry around them and didn't like the giant's chances. Still, they relaxed before the girls, even with all the dying about them.

He then heard the snort of the great hairy elephant and expected to look down the hall and see the beast fall over. No, the creature stood, its bearers having departed in the terror of the mass killing of the hall. However, the elephant wandered from its appointed place where people had walked to see it on display.

Lybeck saw Rogan reach down and pull out two swords from the litter hand-holds. One he threw to his father. No one else seemed to see it or care.

"Come along, Zazaeil," Elisa fussed, walking around the raised dais and letting her painted nails tiptoe down the cushioned mat. "Lay here for me and tell me if you like what you see now."

Zazaeil stood from his reclining bench as Elisa took her other hand and put it behind her head. She undid the clasp at her neck, letting her top fall open and her breasts to be exposed. They didn't hardly move, firm and proportioned to her long body. The demon's manhood bounced, already hard, but more eager at the sight.

"I shall," he said, taking a few steps and then swinging a leg over the dais. He lay back, his member erect and throbbing amidst all the chaos. "You might even survive me, girl. That will be a boundless blessing for you."

The rest of her wrap dropping, Elisa climbed up over him, her lacey gloved hands running down her stomach to just above her sex, which Zazaeil eyed unblinking.

"We shall see," she smiled, then bit her bottom lip and knelt between his legs. Her left hand gripped the long shaft of his long member.

Zazaeil groaned a little, then came back with a stronger tone as he said to her, "Call me lord, little girl."

Elisa suddenly looked shocked. Eyes widespread, she said, "Lord?"

Zazaeil smirked. "Call me master."

"Master?" Again her confusion seemed to reign all over, but for a moment, then her sly look returned. She slapped the long member against her stomach and glowered at him. "Can I call you Daddy?"

Lybeck turned and didn't look back as he left.

*****

Rogan seldom prayed to Wodan or for his family, and he didn't at that moment, either. Conversely, it crossed his mind that if the women and their plan would be untrue, he'd be sitting with Wodan to talk it over soon enough.

As Elisa crawled over Zazaeil, straddling his stomach, Marduk reached to his waist to undo his kilt. Zazaeil's long member sprang out from behind Elisa, slapping her buttocks and lower back as Jarek stepped up closer to Marduk.

Rogan understood that no amount of planning would stop his father from letting Marduk get any closer to Gale.

Their part of the plan was designed this way, as Yana rubbed her hands together and they glowed a dull purple.

"Marduk," Yana said as the two swordsman advanced on either side of the reclining Nephilim.

Marduk almost looked at her, but his curious gaze went to what he perceived as two eunuchs wielding blades. The sight amused him, as his smile grew. Marduk sat up a little and showed no sign of worry in his face.

Yana put her hands together, reared back, and threw the purple ball of light at the giant. She gave out a deep cry that sounded angry and very tired to Rogan.

Instinct took over and Marduk extended his right hand, as if to catch the glowing ball. The orb splattered into his six fingers and then travelled all over his body. He maintained a mauve halo for a few moments. His dark eyes fluttered and goosebumps rose on his skin. He stared down at Gale, still between his legs.

The Kelt girl pulled the long earrings from her lobes that resembled shooting stars and stepped up closer to Marduk's crotch. As her father and brother closed in with their blades, she stabbed the two thin metallic objects into the foreskin of Marduk's penis.

Rogan wondered if she wore that angry face of hers better suited to a warrior boy, but not untypical of a Keltic girl. True to her nature, she dropped as he growled in pain, avoiding his big thighs as he tried to crush her between them.

No rehearsal necessary, Jarek and Rogan had fought together before, so he gave his father the higher shot. Jarek swung Elisa's sword at Marduk's head and Rogan swung lower, swinging at Marduk's abdomen.

Against a normal man, they'd have chopped him into a couple pieces. Marduk, of course, wasn't a normal man or even an above average human. They understood this, and hoped to invoke great damage to his flesh, as Yana promised her spell would weaken his tough god-like flesh.

Marduk, while wincing at what Gale wrought on his member, showed no ill effects of the purple haze and threw both arms out. His move warded off both blades, not even scratching his tough skin as the swords bounced off him. He stood, staggered due to the obvious pain to his groin, but sucking wind hard.

As the two Kelts followed through, throwing shoulder blocks into the giant on each side, Rogan wished the rest of his body was as easily pierced as his foreskin under Gale's earrings. Both men threw all of their might into the moves on Marduk and the rising giant did stagger back a step onto the dais.

Again, the Kelts had been in a fight before and figured on the follow-up move by the giant, who swiped at them with his hands. Both men already had rolled off him to avoid such a move, swung about, took a knee, and brought their blades up.

"Yana," Jarek growled, some anger and disappointment in his words.

"Damn, wrong spell," she cursed, turning to the mound of silks piled up on the end of the litter as Marduk got to his feet.

Rogan glared at his father as if to say, *fine time to figure that out.*

Yana rubbed her hands together, glanced at her daughter residing over Zazaeil's member, and then said, "Need to enchant your blades, not him."

"Shit fire," Rogan roared and spun out of the way of Marduk, who chopped a hand at his blade. Rogan didn't allow him to touch him.

Jarek moved on in closer to Yana and held out his sword in defense. He gritted his teeth, impatient and hung out to dry, as Marduk tried to crush Rogan with blows delivered from balled up fists.

As Yana's hands glowed orange, Elisa poised above Zazaeil member, touching it to the lips of her sex. She smiled and said, "You want me, Daddy?"

Zazaeil trembled all over and nodded.

"Give it to me Daddy."

Zazaeil's chest heaved as he took ahold of his shaft. He tried to stab up into her, but the going didn't go so easy. "Virgin meat are you?"

As the head of the member entered her slow, Elisa's eyes widened and she gasped, saying, "Yes Daddy. Saving myself for you." She then clenched her teeth, working her pelvis in rhythm, then clasping her thighs and trying to force him into her.

Yana released her spell that bathed Jarek's blade in an orange glow.

Marduk turned and backhanded Jarek across the face. The Kelt did bring the blade up, brushing it off the giant's paw. Marduk looked at the back of his hand and at the blood that sprang to light. His eyes opened wide in amazement.

Rogan ran forward, grappling Marduk's midsection, trying to knock him off his feet, but the move failed. The left hand of the giant dropped, striking Rogan awkward on his backside. Rogan fell and rolled, avoiding the follow-up slice down move that would've surely broken his back.

"Yes," Elisa muttered, low, and then a grunt, before she exclaimed, "yes, give it to me, Daddy."

"Split you in half," Zazaeil promised, grinning eclectic, uncaring of the battle about them with Marduk.

Jarek tried the same move as Rogan, but he, too felt the back hand again of Marduk. As he dropped down fast, Marduk backed away from them and cursed the two warriors.

"Piglets," Marduk said, grabbing the edge of the dais and leaning over. "I will shred your souls from your flesh."

The two Kelts rose up but stopped as Marduk's form convulsed, heaving a bit as his back arched. From out of the long back unfolded what appeared to Rogan as two shutters, but they gleamed like steel…then divided again and tried to unfold.

"Wings," Jarek said, stating the obvious. "Sonofabitch."

"Aw, fuck," Rogan declared and moved in at the same time as his father. "Damn it all to hell."

Jarek leapt onto the dais and stepped onto Marduk's head before dropping his glowing blade into the center of the giant's back. The sword stuck where he aimed it, but Marduk rose up, screaming, knocking Rogan away as he tried to hit his back in a lower strike. Jarek pivoted, but fell off the giant, letting go of the blade lodged in between the wings.

Rogan got up again as Marduk turned, seeing Elisa's glowing blade had pierced two of the four appendages appearing on the giant's back wings, crossways. Watching his father fall and reel near to the dais of Zazaeil, Rogan swung his sword up and didn't do much damage to any of the glittering wings. Though distressed deep, Rogan became distracted by the laughter on the other dais.

Elisa cackled as she rode the huge member of Zazaeil. She hunched over more, her arms waving wide, her hilarity out of control as the demon thrust up deeper.

Thinking she had snapped, gone utterly mad, and that her story to them before was a big falsehood, Rogan prepared to attack anew.

Gale appeared in his vision, between the legs of the standing Marduk, grabbing his pierced manhood and swinging like a child on a rope line tied to a tree. She swung out, feet on the dais, then pushed off, swinging back the other way.

Marduk grated and cursed, trying to dislodge her off himself.

Avoiding the hands of the giant, Gale let go and landed on her feet, scrambling toward the other dais and her father.

Rogan used the bent-down giant's calves as stepping stones, jumping on him and hacking fast with his sword at the two wings that the other blade didn't pierce. He hoped the wings not made of as stern of stuff as the rest of Marduk's flesh. His repeated blows did fold in and angle a lower wing. Knowing his time short for the attack, Rogan leapt onto the dais and started to hack at the upper wing.

Then, his sword broke.

Two thirds of the blade forged by his father long ago and far away flipped over and dropped by his boot on the dais. He stared at the jagged hunk of metal left attached to his hilt in disbelief.

Marduk didn't move to strike Rogan, but went down to his left knee, shoulders shrugging, hand reaching back to try and remove the sword Jarek planted there.

Gazing at his father, surely still in a shock, Rogan saw his sire arm up Gale and move about the other dais. "Run, get her out of here!" Rogan yelled at him as Marduk recalled the Kelt and knocked his legs out from under him with a swipe of hand.

Rogan landed on his right hip, face to face with the kneeling Marduk. Their eyes met and Rogan jabbed him in the face with the ruined blade. The jagged edge didn't do much but annoy the giant, who reached out to get after Rogan, who rolled over the other side. Back flat to the dais, he gaped at the other platform, like his fleeing father and sister did from the hall to the kitchen.

Elisa's arms waved in the air wild, but he soon saw that she brought them together over Zazaeil's line of vision. She took off her gloves, revealing what Rogan had seen earlier in the prep house. Her hands, long-fingered, painted, and sure, were malformed…well, that's what anyone might think at first glance. No, they were perfectly fine, for a woman who'd had an extra digit removed.

"That's it, Daddy," Elisa snarled, her hands flat down on the demon's chest. "Give it to me as I give it to you."

Rogan heard Marduk growl and then what sounded like a sword hit the ground. He assumed it was that weapon from Elisa, and moved away from the dais as Marduk stood up. The giant grabbed the broken blade from Rogan and suddenly stopped. The giant found himself struck dumb at what he watched, too.

Zazaeil gagged and cried out, his hands up, trying to grip her shoulders, then her chest, but found his fingers no longer worked.

"Come on Daddy," Elisa snarled, still riding him hard. "Do I make you hard?" She purred and then roared in antagonism. "Gonna make you hard forever."

Rogan stepped away to try avoid any move by Marduk, but the giant watched like they all did, as Zazaeil shook and started to take on a gray hue to his body.

"That's it, that's my daddy," Elisa rumbled and then laughed. "Go on, get out, and go to Hell." She then rose off his huge member that stayed up and erect…well, it had no choice. It had turned to stone. "Burn in Hell, Daddy!"

The insanity of watching Zazaeil's flesh turn to stone struck them all still, but Marduk did move. He picked up the blade and threw it at Yana…who stood by the head of the dais, smiling. The slinging sword piece struck her flat, not piercing her but knocking her down. Marduk moved over and thrust a hand at Rogan, near to braining him, but he moved, broke from the spell of watching.

When Marduk bent down to grab Yana, her body twisted as she struck out at him. The black stone in her grip smashed into Marduk's face and he growled in pain. Yana giggled at him, but Marduk turned back to her and slapped his left hand down, knocking the black stone free and to the floor.

Marduk grabbed the old woman by the throat and raised her up above his head. Both of her hands glowed as if to incite a spell. It spread all about the giant and her, but faded as Marduk's hand closed, crushing the bones in Yana's neck. He threw the old woman at Rogan, who caught her and turned about, laying her almost gently on the other dais.

He stared at her, a woman ruined by a demon so long ago, but who bore a female Nephilim and hid her, taking off the girl's extra fingers & toes…keeping them as a necklace for the span of her long life. That moment Rogan thought about her proved all the giant needed, as Marduk took a step and struck the Kelt hard across the back, sending him spinning down beside the platform.

The world tilted as Rogan went to his knees, his head full of fireflies and the sound of Elisa screaming in victory over the demon turned to stone. He took a few breaths and tried to maneuver away from where he thought Marduk must be. When he peered back, the giant had moved out of his field of vision.

He looked up and Elisa stood, crying in victory, blood running down her pale legs. She shook all over and practically fell to her knees, still poised on the dais over the demon turned to stone. Her gaze found the crumpled body of her mother, her smile disappointed, and then she looked at Rogan.

"Kelt killer…" she gasped.

Hands to his waist, as all he had were his daggers still in the holsters, Rogan looked up at her, not knowing her next move.

He then head the sound of metal scrapping against stone…
of a sword drawing over a rock. It seemed to take a long time.

CHAPTER EIGHTEEN
Symptom of the Universe

Elisa's face still wore a smile of glee, one fitting her victory over the demon Zazaeil, when she looked down at the blade that protruded from the left side of her chest.

Rogan saw her face focus on that piece of bloody steel he raised up again. Her smile, somewhat off a bit, gave way to another look Rogan couldn't quite nail down. Was it recognition, resignation, or a dim understanding that this came as the end of her, a sword through the back at her moment of triumph.

Rogan heard the deep chortle of Marduk, who had taken a knee by the rigid body of Zazaeil to get an acute stab at the victorious Elisa. The baritone chuckle kept undulating and it caused Rogan to feel sick and then livid. Big hands to his belt, Rogan acted.

"With your own sword, little girl," Marduk laughed on and leaned down, his right hand twisting the blade in her body. He softly kissed the top of her head and said, "But well played to slay Zazaeil. Now then, little one, *you* go to Hell."

Elisa's left hand shot up and gripped the curls of Marduk's hair as Rogan stood taller and acted.

Marduk couldn't square up to Rogan and defend himself as

the Kelt drew back and threw both daggers, end over end, into the Nephilim's face. One of the dirks hit the mark, plunging far down into Marduk's left eye socket, but the second dagger missed the other eye, striking his mane of hair nearby his ear. Elisa made a grab for the errant knife, but she tumbled to the floor, all done.

The giant staggered away from the platform, trying to get upright before Rogan approached fast. Marduk swung his left arm out but missed his attacker as Rogan launched himself at the lumbering giant. His right boot met Marduk's face, right on the hilt of the dagger in the eye socket and drove the blade on home, delving the weapon so far in only the butt could be seen.

Up to his feet, spine erect, Marduk howled, both hands on his head, then his many fingers gouging at the eye socket, trying to get the weapon free. He stumbled, his body convulsing, his legs quaking fast as if drunk, but moving too fast to control his actions.

Rogan looked down at Elisa. He didn't hesitate to adjust her body with his boot and pull the sword out of her. The sound she gave out came as a slithering wet belch, followed by an almost ecstatic sigh. It was the sweetest thing he'd ever heard her say.

The move appeared ferocious as the two kings in the corner near to vomited, but Rogan figured she would've done the same to him.

He turned to the shaking Marduk, saw then Aliene move over and near to block any escape the giant dreamed about. Rogan then stabbed the Nephilim in the ass. The blow served no real purpose, he just felt like doing it, as the bum presented itself as an easy target. The next swipe up with the blade connected with Marduk's groin, as he felt the soft tissue via the sword, probably hitting the giant's testicles, take in the edge of Elisa's sword. By the tone in Marduk's screaming voice, Rogan guessed his wrenching moves gelded the furious giant at a wicked direction.

Marduk twisted and Rogan dived to avoid the big hand strike. The giant gave a malicious laugh, then outright shrieked, worse than at the gelding, for the great mammoth moved up behind him. Aliene struck Marduk in the back, one of her tusks driving through his midsection, a loop of guts dangling out the front of him for all to see.

The giant fell to his knees, his right hand on his groin, his left still pawing at his face, his guts unraveling. He couldn't fall down all the way, as the tusk of the mammoth held him aloft like a forbidding prize.

Up to his boots again, Rogan retrieved what remained of his broken sword. The blade slipped out of his hands and Rogan saw that his fingers were trembling. He stepped up to face Marduk, who looked to be taking shallow breaths, and almost shrinking on his knees. A gray slime bubbled out of the giant's ruined eye and Rogan figured it his brains, running out. But Marduk's other eye stared right at him.

"You still in there?" Rogan asked, breathing hard, his body simmering. He bent down and picked something up with his big left hand. "I want you to see this coming."

Marduk's arms flailed a little, but then both hung limp by his sides as Rogan stepped forward and raised up the black stone from Yana. Rogan brought the rock down and smashed it into Marduk's head. He dropped his sword and used both hands as he repeated this act four times until the rock fell from his hands.

Angered more, and seeing the dents in the giant's skull, Rogan picked up his ruined blade once more, as well as that of Elisa. Crying out for his god to help or just to scream the name, Rogan slashed Marduk across the throat with the weapons. The tough hide of the giant resisted the death blows, but the blades did make a gouge in the flesh of the giant's neck.

Marduk didn't resist as Rogan implanted Elisa's sword tip in the gap, wrenched a space open so he could insert the ruined edge of his sword further. He angled his knee on Aliene's tusk and sawed at the head of the giant. Rogan worked a long time and, alas, he fell back, too tired to finish the job.

Aliene pulled back, her tusk out of Marduk's midsection,

and lowered her massive head. Her trunk coiled about the head of the giant, and then she raised up, lifting Marduk off the floor. His own weight combined with Rogan's cuts did the trick, and the head presently ripped free of the colossal body. Marduk tumbled to the floor and Aliene dropped the head, trumpeting loud. The echo in the temple bounded about for a while and sounded better to Rogan than the climax of a hundred whores.

His dropped his weapons and sucked air with wanton hunger. Rogan crawled over to Elisa and took her in his arms.

Rogan's forehead pressed to Elisa's chest. He could no longer hear her breathe, nor did he expect it. A sound did touch his ears, though. He could hear a slow, methodic clapping sound in the extraordinary chamber. His head arose to find the source of the sound and he saw the two kings, Nungal and Kalama-ur, giving mocking applause to what they just witnessed. Their smiles burned in his brain all the way down to his balls.

"Oh good show, young fellow," Nungal said, his clapping hands deliberate and mocking. "A fine performance."

Kalama-ur made a more pattering clap, like that of a woman trying to say a fine performance got turned in by an acting troop. "I concur. Well played indeed." The rough nature of Kamala-ur brought out his derision better due to the flouncing mock approval.

Rogan sat back on his haunches, getting his wind back, hands still on the dead Nephilim woman. "Did I entertain you?"

The ovation faded and Nungal said, "It all came along as satisfactory entertainment. That big girl turning Zazaeil to stone by screwing him and you, your frenzy so lovely in slaying Marduk. My, my!"

"And the help of that ivory beast, bravo!" Kamala-ur grinned.

Nungal hit the table with vigor. "Yes, yes!"

Kamala-ur concurred. "A worthy demonstration, young fellow."

His aching body not acting like he wanted, Rogan made

slow motions as he climbed to his feet. "Glad that entertained you rich pricks."

Both men giggled, but Nungal spoke first, saying, "No reason to be so salty, young fellow. The world is yours now."

"Indeed," concurred Kamala-ur.

"All of the wealth of these fools you can carry and you have bested them."

Looking at his bloody fingers, Rogan thought, *I'll be dead as soon as I step out of those big doors.*

Kamala-ur said, "Well, to be certain, that big girl, she bested the demon, but that might be forgotten in time."

"True enough, there." Nungal nodded fast as he sucked down more wine from his goblet. "You though, the one we hunted for out in the wilds, has become the capstone of the story. Fantastic show."

Kamala-ur feigned worship of Rogan, raising both hands and dropping them. "The killer of giants."

"Elisa slew the demon," said Rogan softly, looking over at the rigid stone silhouette of Zazaeil. The manhood of the demon still rigid, as it would be forever.

"Your barbarous rage took out Marduk," Nungal added with a shake of his head. "Did us a favor, really."

Rogan nodded his head with a sluggish move. "Hell, Aliene ran him through or I might be a dead rat now."

Kamala-ur said, "Who will recall the tale, be it women or a beast? Your name will be remembered."

"Rogan!" Nungal called out loud, to let the name echo in the hall.

"Run with that slight honor and get rich." Kalama-ur's raspy voice turned colder as he stated, "Go on back home to your sweet land of ice and snow now. Be the killer of giants, revered by all."

Nungal grinned. "That story will get you all the women and wine you can stomach for a long spell."

His movements lethargic, Rogan stepped away from Elisa's

body and picked up what remained of his blade.

With great weariness, Kalama-ur sighed and then clicked his tongue on his teeth, "Your sword is broken. Tsk!"

Rogan's fist closed on the leather hilt and he studied the jagged edge of the broken blade. "It's all I need."

As he stepped closer to the two kings, their smiles washed-out, but his grew wider.

*****

As Aliene's head shoved the long double doors open wide, Rogan heard the drawing of swords. Head down, body exhausted, Rogan's eyes did look up to see that outside, in the enormous courtyard, several guards and a company of the Irem army stood in a wide semi-circle. At the sight of the mammoth, they readied their blades, a company of spearmen moving up behind them tight. These soldiers traded looks as the spearmen moved out into the flanks, but they made no move to advance.

A gasp went out from them and the gathered populace when they saw what came out, balanced on the bloody tusks of the mammoth. Each point of the tusks bore a severed head, those of the kings Nungal and Kalama-ur. Rogan held no bridle or rope to guide the great beast, but he did grip the locks of the enormous head of Marduk.

When the head of the Nephilim tumbled off the mammoth and made a wet sound as it bounced, he figured the terror in the crowd thought he spiked it in defiance. Their fear rose at the rebellious savage throwing the head of their demi-god to the intricate stone floor of the courtyard.

In truth, Rogan just dropped it. His hands wet with the blood of the leaders, the Nephilim, and Elisa, couldn't hold tight any longer…that and he felt spent. At least half of those brandishing weapons at him backpedaled and ran at this act, looking back many times as they ran away.

His head lifted slow as he leered at the soldiers that stayed, but soon, they started to recede as well. A few sheathed their blades, a couple even dropped them. As they stumbled into the spearmen and slingers coming up behind them, Rogan glared at them, wishing them death. He took a breath, one probably seen as arrogance or more defiance at them all. In truth, he could hardly stay in the makeshift saddle and felt glad he practically stuck to the hair of the elephant by his legs.

As the rest of the army and guards pulled back, Rogan's father and sister stepped out of the crowd of civilians watching. Jarek and Gale walked to the side of Aliene, gazing up at their kindred. Jarek eyed the receding soldiers, who wanted no more of the scene. He then looked up at his son.

Rogan let out a breath, leaned forward, and dismounted. That's what the bar songs said in later years, but in truth, he pitched forward and fell off Aliene. His father caught him and kept him upright, just so he wouldn't brain himself. As they briefly embraced, something fell from Rogan's grasp. The object hit the stone floor and clattered.

Still bearing his son up, Jarek eyed the object. "You broke your sword."

"You made it very well, though." Rogan rasped a breath and struggled to stand. "It was a very good sword."

"Was," Jarek sighed as Rogan's boots secured on the street. "I'll have to make you another."

"All right," Rogan consented as his sister gave him a pat on the side. "You look well, little one."

"I really need to wash this crap off my face." Gale blinked, scrounging her visage at the makeup. "You look like Hell's poop pot, Rogan."

"Yeah well, that may be so, but I feel good," Rogan chuckled, touching an object on his waist belt.

His sister squinted. "What is that? A torque?"

"Yeah," Rogan confirmed. "Came off of the giant Marduk. Gold prolly. It'd fit on a man's thigh." He touched the holsters on this belt. "My knives are gone, too, deep in the brain of that sonofabitch Marduk or lost."

Jarek looked up at what lay across the rump of the mammoth. He then locked eyes with his son.

Rogan said, "Could you help me burn the big girl, chief? She needs to burn. Elisa needs to be free. I can't do it. I'm about done."

"Never admit that to anyone, even another Kelt," Jarek whispered to him, eyes intense. His manner then softened as he touched the hair of the dead girl down the white tresses of Aliene. "Yeah, we'll send her soul home," Jarek then agreed.

After a single nod, Rogan asked, "Where is Thyssen?"

Gale pointed out of the king's courtyard at the avenue of shops. "Pretty sure he's in the first tavern."

Rogan took a shaky step and his father reached out. Pushing him away and staggering, Rogan said, "If I can't walk on my own, burn me too."

Grimacing, Jarek told him, "I might just do that."

"Get me that sword made," said Rogan in a loud voice as he took shuddering steps toward the tavern. "When you can."

"I'll see you when I see you, son," Jarek sighed, back to him, unconcerned.

Rogan's steps fell in bad rhythm at first, but he improved a little the closer he came to the edge of the courtyard. Not one man stood to attack him or fight him. Their cries of fright, fleeing, echoed down the street, which stood vacant of life in the night. He saw no hawkers or merchants, either and that felt all right with him.

He stepped past a horse tethered outside the tavern. The animal danced a bit, disturbed by all the fleeing people. His sore fingers gripped the post and he felt icy waves tremor over him, head to foot. Rogan pushed the doors of the bar open and took a tentative step inside.

While he made a great effort to walk through his pains, Rogan thought he might have a catch in his step. Head down some, he saw a few older men with great bellies earned by hard drinking peer out the shutters at the street. A few other patrons sat in the shadows, looking at parchment, sipping tall flagons of brew, but a couple men leaned on the bar aside a few painted women Rogan took as whores. One, though, stood out as she dressed plain…Bodyne. Near her, talking shit as always, stood Thyssen.

An empty flagon on his hand, he clattered the vessel on the bar and said, "Yeah, fill me up and I'll tell you another tale."

The bartender, a sun-scorched man for many winters and few hairs on his body, promised, "I might give you one half price if you shut the hell up."

Rogan stepped up to the bar and stumbled, grabbing the edge, head down, no longer able to hide his exhaustion.

The bartender stared at Rogan. "Yer a big fella, so I won't toss your ass out now. Can ya pay for a brew? Or are you just gonna bleed all over my place?"

Rogan's left hand went to his belt and he put the huge torq on the bar. "Drinks for all, many times over, right now." His eyes then drilled into those of the bartender. "I have a terrible thirst this night."

The bartender took the torq and looked him over again. "I bet you do. Beer, brandywine or something stronger? By the beard of the twin gods, you look like you need the meat wagon master's juice."

"Water of life if you have it and a beer." Rogan's face aimed down, his long locks covering his face. "Keep them coming for all."

As some laughs and cheers rippled in the bar, Thyssen said, "You look a mess, Ragnar my friend."

Rogan peered up at him, confused.

"Ragnar," Thyssen patted him on the back, "I was just telling some of these rogue bounty hunter men about my adventures with my late friend, Rogan the Kelt."

Bodyne then joined in, saying, "Yes Ragnar, did you hear

Rogan died trying to free his father from the flesh pots at the Foundry of Dis?"

"What?" Rogan muttered as the bartender sat a cup of whiskey before him, then poured a great mug of warm beer for him.

"Yes, yes," Thyssen chimed in. "Rogan fell trying to free his father and sister, damn shame, he was a great fighter and lover of tremendous capacity. He got burnt up in the ovens after fighting that guardian thing."

Bodyne cooed and rolled her eyes toward the ceiling. "So they say."

Thyssen gave her a dirty look. "What do you know?"

Bodyne patted her tummy. "I'd have his baby if he'd have asked. Quite a fighter and warrior, right Ragnar?"

Rogan drank from the whiskey cup then chased it with a mouthful of the warm beer. He coughed a little and turned to face them. However, between them, he saw a man stand up from the shadows, a figure with a familiar face.

The deep voice of this man said, "Sounds like bar story." His heavy boots echoed in the revelries of free drinks and Rogan heard his sword scabbard knock against a bar stool. "Rogan was tough to kill, so they say."

Thyssen faced the man and said, "It was an entire company of guards, all with mean hounds helping that guardian of the place. He didn't have a chance."

The boots thudded closer as the man walked around Bodyne. "I don't know if I can believe that story. A bunch of drunk guards, scared of their shadows, with a few mean bitches, out-fought Rogan the Kelt? Even with a big guardian to lead them?"

Eyes closed for a moment, Rogan thought he blacked out. In a second, his eyes flipped open wide.

"Rogan died that way?" the baritone voice drawled on. "The man who struck like a god on the battlefield and in the bedroom?"

Killer of Giants

Rogan's eyes met with those of the man from the shadows. As he drank the whiskey again, his hand almost reached to his back for his scabbard, but that was empty.

Drinking anew, Thyssen gave a hearty belch and said, "Maybe it wasn't his day. I hated to hear of him dying that way."

"Maybe it wasn't his day," the deep voice said. "But maybe today is?"

Rogan swallowed a mouthful of beer and said nothing.

The man gazed at Rogan, looking at the blood on him and that his hand rested on his belt, devoid of knives.

After a slow pause, Bodyne chimed in fast, "Who can say for real? I'd say he was dead and burnt up. A man like that would have made himself known hereabouts if he still lived, isn't that right, sir?"

"I don't believe it," the man said, his face full in the light to Rogan.

Already sure of his identity, Rogan cussed the man Lybeck to himself and knew he had him, exhausted, no weapons, dead down to rights as a broke-dicked dog.

Lybeck said, "But I'm on my way to find a retiring life, over in the east where the women have slanted eyes and make your manhood sing." The big man smiled. "Perhaps Rogan ran away that way and seeks the same thing."

Thyssen yawned, "Could be, but I think he's dead."

Lybeck said, "I'll go to my retirement now that my company is gone. I shall cash in my gold and take up lazy living."

Thyssen grinned. "Sounds like a good plan for life at any age."

Lybeck said, "If I ever see that rogue Rogan..."

"Yeah?" Rogan rasped.

"The choice is his if I live or die." He paused for almost a full minute before he said, "I'll also tell him it's not worth all the blood of men or women to kill the gods. What do you think of that, Ragnar?"

Rogan nodded. "I reckon so."

Lybeck smirked and swigged the last of his flagon. He sat it on the bar and turned his back to them. He walked out, and never looked back.

His face near to the bar's surface, Rogan took labored breaths, but in a few moments, started to laugh.

Her hand on his shoulder, Bodyne whispered, "Stop it, he's about gone." She looked to the doors with distressed eyes. "Please be quiet."

The laughter from Rogan grew louder and all of Thyssen's humor disappeared. "All right, shut up, damn it."

"So funny, it is…" Rogan gurgled and then cleared his throat. His head never rose off the bar and all those in attendance gaped at the big man.

Thyssen let out a loud sigh. "All right, damn ya to hell. What in the fuck is so funny, ya lucky jackass?"

"Being alive, you ugly asshead." Standing tall, Rogan raised the whiskey to toast him. "Being alive."

EPILOGUE

Falling Off the Edge of the World

"**S**uck in that sea air, Rogan," Thyssen shouted as he gripped tight to the rigging near the central mast of the ship.

Rogan stayed near the rear of the vessel by where the deck arose. The long ship pitched and dipped, then righted itself many times. He looked at what he held in his hands and said nothing in return.

Sliding across the deck toward him, Thyssen said, "It's gonna clear out in a bit. The sea here is choppy but once we get out into open water, it'll calm down fine."

Nodding, Rogan said, "I hope I don't puke my guts out."

"Not a good sailor?"

Rogan's eyes widened a bit as he glared at him. "I'm from the mountains. We are short on oceans there."

"I figured ya traveled a lot, though."

"Yeah, but I'd rather have the ground under my boots. Damn water." He gazed across the sea and noted that it did start to level out some as they went. "Can't breathe in that crap. You sailor types are crazy."

"Correct," Thynnes laughed, taking a big breath. "Yer just pissy that ol' Aliene went back up north with your dad and sister,"

"I'd have rather of had a horse, but she came in really handy in all this crap, true enough." He thought of Jarek and his sister climbing up on Aliene and how the elephant looked at him as he patted her ear a last time. The white trunk had soothed across his back like the beast cradled an infant. "Just a dumb animal," Rogan dismissed it to him, eyes aimed down at the glistening boards.

Thyssen held his spear tight and grabbed the rail by Rogan as the ship pitched again. "So they say. Some are smart ones. She served yer big ass well, though." Thyssen then eyed Rogan's back. "Hope the new sword Jarek forged back there in that crap smithy works well."

The weight of the new blade on his back felt more apparent at that moment. "We'll prolly find out before long."

"Yeah, but let's hope not. I hope fucking finds us, not fighting."

Rogan gave a grunt of agreement. "Let's hope."

"On the distant coasts let's hope the whorehouses leave us walking like baby giraffe's and hungry for more."

"A baby what?"

Thyssen smirked. "Never mind."

Rogan turned the object over in his hands. "The carving on the bottom of this urn is marked the same way that big-assed man by Azar did his works."

"Ludvig?"

"Yeah."

Thyssen wondered, "Maybe he's crafty, too."

"Melts bodies and crafts urns to sell?"

"Bodies are his business," Thyssen said, eyes darting around. "Think these fuckers have some wine or stronger?"

"They are sailors. I'm sure they do."

Again, Rogan faced the water. "It goes on forever to the south."

Thyssen joined his gaze. "That's the theory. These guys will stay nearer to the coastlines as we travel. They fear falling off the edge of the world."

"You ever seen it?"

"What?"

"The edge of the world."

"No. I've never seen Hell, but I think it's there."

"Why?"

Thyssen gawked at him and made a twisted expression with his mouth. "Gotta be a place for all these bad pricks to go to once we kill them, right?"

"Right."

"And that prick Zazaeil had to come from someplace. Them fuckers never wanna go back there, so, yeah, it's there."

"Are we bad pricks?"

"Sure." Thyssen faced the sea. "Not as bad as some."

"That will have to be enough."

"Sure it is."

Rogan turned over the urn again and stood, mind trying to not think of Elisa, but failing. His lust for her ran about the same as for most women, perhaps challenged a little by her size, but he found her intriguing. He blinked, not realizing Thyssen had left until he returned with a small flask and slapped it against his chest.

"They say it is some stuff stronger than the usual wine but not as powerful as some fine whiskey."

Rogan put the urn under his arm, opened the flask, and took a sip. "Damn, it's about awful and very sweet."

"They said the wine is for later."

The sea had calmed as Rogan said, "Good."

"Thinking of her?"

"Piss off."

"Good thing ya didn't screw her, huh?"

Rogan half laughed. "Well, true, but she wasn't about our simple lives, of staying alive and all that crap. She had a goal and did it."

"Making ya wish ya had a goal?"

"Beyond getting drunk and whoring my way across the world?"

"It's a goal." Thyssen shrugged. "You fight like a bastard. My father could use a warrior like you."

"I thought it was you that didn't care for army life? Being in a mercenary army got me into this deal in the first place."

"So what will it be for you?"

Again, Rogan eyed the urn and then walked away from him, to the railing of the vessel. "I'm not done wandering, not done dreaming about what lies over the next hill." He then stared up at the water. "Or across the fucking endless sea. But there's something over that horizon I must see. Someday, maybe, I'll tire of it and want to sit on my ass, get fat, and look at parchment."

"Yeah?" Thyssen asked as he joined him. "I dunno if I wanna see that. Want me to kill ya if ya get to that place?"

"Please do, if ya will."

"I shall and then remember you in a debauchery afterwards."

"Fine, fine," Rogan said and gazed at the urn. "Now, fuck off, will you now? I want to do this alone."

Thyssen made a slight bow. "Fucking off, your highness."

The spear on the deck thudded away from Rogan as he unsealed the urn. He peered down into the container of ashes and saw a few chips of bone. He frowned, knowing it wasn't an exact science. His mind pondered the girl, and her mother, how they did what they did and understood death would be the payment…and yet they did it anyway. Part of him thought that crazy, but in his gut an admiration burned for them.

He didn't pray for her soul, nor did he know if she had a god, goddess, or didn't give a shit about any of that. For a moment, he considered the ash and how Elisa's ashes indeed even would be magical. He didn't care for all that, either. Rogan turned the urn over, letting the ashes spill out and then dropped the urn into the southern sea.

With unblinking eyes, he watched for a few moments as the waters embraced and carried away the killer of giants.

THE END

Of

KILLER OF GIANTS

But ROGAN will return…

In

BLADESPELL

About the Author

Steven Shrewsbury has had over 20 novels published such as OVERKILL, PHILISTINE, LAST MAN SCREAMING and BEYOND NIGHT. He has collaborated with author Brian Keene on the King of the Bastard Series.

www.ingramcontent.com/pod-product-compliance
Lightning Source LLC
Chambersburg PA
CBHW020544020726
47494CB00006B/1906